The Eighth Veil

Books by Frederick Ramsay

The Ike Schwartz Mysteries
Artscape
Secrets
Buffalo Mountain
Stranger Room
Choker
The Eye of the Virgin
Rogue

The Botswana Mysteries
Predators
Reapers

Other Novels
Impulse
Judas
The Eighth Veil

The Eighth Veil

A Jerusalem Mystery

Frederick Ramsay

Poisoned Pen Press

Poisoned Pen Press
6962 E. First Ave., Ste. 103
Scottsdale, AZ 85251
www.poisonedpenpress.com
info@poisonedpenpress.com

Printed in the United States of America

The faculty at Saint George's College Jerusalem
June/July, 1991

Wherever you are.

Introduction and Acknowledgments

A little over twenty years ago my wife and I had the good fortune to spend not quite three weeks in Israel and particularly Jerusalem as students at Saint George's College. The course of study was entitled, if memory serves, *The Palestine of Jesus.* As students, we traveled about the country and city with the guidance of an excellent international faculty and were taught how to peel away the years and the strife that characterizes that land and its history, to see it as it must have been two millennia ago. To say the experience at Saint George's was life changing would be a gross understatement. During the decade or so that followed, we were privileged to visit Israel another five times, either leading groups or simply touring on our own.

In this book I have attempted to capture some of that experience and depict an Israel as it once was. Obviously it is a book of fiction, but some of the characters did, in fact, walk the streets of Jerusalem two thousand years ago, did see the sun rise and set on its dun-colored limestone buildings, and knew in their time the people we only meet in the Bible, Shakespeare's plays, or films.

When I preached (that would have been in another life, of course) I used to ask the congregation to picture the scene just read from the day's Gospel as if they were present in that dusty street, house, hillside, or synagogue, standing shoulder to shoulder with the people who'd just heard the words for the first time. To grasp the teaching inherit in the reading, I maintained, one must hear it with the ears of the first century Jews living in a Galilee or Judea occupied by Rome and divided by sectarian differences. Differences in what was meant to be Jewish in search of a Messiah, differences in what constituted correct practice, differences in how to cope with yet another conqueror in a long line of overlords that stretched back as far as memory served. Modern readers, I maintain, must strip away prejudices gained over a lifetime of Sunday school and imagine what it must have been like for those first witnesses. What thoughts must have gone through their minds, what fears, what doubts, and what hopes?

I have attempted to do that with this little mystery—to draw a picture of another time and place but with a few familiar characters.

⟨⟩⟨⟩⟨⟩

And, having set the scene, I must now acknowledge the people who helped me do it: Everyone at The Poisoned Pen Press, Barbara, Robert, Nan, Jessica, and all of you who help make my life a delight. Also, thanks to the folks, near and far, who make me look better than I really am; Glenda, who peruses these words and blue pencils my most egregious errors; and Susan, who attempts (and fails) to instruct me in Hebrew but lets me play at being an author anyway.

I want to also send a nod to Tom Stone, who shared a substantial portion of our youth at McDonogh School with me and whose book, *Zeus*, reminded me of the complexities of Greek mythology foisted on us in those days. I have attached notes sections in two places—immediately following, and at the end of the book. I must thank Julie Waskow and Ernie Bringas from the Philosophy Department at Glendale Community College for their help in vetting them. I hope they will help the reader appreciate the times and the personalities of that era, and at least keep some of the characters straight. You might want to fasten a tab or paperclip or two at various places in those sections to serve as a quick reference.

—Frederick Ramsay 2012

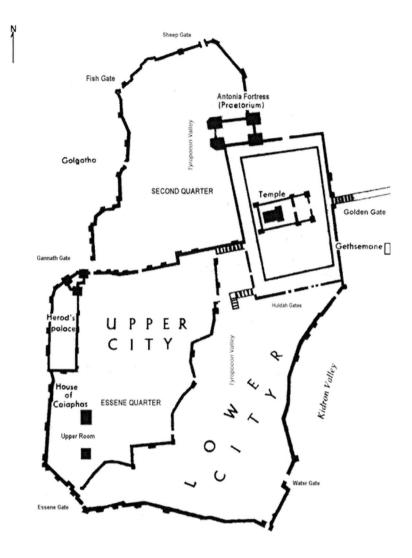

Map of Jerusalem circa 28 CE

Map of the Eastern Roman Empire CA 28 CE

The Line of Herod the Great

The family tree of Herod the Great is depicted below. It is a composite of several similar schemes and should not to be considered as either definitive or necessarily accurate. For the purposes of this narrative the featured players in the book are set in bold.

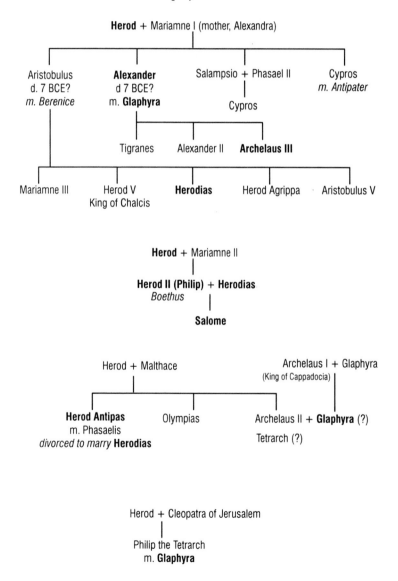

The previous chart represents the traditional rendering and suits the story, but the reader should understand that not everyone agrees with its formulation. Scholars dispute the exact positioning of some of the branches and sub-branches, and clearly, not all of the descendents are shown.

Primary Characters

Caiaphas, Yosef bar Kayafa; High Priest of the Temple, 18 CE to 36 CE. Although removed from office by Caligula, saw his sons succeed him in the office later.

Chuzas: Herod Antipas' steward, married to Joanna who was said to have been a follower of Jesus after being exorcised of demons.

Gamaliel, Gamaliel the Elder, Gamaliel I; served as the Rabban (chief rabbi) of the Sanhedrin, the ruling body of Israel. While believing the Law of Moses to be wholly inspired by God, he is reported to have taken a broad-minded and compassionate stance in its interpretation. Gamaliel held that the Sabbath laws should be understood in a realistic rather than rigorous fashion. He also maintained, in distinction to his contemporaries, that the law should protect women during divorce and urged openness toward Gentiles. Acts 5:38-39 relates that he intervened on behalf of Saint Peter and other Jewish followers of Jesus.

Herod Antipas: One of several male offspring of Herod the great. He ruled, with Rome's sufferance, the areas of Galilee and Perea.

Pontius Pilate: The fifth Prefect of the Roman province of Judaea, from CE 26 to 36. He is best known as the judge at Jesus' trial and the man who authorized his crucifixion. He was recalled to Rome by Caligula at the same time as Caiaphas' removal from office.

Yeshua ben Yosef: Hebrew name for Jesus (Joshua son of Joseph).

Keeping Time

We do not know with any certainty when the rabbi from Nazareth, Jesus, was born. We have fairly substantial evidence that Herod the Great died in 4 BCE. If it was he who ordered the slaughter of the innocents (Matthew 2:16), then Jesus had to have been born sometime before that. The story is set in the year 28 CE on the assumption that the earlier date is correct and Jesus was in his mid-thirties when his ministry was in full flower. But the date is admittedly arbitrary. It should be noted here that there are scholars who place Jesus' birth as late as 6 CE and cite Luke's reference to Quirinius as governor of Syria, an office he held around 6 to 9 CE. But Quirinius is believed to have served in some official capacity in Syria twice: 6-4 BCE and then again in 6-9 CE so the earlier birth date can stand.

Days of the Week

Yom Rishon = "first day" = Sunday
   (starting at preceding sunset)
Yom Sheni = "second day" = Monday
Yom Shlishi = "third day" = Tuesday
Yom Revi'i = "fourth day" = Wednesday
Yom Chamishi = "fifth day" = Thursday
Yom Shishi = "sixth day" = Friday
Yom Shabbat = "Sabbath day (Rest day)" = Saturday

Hours of the Day

A day was divided into twenty four hours—twelve for daylight, twelve for night. Day began at sunup and ended at sunset. The hours were of indefinite lengths depending on the season, shortest in the winter, longer in the summer, but noon, when the sun stood at its zenith, was designated the sixth hour. As there could be no similar reference point at night, the phases of the moon being variable, the night hours had no time divisions except rough notations. Midnight might be described as the night's "sixth hour," but when it occurred would necessarily vary with the speaker and his or her sense of the passage of time.

Speaking the Name

Orthodox Jewish custom prevents a person from saying the name of God. Indeed, some hold to do so is the ultimate and perhaps only blasphemy. The pronunciation of the Hebrew, יהוה (the Tetragrammaton, YHWH) which designates the Almighty is sometimes pronounced Yahweh, Jehovah, or some other circumlocution. Even today, orthodox Jewish literature and web sites will print God only as G*d. In the narrative and because the protagonist, Gamaliel, would have been at least as orthodox as modern day practice, the term Lord, or the Lord, is used instead of God in order to make this distinction. Sometimes a greeting would be even more circumspect and the person initiating it would merely say "Greetings in the Name" (*Ha Shem*, השם).

Pagans, however, did not share those scruples so that a conversation between the two camps would shift from its usage and back again. The distinction is made by the use of a lower case god as opposed to God. The Hebrew conversant would, of course only refer to "the Lord" or a substitute.

This house exhales slaughter,
odors from the open mouth of a grave.

—Aeschylus, *Agamemnon*
456 BCE

Yom Rishon

Chapter I

Her killer straddled her naked and abused body while he held her head below the water's surface he hoped would silence her. Her features were distorted by the roiling water but she seemed to be staring back at him wide-eyed and terrified. Air bubbles escaped from her pursed lips in spite of her efforts to hold them in. Starved for air, she jerked her head wildly from side to side, desperate to breathe, to scream for help, to stay alive. But no one would hear her cry. Not that night, not ever again. The knife slashed through the leather thong and across her throat, as if writing that cry for her instead. The last air in her lungs burst from the deep wound in her neck to mingle with the blood that gushed out with it. Her killer rocked back from his kneeling position with a curse. Disgusted, he shoved her body the rest of the way into the bath and watched as it sank to the bottom and the blood that streamed from her wounded neck like bright red smoke as it carried her life away. He made a desperate grab for the pendant, the item he'd been sent to retrieve in the first place, but too late. It slipped from his grasp and disappeared in a fresh swirl of the girl's blood.

Footsteps echoed against tiled walls weeping from condensation formed by the still heated water vapor against their cooling surface. It would be the only weeping done for her. The murderer crept back into the shadows, and thence the farther recesses of the palace, angry that the amulet, the pendant, his object in the whole adventure, had slipped out of his reach. Another mistake. He had to have it, to reclaim it. With the gods' favor he reckoned it might be possible that whoever was headed this way would not see the girl or the blood and he could slip back and finish his business. A great deal depended on it. He must not fail.

⟨⟩⟨⟩⟨⟩

It had fallen to old Barak to make his rounds at the night's deepest hour when all of Jerusalem should be in bed and asleep. He shivered at the unseasonable chill and hugged himself in an effort to keep warm. This night, because he had done a favor for the king's under-steward, he needed only to monitor the bath and its adjacent atrium instead of the whole east end of the palace, his usual round. This meant he was ahead of schedule and in a few moments would be back in his own warm bed with his wife of fifty years. Barak had served this king and his father before him. Now, in his sixty-seventh year he shuffled through the dimly lit hallways weary but comforted by the fact that he had a roof over his head and a sense of security at an age when many like him were cast out or dependent on children and grandchildren.

The large vaulted room that featured the Roman inspired bath at its center, had only a few flickering torches lighted after the previous evening's revels. "Roman orgy more like," he muttered to himself. Barak had no use for the palace's loose religious observance or this king who seemed determined to dishonor both the Law and the Nation. He'd heard the other servant's whispers about what went on in this place at night. He assumed the worst about what must have taken place earlier. He closed his mind to these thoughts for fear they might lead him where he should not go. The neopagan mosaics of the bacchanal, scenes of half-naked nymphs and satyrs in shameless poses that decorated the ceiling, were in deep shadow. Barak would not have looked at them anyway. He tried, in spite of the lax form of Judaism practiced by the court, to remain obedient to the Law.

He imagined he heard footsteps as he entered, but in the uncertain light, he saw no one. Even if he had, it would not mean anything to him. Courtiers and servants wandered these halls constantly night and day. What they were up to he could only guess at. Undoubtedly up to no good. He accepted the fact that they lived in a different world than he. He did not envy them for that.

Thanks to the gloom, and because of his advanced years, and failing eyesight, he could be excused for missing the body at first. It was something about the water that caught his eye. No longer clear but dim and sullen somehow. Herodias the Queen, he knew, often requested perfume to be poured into the baths, particularly when it was the women's time to use them, but adding coloring, well that would be something new. A second glance and he realized the water's stains were uneven and darker at one end than the other. He wondered if by some accident of plumbing, muddy water had somehow found its way in. The bath, like so many of the city's water sources owed some of its volume to Pilate's aqueduct, a project he'd funded with Temple money much to the consternation of the High Priest and the Sanhedrin. When Barak leaned over and lowered his torch close to the surface, he realized the color was not brown, but red. Only then did he spot the naked woman in its murky depths and realize the coloration had most likely resulted from her slit throat, not the introduction of a vial of madder.

He whirled the klaxon he carried in the event he needed to raise an alarm. Within what he would later describe were no more than five heartbeats, the sound of running footsteps shattered the silence. Palace guards crashed into the room, their short Roman swords drawn, eyes alert and busy. The chief steward followed within the next five beats, and chaos followed him. Barak pointed toward the bloody pool and sat down heavily on a carved marble couch, one of which doubtless had supported a nobler backside hours earlier.

The steward rushed out. Guards were posted at all entrances with instructions to allow no one in or out. Barak sighed. There would be no sleeping this night. What would his Minna say when he did not return to their bed?

Yom Sheni

Chapter II

Shofars sounded their mournful wail from the Temple's pinnacle announcing the arrival of a new day. Gamaliel had already been up for an hour by then. He folded his tallit and placed it on the tall sandalwood chest where he also kept his phylactery, some papyrus scrolls, and a few sheckles he would need when he traveled up to the Temple to see the High Priest. He'd finished his morning prayers and would break his fast. A small court opened off of the room and he stepped out to enjoy its fresh air and the first glimmerings of sunlight seeping over the walls. The cool air held the promise of a fair day, but he did not notice it. A circular cistern in the court's center provided what he needed next. He splashed a little water on his face and hands, an act which required another short prayer, and then another prayer directed at his approaching confrontation with the High Priest. Caiaphas nagged at him endlessly like a strong-willed wife about that annoying rabbi. He could not be put off any longer. He insisted on an answer.

The issue troubled him. It seemed such a petty thing on which to spend time and energy. He did not look forward to the interview. Caiaphas did not like being denied and had a way of making one's life difficult if he considered you to be the root of his disappointment. But Gamaliel would not worry about that just now. The High Priest was always in a dudgeon about something and more often than not he assumed Gamaliel would sort it all out for him. The fact he held the esteemed position of Rabban of the Sanhedrin, and that he had taught nearly all the

Pharisees and important rabbis who now held sway in Judea as leaders and interpreters of the Law, meant Gamaliel had acquired a layer of political insulation not enjoyed by his colleagues and lesser men. Still, making an enemy of the High Priest could prove inconvenient.

Gamaliel did not share the High Priest's discomfort with the Galileans or their simple rabbi from Nazareth whose preaching hardly qualified as either scholarly or perilous; certainly not like that of the Essenes or the Siccori, both of whom were considerably more insistent and dangerous, each in their own way. Was this Galilean preaching heterodoxy? Probably, but not more so than many of his contemporaries who wandered the streets of Jerusalem and countryside declaring the "Year of the Lord." It was said he appealed to Gentiles especially and, as a generality, that must be viewed as a good thing. The Nation would never survive if it did not accommodate to the rest of the world in at least some important areas.

Would this man emerge as the Messiah, as a few of his followers claimed? Who knew? Lately there had been no dearth of claimants to that status, and some espousing far more radical views than this one, if one was to believe what people said. Time alone would tell if the Deliverer were among any of them. Personally, Gamaliel doubted it. Of course, this person's relationship to the Baptizer had to be accounted for. Well, not so much anymore as Herod Antipas, in a moment of monumental stupidity, had beheaded the "Angel of the Desert," as his admirers sometimes called him.

Gamaliel had not yet witnessed the man in action nor had he any wish to do so. Perhaps during the Feast which began the next day he would, perhaps not. Rabbis from all over the Nation usually converged on the city during the Holy Days. Perhaps this one would too and he'd get his chance. On the whole, he thought Caiaphas to be overreacting. It was his right to do so, of course, but Gamaliel did not wish to be party to a program aimed at hounding illiterate fishermen and farmers who at least followed someone, even if, strictly speaking, not someone correctly trained or ordained. He would leave persecution to ambitious clerks like Ehud or the new one, Jabez ben Ratzon. There were far more important things needing his attention than harassing this rag-tag group of would-be reformers and apocalyptic busybodies.

The High Priest had expected him at daybreak. Why such an early hour he could not fathom, but the High Priest had, of late, seemed unduly agitated about most things and he guessed meeting at such an early hour secured some measure of privacy not normally accorded the man. He would be disappointed. The Lord created all things in an order that not even the High Priest could alter. It is the nature of Pharisaic thinking, that order should be in all things and all things should be in order. The Lord provided the Law. The Law provided the order, and the Pharisees provided its correct interpretation. Nothing more need be said. It was the lesson he pounded into his students and, if and when they would take the time to listen, the other members of the Sanhedrin. They, however, were not as teachable as his rabbinical students.

A bowl of dates, a jug of goat's milk, and a small loaf of freshly baked bread awaited him on a rough wooden table that he'd insisted be placed in the archway leading to the street. He wanted to absorb the sounds and scents of Jerusalem as he ate. He also wished to have a few more moments to frame his answer to Caiaphas. He ate slowly measuring time with his chewing and watching the mass of humanity moving back and forth on the street beyond, a street that led to the Temple. Satisfied at last that he could withstand the High Priest's ire and fortified by prayers and his morning meal, he stood and made for the gate. The blended scents of camel, donkey, cooking oil, and sweaty travelers washed over him like a warm bath and required him to pause a moment to adjust to the city, his city, David's city. At the doorsill he paused to let a group of pilgrims newly arrived in Jerusalem for the seven-day-long Feast of Tabernacles pass by. He wondered idly where they had come from, north, south? Then, he stepped gingerly into the street prepared to confront the High Priest, his students, and anyone else who proposed to challenge him this day.

A young man stepped in his path.

"Honored sir," he said. "Are you Gamaliel, Rabban of the Sanhedrin, teacher, and most noble man of the Law?"

"I am he. I am not so sure about some of the other titles you have bestowed on me, however."

"Sir, I am bidden to tell you to come at once to King Herod's palace. I am to say it is a matter most urgent and—"

Gamaliel held up his hand. He studied the youth's face. If there was any guile in him, he would detect it immediately. He had acquired a faculty over the years for discerning the truth from a man's face, any disingenuousness in his soul, if such existed. It had served him well over the years particularly when screening pupils and dealing with his colleagues in the Sanhedrin. Many young men wished to study with him, only a select few would.

"And what is this matter that is of such great importance that the king summons me?"

"It is not the king, sir, who summons. It is the Prefect who requires your presence."

"Pontius Pilate summons me to Herod's palace? This cannot be true. No Roman willingly sets foot in the king's palace, nor would he be welcome."

"Nevertheless, it is the message I bear."

"I am sorry, but I have an appointment with the High Priest at this very moment. Tell Pilate he must wait."

"Sir, he insists. More than that, he has sent his soldiers to accompany you. It will not do to refuse."

Gamaliel looked up and realized all activity on the street had come to a near halt. Passersby stood and gawked, first at the guards in their ornate garb and half armor, then at him. He wondered what must be going through their minds. How often did one travel up to Jerusalem and see the Rabban of the Sanhedrin taken into custody by a clutch of legionnaires?

"Very well, young man, as I have no choice in the matter, you may take me to Pilate, but it will be against my wishes and better judgment."

Chapter III

Pontius Pilate, the Prefect to Judea and Palestine, stood in the retreating shade offered by a portico at the entrance to Herod's palace. The Prefect, Gamaliel noted, had not entered it after all. He stepped carefully to avoid some camel offal left by a small caravan that had passed down the street only recently. He kept the Great Man, Rome's anointed overseer, the famous and universally hated Pilate, in the corner of his eye as he did so. He had a fleeting, unkind thought that given the choice, he'd rather take the offal and avoid the Prefect. Then, he reflected that perhaps he was being too harsh. It wasn't just a matter of distrusting gentiles. He had stated publically and frequently the Nation's need to soften views of those who did not share their beliefs. But this particular specimen of humanity…Somewhere, someone must approve of this man. He must have a mother at least, and the emperor thought enough of him to give him this posting. Of course, that would have been Tiberius, and everyone knew that aging old man was prone to mad flights of fancy and other peculiarities.

As Pilate lounged against a pillar, his eyes darted back and forth impatiently seeming to search the street. Clearly, he did not know what or who to expect as the famous Rabban. The two had never met. Gamaliel had seen him once or twice, from a distance, when the emissary from Rome had addressed the people on the occasion of the removal of the Legion's standards from the Temple Mount, and again when he made his pathetic triumphal entrances into the city before each of the High Holy Days. A proud and arrogant man, given to fits of brutality, he'd been told. He was of above average stature, lean and quite dangerous looking. Not a man to be trifled with.

Gamaliel greeted him and bowed his head marginally. If the great Pilate expected more in the way of obeisance he'd need to say something.

"You are the Rabban?" Pilate asked, as if there'd been some mistake.

"I am, Excellency. I have been summoned? To what purpose, may I ask?"

"I expected you to be older. All your people in positions of power, it seems, must achieve the age of your Moses at least before they are considered trustworthy. Well, never mind about that. You may well ask, 'to what purpose.' It is your king and his household that require your services in resolving this sordid matter, not I. It is only my duty to bring the authority of my office to assure you will comply with their needs, and mine."

"Sir? A sordid business, you say? I am at a loss."

"Ah, I take it you have not heard, then."

"I have only just made my morning prayers and eaten my first meal of the day. It is early yet and I have not been about to hear anything. What, may I ask, should I have heard?"

"Murder, Rabban. There is a dead woman, a young girl of questionable status in the palace and it may signal a scandal. For me, I do not care a bowl of dates for the business one way or the other, but it has been done in this place under the king's nose. And as he is the king and rules because Rome decrees it to be so, it will not do to have a scandal involving this family. No, it is not allowable."

"A scandal in the family of Herod? Surely you cannot be serious, Prefect. You must know the history of this royal line? One more death, one more scandal involving one woman or a dozen would hardly be noticed much less a cause for concern. The people over whom this king rules have little regard for him.

We view him as only slightly less trying than yourself, Prefect, with due respect."

Pilate's face blazed and for a moment Gamaliel thought he would lash out at him with his fist or even his sword. He didn't. Blunt speech had its place in the Sanhedrin and with students. With the Prefect, however, it didn't sit well. For this Roman bully to have resisted an opportunity to drop one more upstart Jew in the dust must mean the situation was truly serious.

"I will overlook that remark, Rabbi," the Prefect said.

Gamaliel tensed and then relaxed. So, now only Rabbi. Not Rabban. A mild rebuke surely.

"My apologies, a slip of the tongue, but you understand no one likes a conqueror however sublime. How can I be of service to your Excellency?"

Pilate harrumphed and swung one long muscular arm in an arc. "Follow me."

Pilate led Gamaliel through the portal and swerved to the left, avoiding the palace proper and turned into a small atrium at one side. He sat on a bench and indicated Gamaliel should do likewise.

"You know the torturous history of this family, these Hasmoneans favored by Julius, is both complex and marginally incestuous."

"It is the nature of royalty, Excellency, to interbreed so as not to share power, wealth, or position. Your own Caesars, for instance—"

"Caesar is yours as well, Rabbi. Best not forget that and you will do well to keep your opinions of Rome's ruling house to yourself. Please do not interrupt me again. I have much to tell and little time to tell it."

"Again my apologies. You were saying the lineage of our late great king seems complex."

"A Gordian Knot, more like, but an Alexandrian solution to unraveling it is not available to us so we must struggle through it as best we can. Since you know it better than I, I will skip to the branch of that thorn-encrusted tree that concerns us today.

You are aware, doubtless, that this King, Antipas, has acquired his brother's wife."

"Indeed. It is a matter of concern for the rabbis and for many others. It is held to be a sin to marry one's brother-in-law under these particular circumstances. Not a few critics have pointed that out. John the Baptizer comes to mind"

"Your holy man who lost his head to the king's whims and weakness. Yes, him of course. At any rate, it is reported to me that the liaison with his new queen began well before his brother, Herod II who is variously called Boethus or Philip, died and set her free to remarry."

"That would not surprise me or any perceptive person, Excellency. The house of Herod is not given to subtlety. Your point being?"

"My point? Indeed, to the point, I must back up a bit. The first Herod, Julius Caesar's friend, executed his two sons, Alexander and Aristobulus."

"Among many others including a wife and her mother, Alexandra."

"Exactly. Alexander had married a princess of Cappadocia, Glaphyra, who was his niece, I believe."

"Somewhat removed, but yes."

"She bore him three children before he found himself accused of plotting to oust Herod and was strangled with the cord."

"With the permission of Augustus, yes I know, but three? I know of only two, both of whom eventually fled Judea after Herod died. There they renounced the one true Faith and now live and prosper in the land once ruled by their grandfather."

"Ah, yes, but there was a third, a son, Archelaus, named after the grandfather, who—"

"Who was alleged to be descended from Mithridates but was deposed by the emperor, moved to Rome and died there a decade ago. It is confusing because the same names keep popping up. That is to say, both that of Glaphyra and Archelaus. I am sorry. I have untracked your course. You were saying?"

"Very well, you know your history. At any rate this Archelaus, the grandson, may or may not have also fled to that place with his brothers. And what they are up to in the absence of a king is not clear, but Cappadocia has always been a hotbed of intrigue and rebellion. It is lately rumored this youngest son is here in Jerusalem, not in Cappadocia, perhaps even in this very palace, why or how I cannot imagine, but where there are princes, there are plots and intrigue." Gamaliel resisted the temptation to interrupt the Prefect again and waited for what came next.

"Antipas would be his uncle, after all. So, to continue, there is also Menahem, the late king's adopted son, or so they say. He is here as well. It is not as clear why this man received such favor from Herod. I suppose he could be one of the first Herod's bastards by some member of his court. I presume his ancestry made it advisable to treat him as a son rather than a foundling. Your Herod is a puzzle to say the least."

"Puzzle hardly does him justice. His tree is so twisted, its branches so tangled, and the roots so decayed, that foster brother might have seemed the best or only choice. If he had offspring, it inevitably raises the issue of inheritance. At any rate, I assume all this relates to the murder in some way. But here, a son of Alexander? Do you have any idea where he might be staying? He is kinsman to the king. Surely if he were here in the palace, we would know of it."

"Yes, so I imagine. Do you suppose this man, who might by now be named anything other than that with which he came into the world, is hiding in plain sight? It is rumored he was involved somehow with Herodias and her daughter, the dancer who, as you know was a willing accomplice in the death of your scruffy holy man."

"Involved? In what way? And this relates to a murder, how?"

"I have no idea. I am merely arranging the game pieces in the circle. You will cast the stones to see where they move next."

"We are playing the King's Game, you think? That is interesting, surely. But would not Philip have known and would he have welcomed him into his house?"

"I have no idea, but I assume if he felt any threat, he would have acted as his father and ridded himself of the unwanted interloper with dispatch."

"Yes that makes sense, if any of this makes sense. Of course, there is the princess, who by all accounts lacks something in judgment."

"An understatement at best."

"One wonders what John's fate might have been if the Princess Salome had possessed the foresight to equip herself with eight veils instead of the alleged seven, and enough discretion to retain the last."

"Pah! Once again you are interrupting, Rabbi. Do not do so. To continue, as I said, this Archelaus had been exiled. My informants tell me of rumors that suggest he committed acts that could be neither tolerated nor condoned and would have been put to the cord like his father, were it not for the fact he was of Herod's line, had allies in the courts in this land, and as such retained some measure of immunity, Cappadocia being, as it stands now, a rich country but still a Province of the Empire, not an independent nation."

"What sort of crimes would that be, I wonder? Ones similar to the one perpetrated here, perhaps?"

"You are astute Rabbi. It was so intimated to me and that is why I have summoned you."

"Of course any negative rumor attached to a royal on the run must be taken with a grain of salt."

"Of course, you would know that, I assume. To the point, then, Antipas will not trust my people in his court or in his presence to sort out this crime. I do not trust his people to do anything more than cover up this mess. We, the king and I that is, have settled on you as a neutral, objective, third party."

"Me? I am a scholar and teacher of the Law, not a magistrate, and certainly not an investigator of crimes."

"Precisely. Any judgments you may make will be treated with the greatest respect because, as you are well aware, your voice carries the authority of your law. A caution, however, all the information I have just supplied cannot be verified and may not bear in any way on the circumstances of the girl's death. My spies in this matter are less than trustworthy and their reports often contradictory. It is the nature of the politically motivated to spread misinformation more readily than the truth. So, everything I have just said may be completely false and misleading and deliberately so." Gamaliel opened his mouth to speak. Pilate stopped him with a gesture. "Before you ask me why I gave it to you, I will say it sets the tone for your task. At the risk of being redundant I must warn you again that anything a palace luminary says to you during the course of your probing must be weighed against what I have told you and must never be taken at face value. You see?"

"I see, yes. I am not happy about it, but I see. I was just about to ask you why climbing the branches of the late king's family tree is relevant?"

"Sorting out this tangled family will be difficult if not impossible. Yet it may have to be done to get at the murder, I think. Perhaps not to the extent I have laid out for you. Beyond that, I have no idea, but my sense of the thing is this, if you can pry out a motive for the murderer, you will be that much closer to knowing who he is, and it is in this conspiratorial milieu that you will find it."

"Again, with respect, I am singularly unqualified to carry out this task. Do I have a say in any of this?"

"None. I have already sent a message to your High Priest, foolish man, and requested that he so inform the Sanhedrin of this commission. The king has kindly provided this man here… What is your name?"

"Barak, Excellency."

"Barak, will serve you in whatever capacity you may require." Pilate slipped a ring from his finger. "This you will show to anyone who questions your authority to act in this matter." He handed the ring to Gamaliel. "Wear it until you have completed your commission. I will expect to hear from you daily."

"But this Archelaus. Is he or is he not in the palace?"

"Have you been listening, Rabbi? I have no idea. He may not even exist. I have only rumors and hearsay, the veracity of which, as I have just explained, is less than reliable. You people have a talent for obfuscation and complex thinking that quite dismays me. You should be able to sort through this tangle as well as anyone. Do that and who knows, you may have your killer."

"But—"

"There is no *but*, Rabban. Your Holy Days will last seven days and have just begun. You have Shabbat coming and I understand nothing will be accomplished on that day. A foolish rule in my view. What do you do if you are under siege? At any rate, because of your Sabbath, I will give you an octave. Eight days, Rabban, and then I expect a solution."

With those words, the great Pilate stood and stalked away, leaving Gamaliel to ponder what he should do and, more importantly, what he should not do. His issue with Caiaphas faded away with the morning mist.

Chapter IV

Gamaliel stood immobile in the center of the atrium and watched Pilate disappear into the clamorous streets of Jerusalem. Somewhere nearby a late blooming tree dropped its petals and they, borne on a soft breeze, fell like early snow. A string of servants passed him on their way to the kitchens carrying bundles of foodstuffs. The king did not stint on comfort, not even in a palace he rarely used and irrespective of the occasion. Gamaliel wondered what would have been in the bundles the previous week during the Day of Atonement. Judging from this king's demonstrated spiritual inertia, probably pretty much the same.

He had stood at the Prefect's departure. Now he sat again. What an odd assignment to task a Talmudic scholar. What should he do next? His expertise was in divining the mind of the Lord from dry and dusty ancient scrolls. He had little or no experience in sorting through the cluttered minds of humans. The old man assigned to him waited anxiously in the shade of a small date palm shifting his weight from foot to foot like a child who needed to excuse himself. A pair of beaded women's-sized sandals, evidently hastily abandoned by their wearer, lay beneath the same palm. If he were truly a solver of human mysteries rather than the witness to spiritual ones, he might have thought they were a clue. Since he wasn't, he didn't, and they weren't.

"Barak, you are a servant in the king's palace, I presume. Tell me what you understand of this business."

"Yes, sir. I am. I can tell you all there is to know. You see it was I who found the unfortunate woman there in the bath." He shivered at the memory and pointed to his right at an archway set in the palace's wall. Gamaliel assumed it must lead to the previously mentioned bath.

"Through there? Suppose you show me this place and tell me what happened, how you came upon the murdered woman and what happened next." For better or for worse, his inquiries into the death of the servant girl had begun. Where they would ultimately lead, he could only guess but he wasn't optimistic about their eventual outcome.

The old man led him through the archway into the bath. It bore no resemblance at all to the *mikvah* Gamaliel expected, or rather hoped to see. Instead it more closely mimicked the baths common to Romans and pagans he had heard about, but had never visited. The air, heavy with water vapor, still bore the pungent scents of olive oil, cinnamon, and exotic perfumes from the east, the residue of the previous evening's bathers. His experience with scents of any sort was extremely limited, the product of a self-imposed ascetic life. He cast his gaze upwards and took in the mosaics on the ceiling. A cascade of nymphs and satyrs cavorted across the heights, their intentions clearly not a thing the Rabban wished to plumb. Greek pantheism and its complex, erratic, not to mention erotic relationships stubbornly refused to make sense to him. Joining them in their antics were men and women all of whom, judging by their attire or lack thereof, were fully prepared to join in the same behavior. His direct knowledge of activities at places like this was limited to what he'd read and heard and he shuddered at the thought that the King of the Jews, even this attenuated branch, would condone it, much less support it in his palace. Gamaliel did not consider himself a prude or squeamish about most things, yet for this display of crass nudity and sensuality, an obvious pagan scene, to be included in a Jewish residence, palace or not, bordered on the blasphemous. What sort of king had we here?

He knew, of course. Everyone knew that this Herod Antipas had no more faith than his father, which is to say his religious practice was strictly a political and public undertaking. He was, after all, only one generation from the pagan practices of an Edomite. Gamaliel sighed in the sure knowledge that the king was not alone in that paltry level of belief. Many of the Sanhedrin, though they would deny it vehemently, shared it with him. He blamed it on Alexander the Macedonian who had Hellenized the country centuries before and even now there seemed no way to eradicate his continuing influence.

"I came here in the sixth hour of the night," Barak was saying, "And I noticed the water in the bath is not quite right."

"How, 'not quite right,' Barak?"

"Well, sir you can see for yourself. It's all discolored. Red it was. That's why I didn't see the girl at first. Because of the water being red-like."

Gamaliel pivoted and took in the scene. The bath water steamed as the cool morning air wafted through the arch from outside. He stepped to the edge of the bath to look at it. It was discolored certainly. Across from him on the pool's lip the body of the girl lay under a sheet of some sort.

"Where was this dead woman, when you found her?"

"Why, in the bath, of course. How else could blood have filled the water?"

"I can think of several ways Barak, but that is not important just now. So, you came in at the sixth hour, midnight, you say. Was that your duty, or were you simply wandering about in the middle of the night?"

"Oh no, sir. I had the watch last night. I was to check this room and the adjoining atrium. Check the lamps for oil, pick up any debris from the evening's revelries, and so on."

"Revelries? A Holy Feast is upon us and Shabbat just over and the king is not fasting and preparing to celebrate Tabernacles?"

Barak barely suppressed a smile. "No, Rabban, he is not. Not in this house. Most nights there was feasting and music and later many of the court would repair to this place and—"

"Men and women together?" Gamaliel had heard of the license taken by the occupants of the king's court but he'd always supposed it was mere gossip, the product of envious men. It appeared to be true. He shook his head. "Continue with your narrative, Barak. You said it was about the sixth hour. Measured how?"

"The guard makes a circuit of the palace. Three circuits take an hour, he says. When he said he'd done eighteen of them, I was sent on my rounds. Well, there is not much more to tell. I came in here, saw the water, saw the girl, and raised the alarm."

"And then?"

"Then the guards came and so did Chuzas, the king's steward. They sealed off the bath, set the palace guards to seal off the bath, and pulled the body out and laid her over there," he pointed to the shrouded form, "and went away leaving me to watch over her until morning." Barak shuddered at the memory and tilted his head toward the three men standing at the three entrances to the room, one to the atrium from which they had just come, and two at the arched doorways leading to various parts of the palace. "The guards are still here as you can see."

"No one has entered since?"

"Only yourself and the Prefect, of course. It is as it was when I found her."

"Nothing removed, no one tried to come in?"

"Not that I am aware of, no sir. Wait, I forgot—the man Graecus looked in, I think, but did not enter. The steward's orders, you see."

Gamaliel stared at the murky water. Aside from the fact it impeded his ability to investigate the bath further, blood in the water raised some serious questions about purity. It could not remain this way, obviously. "Can this pool be drained?"

"Indeed, yes. There is a clever hole in the bottom that can be unplugged and the water will flow away into the valley. It is drained when the king is not in residence."

"I want the plug pulled. Can you do it?"

Barak frowned uncertainly. "There is a device, I believe, that allows it to be pulled somewhere about, but I do not know where it is kept. Otherwise, I will have to climb in the bath and pull it by hand,"

"It is unclean. I do not want you to do that. Send for someone to find the device and empty this pool. Let us hope that a spate of bloody water appearing in the valley does not start a panic and a call for Father Moses to appear and strike it with his staff. Now, let us have a quick look at the corpse."

"Sir, must I?'

"I need you to witness everything I do, Barak, so that later, if there are questions, you can verify my account of things. Yes, please pull that sheeting back so that I may see for myself."

Barak did as he was asked but Gamaliel noticed he averted his eyes from the woman's nakedness. Gamaliel had no such scruples. The woman was dead. Were she still alive, it would have been different, of course. He bent closer and inspected the body. Her throat had been slashed, he could see that. There did not seem to be any other obvious marks on her.

He stood erect and scratched his beard. What to do next? Interview the household, of course. The King? Queen? Princess? This Menahem person, and what of the ubiquitous Archelaus? Would anyone admit his presence? Did anyone know of it? Did he, as the Prefect implied, even exist?

"Barak, I want you to do two more things for me. After you find someone to empty the pool, go up to and through the Sheep Gate. Ten paces on your right you will find the dwelling of the physician, Loukas. Tell him that I require his presence immediately. If he demurs, describe this ring to him and tell him who currently wears it." He held the ring out for Barak to see. "Then I wish you to summon the king's steward for me."

Barak scurried off. Gamaliel replaced the sheet over the dead woman and began a careful reconnaissance of the room. If Barak told the truth, the room would be as it was when the body was found. Perhaps there would be something left here to indicate how this terrible thing came about.

He circled the area and the entrances several times picking up odds and ends and memorizing where he'd found them. A pile of clothing, probably the dead girl's, lay in a heap under a bench. There were palm fronds, empty jars still sweet smelling from the ointments they once contained, but nothing he would describe as significant or lacking an explanation for its presence. He was still at it when Barak returned with Loukas the physician.

Chapter V

Barak scurried off to find the steward. Gamaliel escorted the physician to the body. He slipped back the sheet. The woman, he now saw clearly, was a young girl, almost a child.

"I have been tasked by our Prefect to discover the nature of this death, Physician. I do not know why, and I do not know how I am to do it, but there it is. I will need all the help I can get and I immediately thought of you. So here is the victim. I know nothing more than what you can see for yourself except I am told she met her death around the middle of the watch. Tell me about this murder. What can this unfortunate girl say to us from the grave?"

Loukas shook his head. "Such a pity, she can't be more than fifteen or sixteen. I need to place her on a table where I can examine her more closely. Can I use that one?" He indicated a broad marble table that more than likely held food and drink in better times. Gamaliel nodded his assent but made no move to help lift the body onto the smooth surface. The physician made no comment. He knew enough about observant Jews to appreciate, if not completely comprehend, the complex laws regarding food, corpses, the living, and the dead.

The king's steward arrived and Gamaliel turned his attention to him, leaving the Greek to do his postmortem study of the dead girl.

"Steward, greetings in the name of the Lord. Am I correct in remembering you are called Chuzas?" The round little man nodded his assent. "As you have surely heard by now, I am commissioned by the Prefect with the concurrence of your king, to investigate the death of the girl in this room last night. Why that is so will have to be a question for another day."

"I heard, Rabban, but neither do I understand why, with respect to yourself, of course. She was no more than a servant girl, not even one of ours, strictly speaking, but brought here from some other land. And of another faith." Chuzas shrugged his dismissal of the whole notion of wasting anyone's time and particularly that of someone as important as the Rabban of the Sanhedrin on a matter into the death, however violent, of a foreign servant girl.

"That may be so, Steward, but hers was a life, nonetheless, a life taken before its appointed time and, more importantly, a life taken in the king's palace. The latter elevates its significance and therefore, we must account for it. Can you tell me what you know of the events of last night? Who feasted, who bathed, who seemed to be behaving suspiciously, and so on? I have only Barak's testimony but he had no part in the festivities, if that is what they were. He was only the poor soul who found the murdered girl."

"In truth, Rabban, I cannot tell you much more or recall anything beyond the general state of things. The court assembled as usual and dined. Musicians played, dancers danced..."

"Perhaps the dead girl was among the dancers?" Visions of a lissome Princess Salome whom he'd recently discussed with the Prefect, resurfaced. He pushed the image aside.

"The girl? I do not think so. No, she served at the queen's table, I believe."

"You believe? Surely as the king's steward, you would know the location and duty of every person in service to your master."

"Yes, but you see..." Chuzas looked away and shuffled his expensively sandaled feet against the floor tiles.

"What are you not telling me, Steward?"

"In point of fact," he said, looking extremely uncomfortable as he did so, "she is not of the king's household."

"Not?"

"This is awkward." Chuzas' gaze drifted away again to inspect the fresco on the near wall. "She is in the party of the queen."

"Herodias, the Queen, is not considered part of the household? I think you must have misspoken."

"It is complicated, Rabban."

"Most of life is, Steward."

"Yes, of course. This girl came to us when the queen…when the first…I do not wish to forward scandal or speak ill of the royal family—"

"Let me guess, then. What you are suggesting is this girl might have witnessed the adulterous liaisons of Herodias and Antipas before the separation, divorce, and remarriage and so had to be brought along from Philip's court to keep the secret safe. Servants talk, do they not? Am I close?"

The steward seemed to be sweating and Gamaliel did not think it had as much to do with the steamy ambiance of the bath as with the subject matter under discussion. He cleared his throat with a great deal of huffing and heaving. "I honestly do not know, Rabban. It is a delicate um…yes, near enough, I don't know." he finally murmured.

"So then is it reasonable to suggest that this girl was in fact part of the entourage of the prince, Archelaus, who, it is rumored, traveled from the north somewhere to Herod Philip before he subsequently dropped out of sight in Cappadocia?"

"Who? Archelaus? I have no knowledge of Philip's court or… Archelaus? Why would you think that, Rabban?" Actually, I am guessing, Gamaliel thought. A stab in the dark but it did not strike home. Well, so much for international intrigue. Why did Pilate even bring up the man's name? "With respect for you and your office, no one can say what the circumstances were before our king took his new bride. I never served the king's half brother so I cannot say whether this, who did you say…Archelaus?… Certainly not him, I should think. I have no knowledge of who may have come or gone to Caesarea Philippi."

"Of course not. Very well. I only ask because the Prefect tells me he heard the man in question may be in Jerusalem now and the logical conclusion would be that he would be here with his uncle and if so, he suggested, it could help solve this mystery."

"Could it indeed? I am afraid the Prefect is mistaken. He is not one of us, and certainly not native to the area, so he could not know. It is, after all, my responsibility to know who comes and goes and when they do so in the palace. There is no Archelaus here, prince or otherwise, not now, not ever."

"Yes, I see. Well then, is it remotely possible this girl met her end because she knew of the king and queen's illicit liaison and possession of this knowledge, if shared with the wrong people, could someday embarrass the king?"

"Surely you are not implying the king had anything to do with—"

"I am only speculating, Steward."

"Of course. I suppose anything is possible, but who would credit the gossip of a servant girl?"

"Who indeed? But that works both ways, does it not?"

"Sir?"

"If she did in fact possess this sordid knowledge and were killed because of it, who, as you indicated in your own reaction to her death, would care? And then there would be an end of even the possibility of a threat to the throne."

"I see. Put that way, it is possible. That assumes there was such knowledge to be had and I do not think there was."

"Really? Very well, that brings us back to the royal couple and their marriage. Steward, I believe you are not a fool. Therefore, do not assume others are. It takes no perceptive skills to put the truth together in the matter of the king and queen and how they came to be married."

"Truth is sometimes difficult to discern."

"Nonsense. Balaam's ass discerned the truth. Any person with his eyes open and his ears clear of wax can tell you the truth of the matter. No, Steward, truth is not difficult to discern.

Falsehood, on the other hand, can be very confusing. So why are you attempting to confuse me?"

"Rabban," Chuzas fluttered, "I am not...you do not think that I—"

"Enough. You have things to sort, it appears. Details you wish to present to me in a different light perhaps, after you have thought them through. I will end this interview and ask you to return here tomorrow. In the meantime, please send to me at intervals any and all of the serving staff, musicians, and so on, who might have been party to the events of last night beginning with the dining. I wish particularly to speak with anyone who may have ended their evening in this bath. When I am finished with them I will ask you to introduce me to the king, the queen, the Princess Salome, this Menahem person thought to be the king's foster brother, and anyone else staying in the palace as the king's guest."

"Yes, sir. Will there be anything else?"

"No...yes, I want the dead girl's things gathered together and placed in safekeeping until I have a chance to go through them."

"That may be difficult. They will have been rifled and expropriated by the other servants by now."

"Then you will take one or more of the palace guards and retrieve all of them. I must have everything as it was if I am to unravel this snarl."

Gamaliel sent Chuzas away and turned back to the physician.

"What have you for me so far, Loukas?"

"Ah, it is most interesting. Tell me, Honorable Sir, what is the left hand used for?"

"The left hand? It is the dirty hand, of course. It is used for all those functions not fitting to be discussed or of an impure nature."

"Precisely. Whoever killed this young girl was *sinistromanual*, an unusual state in this day."

"My murderer was left-handed? That is most unusual, I agree. How do you come to that finding?"

"Observe the cut. It has been made from the right to the left. A right-handed assassin would have slashed left to right."

"That is most interesting. You can tell this from the cut?"

"I believe so, yes, from the depth and direction. Here is another question for you. If the killer felt what he was doing or touching qualified as impure or dirty—your words—would he not use his left hand to do it?"

"That is very possible, and suggests other possibilities for our murderer. He is a low person who does not quibble about which hand is used for what and is naturally left-handed. He is scrupulous and deigns not to use his right hand in this dirty work. Or..."

"Or?"

"He wishes to leave us with a message."

"A message?"

"Yes. It is most interesting, is it not? There is another possibility, of course, but I can hardly accept it."

"That being?"

"Our killer is an Ehud."

"A what?"

"Ehud, the son of Gara, and a left-handed man sent by the Lord to deliver the children of Israel from the Moabites. He killed Eglon, their king, by stabbing him with his left hand. One expects to see a weapon in a warrior's right hand, not his left, you see? The king was taken unawares. So, an Ehud."

"You might wish to add one more. Your killer is an outsider, a barbarian who does not value or care about your laws or your traditions."

"A barbarian? I think not, Physician. Not in the king's court and unknown to us," He paused and thought a moment. "There was mention of a man called Graecus. Perhaps...This speculation assumes our killer faced the girl, but could he not have stood behind her when he drew the knife?"

"No, I don't think so. There are bruises on her right shoulder that suggest he held her facing him when he drew the knife. You see," he pointed to a bluish mark on the girl's upper arm, "this could very well be the mark made by his thumb. There are four similar, but smaller marks on the back of her arm that would be from his fingers. But more importantly, note the direction. If he faces her and slashes, the knife moves across and down. If he stands behind her, the knife moves across and up. Here is the next piece of your puzzle. Your victim was murdered in the pool."

"We know that. The water is discolored with her blood, you see."

"Yes, but that is not what I meant. She was held under the water, then had her throat slit. The cut is deep enough so that she would have died anyway, but she drowned because of it."

"Had our villain removed her from the bath and not cut her, she might have lived?"

"Possibly."

"She drowned because she was slashed, or instead?"

"Who can say whether the drowning was cause or effect? But it is another reason I think he did not stand behind her. He would need to hold her head underwater. One last thing for now, more detail can only come after I take her away and inspect her more closely in the privacy I require." Gamaliel raised his eyebrows at that. He guessed, but did not wish to have confirmed what he would do to the girl's body. He'd heard rumors about dissection and assumed this man knew them too.

"That is?"

"She was only just recently relieved of her virginity."

"She was still a maiden, forced, and then killed?"

"So it would seem."

"Interesting."

"No, Rabban, sinister."

<>◇><>

Gamaliel left the humidity of the bath and seated himself outside on a bench in the atrium. He wanted some time to think through what he'd learned thus far while he waited for the first of what would be a long string of servants, cup bearers, dancers, and slaves of indeterminate occupations, age, and race.

Then there would be Chuzas' staff, plus that devious little man himself once again.

The task of interviewing the king's entourage took the entire morning through the sixth hour. Gamaliel managed to refresh himself with a crust of bread and some broiled fish that he washed down with a cup of passable wine at midday. He resumed his interrogations on into the afternoon, ending them toward the tenth hour as the sun began its long descent to the west and his voice began to fail. The steward had outdone himself in ordering the interviews. He'd organized them by groups sharing the same or similar functions, dancers, servers, players of music and singers, cup bearers, table clearers, and some whose occupation he could not remember. The most difficult interviews were the concubines. Gamaliel thought of himself as moderately current in the ways of a world regrettably driven by a Greek culture and tempered by Roman proclivities, but the frankness, dress, and demeanor of this last group left him deeply disturbed. How could anyone sift through this household for the presence of a single evildoer, when it seems it lurked in every corridor and during every night in the persons of these women and the men or man who kept them?

"But what of Solomon and his thousand?" his students would have asked him, to which he would reply "And what of David and Uriah the Hittite's wife? 'It is a matter of intent. Unfortunately the Law does not spell that out, so we must.'" He knew, as everyone did, that there were political necessities that gathered wives to a king, and then there were the strictly lust-driven liaisons that kings also enjoyed. No one, he thought with some annoyance, should ever confuse the two.

Before he made his weary way back to his quarters west of the Temple he called Chuzas to him.

"Steward, aside from the royals, have I seen and interviewed all of the people I need to see?" Chuzas hesitated. Gamaliel knew in that moment that the steward would soon tell him a lie. He had not developed this ability to smell out mendacity just to vet potential students. "Again, Steward, what are you so reluctant to tell me? I must get to the bottom of this matter and I do not wish to waste any more time at it than absolutely necessary."

"On my—"

"Do not swear an oath to me, Chuzas. You have enough to answer for without adding that to your list."

"I…" Chuzas obviously wrestled with the desire to deceive on the one hand and the realization he could not fool the Rabban. "There may be one or two others who were not available. He…that is to say, they were not available, they were away temporarily."

"He has a name, Chuzas?"

The steward rolled his eyes in desperate search for a way out of his predicament. Finally he swallowed and blurted, "He is called, Graecus."

"The Greek? He is Greek."

"Yes. At least it is what he claims."

"But you are not sure?"

"It is not my place, Excellency."

"Not your place? This man alone escapes your notice and responsibility? You are the king's steward and you say 'It is not my place?' Very well. Then hear this, I will interview this man immediately on his return. See to it, Steward."

Gamaliel turned on his heel and stalked home. He arrived just as the third star appeared in the east. He signaled for his servant not to speak until he'd made his ritual cleansing in the *mikvah* and had some time to pray. After this day and the company he'd been forced to keep, he would need to spend more time in the living water than usual.

Yom Shlishi

Chapter VI

The next morning he sent a simple message to Pilate informing him that he had nothing to report and that there was no sighting of the phantom, Archelaus. Furthermore, as he was convinced the man did not exist, at least not in Jerusalem, he had no intention in pursuing that line anymore. Finally, he guessed he would need much more time than either had supposed necessary to track down the girl's killer.

He also assumed that Pilate would not grant it.

He dreaded the trip back to the palace. Murder, rape, and palace intrigue were as far from his normal life, the one he desperately wished he could return to, as the moon is from the sun. Were it not for Pilate's reputation as an implacably brutal man who brooked no dissent, he would have folded the whole business up as an unsolvable mystery and returned to his scrolls, books, and students. As that did not appear to be a viable option, he trudged on to the palace, his timeline now reduced to seven days, one of which would be Shabbat when nothing of substance could be done. Barak met him at the gate and escorted him once again to the bath house.

He had fulfilled his order; servants had been tasked to drain the bath. They had done so during the night. They had also been instructed to leave anything left in it undisturbed. Gamaliel stood at the bath's edge and contemplated how best to proceed. The area was not deep and he would have no trouble entering or leaving, but there remained puddles of bloody water and all of the items in it, if any, would be similarly befouled. He sighed with resignation and lowered himself into the now empty but fetid space and began to scan the bottom. What appeared to be a scarf of some sort lay in one corner, still soggy and stained with blood. He used a stick to spread it out. The folds revealed nothing. He lifted it to the pool's rim with the stick and resumed his search. He moved carefully across the width of the pool, back and forth, and at each transit moved one pace closer to the opposite end. He found a handful of coins of various origins and denominations which he placed in a leather pouch he wore beneath his cloak. Further along he found a ceramic medallion of foreign design. A cubit farther a cut leather thong still knotted at one point along its length lay like a soggy snake against the pool's edge. In one corner he discovered a small cloth that served as some sort of undergarment, perhaps belonging to, and more likely lost by a woman, probably the dead girl although there was no certainty as to that. As it seemed unlikely the bathers and frolickers were segregated by gender, the Law's proscription of sharing water with the opposite sexes had not applied to this bath, at least not on the night of the murder.

At the far end lay what he hoped for but did not expect to find: a knife of foreign design glittered against the tiles. Judging by the gold inlay and semi-precious stones set in its handle he surmised it to be valuable and that caused him to frown as well. He lifted it carefully and set it on the ledge of the pool with the other items. It might or might not be the weapon used to finish the girl. It seemed unlikely a knife, any knife, would be left to corrode in the water on the one hand, and what sort of killer would leave the murder weapon at the scene of his crime? He also had to concede that he knew little or nothing about criminals, criminal behavior, or the likelihood one would or would not leave incriminating evidence behind. But it did seem unlikely.

Barak announced the arrival of the steward. Gamaliel sighed again and climbed back to floor level.

"Let us speak outside in the atrium, Steward. It is uncommonly hot and sticky in this place. Do you suppose we could have some incense burned in here until we are finished with this area?"

Chuzas nodded and told Barak to see to it. He paused on the way out and stared at the knife. "Is that the weapon used to murder the girl?"

"Possibly, I don't know. Is it likely? I will not be able to say one way or the other until I have made certain tests on it."

In truth he had no idea how to determine if a knife, any knife, were the one that had slashed the girl's throat. He rather hoped, but he guessed in vain, that Loukas, the clever physician, would know how to do that. In any event, he intended for the steward to believe him capable of accomplishing such a feat. The steward, he assumed would soon spread that belief among the servants, and thence throughout the palace. If the right person heard of it and believed such a test were possible, it could cause that someone to panic and make the move which in turn would relieve Gamaliel of the need to continue his detection.

"Was there anything else in the pool that could help identify a murderer?" The steward looked hopeful.

"A few bits and pieces only. A medallion, something I took to be a scarf but now realize must have been the girl's headdress, some coins, and some discarded clothing. Tell me, Steward, is it the king's practice to have women share his bath with men?"

Chuzas reverted to hemming and hawing. He obviously knew the proscription in the law about such an arrangement. Gamaliel waited patiently for his answer. How would this conflicted man wiggle out of this one?

"It is the king's wish," he began, hesitated, and shrugged. Gamaliel understood. The family of Herod, father and sons, descending from Idumean stock through multiple pairings, were Jewish only to the extent they needed to be. In reality, they were nearly as Latin as their overlords. Their princes were sent to Rome to serve as hostages against a possible attempted break with Rome, but at the same time to be schooled with the sons of Senators and Caesars. They took their names from Roman and pagan heroes. Brides were secured from other countries, other cultures, other faiths. How long the Lord would permit this apostate intrusion in the line of David remained a constant source of irritation and debate between Gamaliel, his students, and the nation as a whole. But it had been a long time since the line could be described as legitimate and the prospects for restoration any time soon grew less likely with every passing year.

Chuzas shuffled his feet and mopped his brow with a scrap of linen. "Perhaps if I were to view the items you found in the bath, I could identify them and that would help determine who might have…" The steward's voice trailed off. Gamaliel wondered about that. Why this sudden shift in willingness to find the culprit from the man who earlier seemed anxious to see the whole business covered up? If he grew as old as Methuselah, he would never understand these royal sycophants.

"Later possibly, Steward, now I wish you to tell me, with as much precision as you can, the events of the night before last. What happened, where, with whom, and finally, who and/or what went on in the bath."

The steward rambled on for nearly an hour providing details Gamaliel did not need and, he assumed, omitting those he did. The upshot of the discourse was Chuzas had nothing of substance to add to what Gamaliel, indeed everyone, already knew. The king allowed his court to consort openly in the bath with both sexes present and uncensored. It remained unclear if the king may have done so himself in private with the queen and/or his concubines. But the latter was of no immediate consequence, unless the matter of the king's standing with the Lord was to be taken into account, and that was not part of Gamaliel's immediate charge.

He dismissed the steward with a caution and the request to arrange his interviews with the royals.

Chapter VII

Caiaphas, High Priest in the line of Aaron, Arbiter of Israel, and proud bearer of the symbols of high office when permitted access to them by the Prefect, owed his position to the beneficence of the emperor and the sufferance of Pilate. The former ruled far away in self-imposed exile from the Isle of Capri and even then as only the latest in an ever changing kaleidoscope of monarchs whose personae shifted, sometimes wildly, in attitude, temperament, and mental stability. Thus, Caiaphas lived in a perpetual state of malaise. He knew that at any moment and at the whim of either the Prefect or that distant sovereign, he could find himself relegated back to the ranks of the serving priests whose numbers were far too great to offer him much in the way of influence or precedence. His father-in-law, Annas, had suffered such degradation, and he, Caiaphas, determined he would avoid a similar fate whatever the cost.

In addition to these politic concerns, there were frequent questions raised among the people regarding his legitimacy as High Priest. His Sadducee leanings did not sit well with the populace in general and Pharisees in particular, whose support the theocracy he oversaw required. The people expected their Priest to have derived from the line defined by Leviticus, not be thrust on them by a ruler they despised and a Prefect they feared. When combined, these shifting uncertainties made him chronically dyspeptic and suspicious of those around him. He saw plots where none existed. He spent hours uncovering and dismantling those that did. He surrounded himself with cronies and sycophants, who alternately supported him, plotted against him, and advised him, not always in helpful ways. He did not trust the Prefect and he realized the Prefect did not trust him in return, a situation that daily ate at his spirit.

This state of affairs undoubtedly explained his obsession with his critics real and imagined. The late Baptizer, for one, had been a major thorn in his side. He might have been the only person of note to have applauded Herod's bloody end to the "Angel of the Desert," as a few Galilean romantics had taken to calling him. Now, there were these would-be Messiahs popping up, chiefly this eccentric but increasingly popular rabbi from the Galilee who, incidentally, could claim a connection with the Baptizer as well—a situation which severely compromised the High Priest's ability to deal directly with him. So many people had foolishly believed the Baptizer to have been a true prophet. Because this new rabbi had received the dead man's endorsement as the Coming One, Caiaphas desperately needed someone of Gamaliel's stature to challenge him and put an end to his teaching and criticism of the Sanhedrin, the Temple, and common sense. This self-proclaimed rabbi's growing popularity, Caiaphas believed, posed a threat aimed at him personally, at the Temple, and at the Nation in general.

Gamaliel had thus far shown no inclination to accede to the task he'd asked of him—to take this upstart down— and now he had been co-opted by the Prefect to settle some inconsequential business at the palace. He claimed this assignment prevented him from pursuing the High Priest's matter further. It would not do. He needed the Rabban to act and he didn't care what the Prefect wanted. There were the demands of Rome and there were those from the Lord, he thought. The latter should take precedence.

After a day of fuming at what he believed to be a deliberate slight, however instigated by Pilate, he determined that if the Rabban could not come to him as requested, he would go to the Rabban. Such a move could be viewed by the Temple staff as a reduction in his position and certainly unusual to say the least.

The High Priest did not wait on anyone. But he must make this exception. All this he explained in detail to Jabez ben Ratzon, his newest aide, who nodded and agreed, rather too obsequiously Caiaphas thought. He also caught the look in Jabez's eye when he thought his back was turned. This young man had ambition but not much in the way of intelligence, a not particularly promising combination in any young man so awkwardly gifted. Was he yet another potential threat to the High Priest? Caiaphas felt acid spike in his stomach.

In the end, he sent messengers out to locate the Rabban. It was enough that he would go to Gamaliel, but he refused to be seen wandering about the city in search of him. The messengers would locate him and keep him in sight. Caiaphas would then be led directly to him. He hoped that would allow him to maintain some small measure of dignity.

⟨⟩⟨⟩⟨⟩

Gamaliel sat in the atrium of Antipas' Palace deep in thought when the High Priest announced his presence. He'd brought with him only a small entourage. Hoping, Gamaliel supposed, that it would draw less attention and at the same time provide fewer witnesses to what could be an embarrassment to him at the hands of the Rabban.

"Rabban, greetings in the Name."

Gamaliel stood and bowed. "High Priest, I greet you equally. I regret I could not attend you as you requested but, as I believe you have been told, the Prefect had enlisted me in this affair and I could not refuse. Be assured, this employment is not of my choosing or liking."

"Of course, I understand. The Prefect can be very insistent."

"And the task important, at least he believes it to be. I am of a different mind but —"

Caiaphas waved off these last remarks and signaled Gamaliel to resume his seat presumably to consider how best to convince this man of the danger the rabble surrounding the troublemaker from Nazareth posed.

Gamaliel settled in to hear the High Priest out. He knew what would be forthcoming and why the High Priest thought it so important. He would listen with half an ear and the same time could be used to think through the events of the last two days and try to make some sense of them. The steward had been far too eager to inspect and identify the odd bits and pieces he'd removed from the pool. He wished he knew why. Barak's telling of the events he assumed to be the most accurate because he had the least to hide. Thus, every account from the others he'd heard should be measured against that of Barak. The royals, he admitted to himself, would not tell the truth. It was their nature to dissemble if they felt threatened and often they did so simply out of habit. Certainly the Prefect's interest in the events would be taken as a threat to them, so they would position themselves carefully.

Often, he thought, the truth could only be found in the spaces between the words, not in the words themselves, like the mortar between bricks. If anything useful would come from their accounts, it must be pried loose from the discontinuities in their stories. Still he would need to query them and then search the interstices and crevices.

Caiaphas droned on. "You see our position?" he'd said and seemed to be waiting for a response. Gamaliel did, indeed, appreciate the High Priest's position and thanked the Lord he did not share it, or ever would. The High Priest lived in a constant fear of being deposed—by the emperor or by the Lord. Perhaps by both and perhaps justifiably. No one of his acquaintance would be upset if he were. So in the case of this annoying rabbi, what should he say to Caiaphas? What could he say? Like a stubborn captain of a ship, Caiaphas had set his course and neither threat of storms nor becalming would persuade him to alter it.

"I believe, High Priest, that your best course, our best course, is to do nothing. If this man is a fraud, as you and I both believe, he will eventually blow away like sand in the desert."

Caiaphas scowled. Clearly this was not the message he wished to hear.

"Hear me out, High Priest. If he is what he claims to be, then you cannot stop him no matter what you or I will do, nor should you. Moreover, if his movement takes hold, we will have our hands full trying to catch up, will we not? My advice is, stay calm and wait. And in all events, ignore him. It is a maxim that the opposite of love is not hate. The opposite of both is indifference. If you wish to destroy an idea, ignore it. Attacking it will only draw more attention to the subject and have the reverse effect to the one you envision. Reportedly, this man is barely educated, mildly to extremely heretical, but no threat to you or the Nation at the moment that I can see. I admit I have not heard him myself and am relying on students and friends to guide me here. But, having said that, I urge you do not give him *gravitas* by persecuting him. No good can come of it. Trust the Lord to manage the heresies, his followers, and his lack of depth. My students track him almost every day. I will let you know if and when he crosses the line."

Caiaphas did not seem pleased. His face turned bright red as if he'd spent too many hours in the sun.

"This will not do, Rabban. I must have this matter settled."

"I cannot see why, High Priest. The man has done nothing more or less than a handful of others have done before him. You can see the results of those claims. How is this one any different from, say, Judas of the Galilee, who at least fought and eliminated a small contingent of Roman soldiers before he ended up on a cross?"

Caiaphas sputtered and stood. "I am not done with this, Rabban. I need someone to pursue this. As you are not willing, perhaps the Temple requires a stronger Rabban."

"Perhaps it does. The Sanhedrin can always choose to replace me and it can do so at anytime. Since you are determined to see this through, I would suggest that you might put young Jabez or Ehud on it. They are both extremely clever and able. I am certain one or the other will find a solution to your problem."

"Jabez ben Ratzon has red hair. People like that are unreliable and I do not trust him."

Gamaliel let this *non sequitur* pass. What a man's hair color had to do with anything he could not imagine. Caiaphas rose, obviously ill pleased, made his farewell and huffed from the atrium. The poor man, he thought, has too much on his mind, and his problems so many and varied and all compounded further by the fact he is an unreconstructed Sadducee. Not that being a Sadducee presented a problem in and of itself. There were days, indeed most days, when Gamaliel's own position might fairly be described as that of a Sadducee. He would deny it of course, but he knew the value of integration with gentile society. There was a line that separated Greek practice and Judaism as delivered in scripture that needed to be observed. That line should not be crossed and Caiaphas, of late, often crossed it. Centuries had passed and yet Alexander's Hellenism continued to color the culture and divide the Nation. Ironically, for the most part most people did not know how they thought about it personally, but they knew what they wanted their High Priest to think.

Gamaliel watched his colleague and sometime nemesis leave the court. He sat down on the bench once again and turned his thoughts back to the problem at hand: how to question the royals. Could he truly expect any hope of hearing anything of value from them?

Chapter VIII

The king's steward arranged the interviews with the royal family to begin with the Princess Salome. In spite of Gamaliel's objections, the king had insisted that Chuzas also sit in on each interview. Furthermore, he required an hour to elapse between each interview. The ploy was as transparent as the wrappings on one or two of the resident concubines that Gamaliel had interviewed the previous day; he could object but even the threat implicit in Pilate's ring did not provide him with the means to forestall it. The interviews were to proceed as the king insisted or they would not take place at all. Gamaliel agreed, but made a mental note to describe this process to Pilate if, and he assumed when, the investigation sputtered to the unsatisfactory conclusion he expected.

A private room had been set aside for his meetings. Gamaliel noted sourly that the walls were paneled with latticework painted a dark red. He felt sure that behind some part, perhaps all of it, someone could, and undoubtedly would, sit and eavesdrop on what transpired and they could do so easily and anonymously. Not for the first time he wondered what the purpose of this exercise was: certainly not justice for the girl. To avoid a scandal? In this palace with this king? A ridiculous thought, surely.

This day's work, he decided would not offer up much in the way of useful information. Clearly all the interviewees would be briefed by the steward or listen at the wall or both. Their stories would jibe in every detail and reveal nothing useful. The only way he could see to get around that would be to couch his questions in such a way that at least some of them would not be anticipated. Then, he reminded himself, he would search the "mortar between the bricks."

The Princess Salome swept in and took her place in the chair provided. Gamaliel had not seen the young woman up close before. His previous sighting of the girl allegedly responsible for the death of the Baptizer had only been from a discreet distance. She was a beauty, no denying that. And seeing her close up he understood how easy it must have been for her stepfather to lust after her. When he looked closer he saw that she had the physical makeup, probably inherited from her mother, to go to plump early. Salome, Princess of Judea, should find a husband and quickly for she was destined to become as broad across the middle and as heavy as a Judean merchant's wife. The signs were there.

He cleared his throat, as much to rid it of the overpowering scent that surrounded the princess like an invisible nimbus as from nervousness. "Princess, I will be brief. What can you tell me of the events that took place on the night of the murder? I assume you were there for some of them, is that not so?"

The woman, eyes downcast in a theatrical rendering of ingenuousness, murmured her answer. He could not make out any but two or three words. "I must apologize, Majesty, I am old before my time, it seems, and my hearing is not what it should be. We are in a private room so no one but I will hear what you have to say." He knew it was a lie, and she knew it, too, but he preferred to let the court, or whoever might be lurking behind the lattice, believe he'd not uncovered their sham.

"I am sorry, then, as well, Rabban. I said that I attended the dining and stayed for some of the music. My poor head hurt so that as soon as I thought it proper or sufficient, I left and went to my chambers to lie down. I must have fallen asleep because the next thing I remember is the klaxon sounding and shouting and many men rushing about."

"Did you go to the baths either before or after the dining or the alarm sounding?"

"Rabban! No of course not. It is not my place to bathe in such a public manner."

"I see." The image of her reported nakedness or nearly so before the entire court crossed his mind and he wondered at this assumed modesty on her part. As to her statement, in truth, he did not see how it could be she knew nothing. Her painfully apparent dissembling annoyed him so that even if he wished to believe her, he could not. He reached for the cloth he'd retrieved from the pool the day before. It had dried and he spread it out for her to inspect. It looked fresh and hardly used. "Do you recognize this bit of cloth?"

Salome's eyes dilated briefly. Clearly she did. "No. I don't think so. What is it?"

"What is it? I would have thought you could tell me. I believe, but I am not certain—there are some things not permitted for me to know—that it is a cloth used as some sort of private garment, a small one, in fact. It might have been worn by a boy or a young woman. You don't recognize it now?"

"Where did you find it?"

"Ah, that is the thing, you see. It was in the bath. Whoever wore it that night lost it somehow and it sank to the bottom." He stretched the cloth towards her. "Look again. Perhaps if you see it more closely, some remembrance may occur."

She reached out and took it in her right hand and inspected its edge. "It is not one that belongs to anyone I know," she said and handed it back.

"And you know this how?"

"We mark all our everyday things, *everyday things* you understand, with an initial or a symbol on the edge where the cloth has been hemmed so that after it has been laundered, it will be returned to its proper owner. There is no mark on this piece anywhere."

"I see. Could it have been worn by a guest and left by mistake?"

"I wouldn't know. I told you I was not at the bath. I went to my chambers and fell asleep."

"Yes, so you said. So, you would not have seen a boy or young woman wearing this scrap of cloth. Yes, I see."

The princess stared vacantly at Gamaliel. If he let his imagination run, he would have said she had just the hint of a smile, perhaps a smirk, at the corners of her lips. His experience had only been with sons—his late wife handled their daughters—but he knew adolescent disdain when he saw it.

"One last question. Did you know the dead girl?"

"Cappo? No I did not, well not really. I may have seen her, you know, she served my mother the queen sometimes, but not to speak to. There are protocols, you know. She was only a servant."

"That was her name, Cappo?"

"It is what we called her, so I suppose so."

"Yes, of course. It has been reported to me that the girl was part of your father's, that is to say the king's brother's household, originally. Is that so?"

"She might have been. We don't pay attention to servant girls unless they are part of our personal attendants. They come and they go, so it is difficult for me to say."

"I see. Is there anything you can think of that can be of help to me? I have no doubt the court would like to see me gone soon. I need your help to make that happen."

"Sorry, no. As I said—"

"You retired early, yes, Thank you, Princess. That will be all for now."

She swayed from the room, trailing her scent behind her like a fisherman's lure.

The woman was a liar. That much he now knew for a certainty. She lied about knowing the dead girl and she lied about the cloth, about who wore it, and probably how it came to lie on the bottom of the pool. But whether the lies were important, he could not say. He watched as the young woman, the princess, whose body had caused one man to die and no doubt would bring about the same fate for others before age and childbearing made her heavy and slow, disappeared through the door at the far end of the room.

He would try the mother next. He was sure that if the child could lie with such aplomb, the mother would as well—and doubtless with greater skill.

Chapter IX

The steward escorted the princess out and the door closed on them with a soft thud. Gamaliel waited alone and, he was sure, under close surveillance. Moments later, Chuzas re-entered the room and resumed his seat.

"The queen will attend you shortly. Be forewarned, she is not a patient person and will not likely answer questions she deems too personal or inappropriate to ask of her personage."

"What exactly does that mean, Steward? Are you telling me she will defy the direct request of the Prefect? It is a fact that technically his jurisdiction does not extend into the area ruled by the king, but that rule exists only at the sufferance of the emperor. Surely this household knows from whence its power derives and how tenuous it is. So, she must be aware I am the Prefect's agent in this, and I am no more eager to interrogate her than she is to be interrogated, but it is Pilate's command that I do so, and it is equally her responsibility that she comply. I wish to have done with this onerous task as soon as possible. I would think the royal family would appreciate that and even share it."

"Yes, but you see—"

"I see nothing, but I have no doubt your queen does even as we speak." He turned toward the screens, which one to address he didn't know, so he spoke in both directions. "I would say to her, if she were here, 'Highness, please make both of our days easier and the duration of this investigation shorter and be as forthcoming as you possibly can.'"

The steward sat back in confused silence and glanced anxiously at the wall to the left. So that is where the observers sat—good to know. Who else, Gamaliel wondered sat with her? He guessed his plea may have fallen on deaf ears. He also knew that royalty danced to a different tune played on the *asor* than the rest of humanity. Nothing stirred. He did not expect a response. The queen would not acknowledge the fact she'd eavesdropped in any event. He waited.

"So tell me, Steward, are you married? Are there children in your household? We must keep each other company for the next several days so I would like to know something of you."

"I am, Rabban, married that is. Joanna is my wife. Perhaps, as Rabban, you have heard of her?"

Gamaliel thought he heard the scrape of a chair being moved and furtive footsteps behind the lattice but he could not be sure. He felt a momentary draft on his feet as if a door had been opened and shut somewhere. Cool air with a hint of damp. From where? Some other part of the palace perhaps, but how could that be?

"How would I have heard of your wife, Steward? I get out but seldom and never to the King's Court."

"Not from the court. No, I thought it may have been brought to your attention by the authorities in the Temple. She is one of those who have thrown in with the Galilean rabbi. She was not well and…disturbed you could say."

"Disturbed? What exactly does that mean?"

"She behaved oddly. She attributes her healing to the rabbi. So now, she supports him with her time and my money."

"Does she indeed? And how do you feel about that? Have you so little money you cannot forfeit some of it in that way?"

"To give money to a rabbi is a good thing so we are taught. Is it not written that you do the Lord's work when you pay the teachers? How can I object? It is not so much the money as… the other thing."

"The other thing? First, it is true enough that the teachers deserve your support, but why this one and not some other more noteworthy, more acceptable rabbi, one closer to hand than a Galilean?"

Chuzas only shrugged.

"Did not Solomon tell us, 'Two things rob a man of peace, a yelping dog and a forward woman,' Chuzas? Is that the other thing of which you spoke?"

"Yes and, well is it not also written, Rabban, 'A wife of noble character is her husband's crown.' Yes?"

"Yes, 'but a disgraceful one is like decay in his bones.' Be careful with your words. Wisdom has to be discerned, Steward, before it is dispensed. Are you content with her divided loyalty?"

"Divided? How so?"

"Steward, many may wish to dispute it, and I for one have reservations as to the extent of it, but we hold that a wife must first follow the lead of her husband. A woman may not feel this dictum is just, may rail against the imposition it forces upon her, but it is our way. I would soften it if I could. Perhaps someday, I shall. But for now it is as it is. If your Joanna follows a rabbi not of your choosing, her loyalty is divided in three ways. She will be following this rabbi, following her own will, and only lastly following you. This last is highly debatable, but in any event, one third of a wife is no wife at all."

Chuzas face reddened. "What can I do? This man is persuasive and the little I hear of his teaching, attractive. He has other followers in the court, I am ashamed to say. They have the ability to sway the interests of some, in a general way, of course. There is, after all, the Law and so on."

"Yes, and so on…you have a problem to struggle with, my friend. It is a problem that causes you much distress, I gather. That is what I hear in the tone of your answers at any rate. My advice to you is to deal with it directly and soon. Your wife may admire her rabbi, but her loyalty must remain with you."

"You are right, of course. But still, it is not so easy. I am not unaware, Rabban of my position. It is not fair to say I have nothing."

"Indeed? You will tell me of your measures?"

Chuzas looked away and said nothing. Gamaliel studied the man for a moment. "Very well, then tell me, who are these others in the king's household that are in sympathy with this man?"

Chuzas looked uncomfortable. "It is not for me to say, but there are some."

"Not of the king's company?" Chuzas only shrugged and any further thoughts he might have advanced about the rabbi and his putative followers evaporated at the appearance of the queen. The two men stood and bowed.

"Majesty," Gamaliel said. "You are most kind to grant us this hour of your time. I will do my best to be brief and to the point."

Herodias nodded and took her place on the chair prepared for her which, because of her position, had been placed on a low platform so that her head and shoulders were higher than those of the two men.

"Ma'am, can you describe for me the events of the evening in question, that is to say, the night of the murder of the unfortunate young woman?"

"I can add nothing to what I am sure you have been told by everyone else. We dined, there was music, and then the king and I retired. Whatever happened in the baths is not known to us. Had we been aware that some members of the court had adopted the ways of the Romans and the Greeks before them, we most certainly would have put a stop to it. It is a blasphemy, is it not?"

"It is a breach of the Law, certainly. Then you are telling me, Majesty, that neither you nor the king had any knowledge of the events that took place after the evening's dining and entertainment, that is to say, in the baths?"

"Of course not."

"Excuse the impertinence, but how can that be? Everyone in the court seemed to know and many have testified it was a common occurrence. Even Chuzas, your steward knew. Are you saying he did not tell you?"

"I am." She turned on the steward with a scowl. "You were remiss, Steward. Your negligence in this will be punished."

Well, Gamaliel thought, that's neatly done. Indeed, the mother is not only bolder in her lies than the daughter, but foolishly so. Only someone protected by the royal seal would dare to disclaim what everyone else knew and knew she knew as well.

"I see." He lifted the medallion from the table at his side. Herodias seemed briefly nonplussed. She must have assumed he would ask about the cloth. "Do you, by any chance, recognize this Majesty?" He held it out to her. She took it in her right hand. As she brought it towards her, it slipped from her fingers and fell onto the tiles. Gamaliel reached and retrieved the medallion and did not offer it back to her. Something had changed in its appearance.

"I do not believe I have ever seen the thing," she said.

"No? Well thank you then for your time, I have no further questions."

"Indeed? You summon me from my chambers to ask if I know of this bauble and that is all?"

"For now, yes. You have been most helpful."

She rose and with as much dignity a short and slightly plump woman could manage, swayed from the room. When she had cleared the doorway, Gamaliel leaned to Chuzas and said, "We will see the king after the noonday meal. I have an important errand I must attend to. He rose and left a thoroughly befuddled Chuzas in the center of the room and he guessed several others behind the screen as well.

"Oh, and one more thing, I wish to speak to this man, the king's companion, Menahem, as soon as possible after his Highness."

The beaded curtain rattled behind him as he made for the street.

Chapter X

One could buy nearly anything from fish to furniture in the market street that ran from the king's palace to the temple. Located along its length as well were the craftsmen, molders of clay pots, silver and goldsmiths, and fabricators of jewelry, armor, clothing, and weapons. It was to one of the jewelers that Gamaliel now hurried. He had less than an hour to speak to his man and return to the place for his interview with the king. Enough time, surely, if the jeweler could answer his question. If he could not, tomorrow would be spent elsewhere in the city seeking one that could.

Agon he knew from having briefly taught his son. He was a better jeweler than his son was a Talmudic student and by mutual agreement the son, after his very brief stint as a student, went to Caesarea Maritima to learn a more suitable trade. Study of the Torah was beyond his reach in spite of his genuine enthusiasm, and both parent and teacher knew it.

"Agon, my friend, I have a question for you and I have precious little time to ask and receive your answer."

At the sight of the Rabban of the Sanhedrin, the three customers already in the store bowed and exited, whether from awe, fear, or respect he did not know.

"Rabban, I am your humble servant as always. What is it you wish to know? I will answer if I can."

Gamaliel retrieved the pendent from the leather pouch at his side and laid it on the counter. "You see this pendant?"

"Yes. What is it you wish to know about it?"

"In the process of handing it to someone who shall be nameless, it accidently fell to the floor. You see here, at this point, some of the glaze has been chipped."

Agon picked up the piece and scrutinized it carefully. "Yes, I see that."

"You also see there appears to be metal beneath the glaze and something else as well?"

Agon turned the piece over and back again. "May I inquire where this came from?"

"My friend, for the moment my instinct tells me to withhold that information. There is a story, a bloody story, I fear, which is attached to that item. For your protection, it would be best that you not know where you saw this or what you may discover about it subsequently."

"I see." After such a warning a lesser man might have shown at least some small indication of nervousness, but Agon had served as a soldier in one of the many noncitizen legions, the Roman Auxillae, before he took up the manufacture of precious trinkets. A painful limp and an ugly scar on his left leg attested to his service and its premature end. Gamaliel knew this and enough of the rest of the man's life to know he could be trusted with the task he'd soon be handed.

"What do you want me to do with this thing?"

"I want to know everything about it that can be discerned from it. What do you see?"

"The area where the glazing, if that is truly what this is…I doubt that, by the way…seems to have been engraved with some characters, possibly an inscription. I will venture a guess. It is only a guess, Rabban, be sure of that. This piece has been deliberately covered to disguise it from what it really is. Why, I cannot say. If I could read, I might be more specific. But it begs the question, does it not?"

"Which is?"

"Why would someone cover a golden pendant with this imitation glazing?"

"Why indeed, unless, for some reason, he wished no one read what it says. If we uncover it, we may discover why."

"You wish me to remove this paste covering?"

"Paste? Is that what it is? Maybe, a question first. Are you in possession of the skills necessary to replace it, exactly replace it, if I need to have it done?"

Agon pulled the pendant closer, almost so that it touched his nose, and squinted at the break in the covering once more. "Near enough."

"Then let us peel it away and see what we have stumbled upon."

<>◇<>

Herod Antipas had, by all accounts, his father's imposing stature. His personality, however, could not match the genius of his mad parent. Where the elder was decisive, if emotionally erratic, Antipas waffled and wavered. He shared his parent's lust for women, but had not the will or strength to cast the objects of his desire aside when they no longer pleased or were necessary. Thus, he now lived unknown and unloved in shadows created by the sheer magnitude of his late parent and exacerbated by the vaulting ambition of his new queen, his late brother's wife, and mother of the now infamous Princess Salome.

Gamaliel had returned to the room set aside for his interviews only moments before the king arrived. Unlike the queen and princess, his demeanor was surprisingly open and forthcoming. Because it was so, Gamaliel assumed the king knew absolutely nothing about either the murder or the circumstances surrounding it. It would be a safe wager that he would not be able to distinguish one servant girl from another as well. That observation alone convinced him that if he were to be told anything useful, it would be from one or another of the women. He doubted either would volunteer anything. There was one point, however, which he needed clarification on and that must come from the king. Who was the missing Graecus? Surely he would know.

Herod entered with a necessary but modest show of pomp, not the sort one would expect in more public settings, but enough to remind the Rabban, if reminding were needed, with whom he was dealing. Gamaliel noted he seemed considerably older than his queen, perhaps by as much as a decade or more. Gamaliel reckoned it was an age when a man's eye tended to wander and that would explain his ridiculous behavior with the princess and the aftermath of her performance. Lust outside his marriage was not something Gamaliel had experienced personally, or guessed ever would, but he knew from the confessions of others how the phenomenon made fools of men and harridans of their wives. Old men with failing…who were no longer…well, it was not a mystery why they behaved foolishly at a certain time in life. Gamaliel's opinion of the king softened marginally.

He struggled with how he should frame the question that had agitated him since his time with Agon, the jeweler. How to state it without revealing what he'd discovered and further tipping his hand as to the direction he planned to proceed in his inquiries. Before he could speak the king made the decision for him. He had a question of his own.

"Honored Rabban, you are in possession of an amulet, I believe. It is of unusual design and construction I am told. May I see it?"

Gamaliel had not expected the question, but years engaged in disputation on the more difficult interpretations of the Law had trained him to never let his expression reveal his thoughts, much less any surprise at being caught out.

"You are correct, Highness, I am. Unfortunately, I cannot share it with you at this moment as it may be an important, nay a vital bit of evidence in our inquiries. I have secured it in a safe place until such time as I can make a determination as to whom it belonged and whence it came. Your wife the queen has seen it and disclaims any knowledge of its ownership among other things. Perhaps I can show it to you later."

"I see," the King replied, decidedly uncomfortable.

"Is there something I should know about the pendant?"

"About it? Umm, well I was thinking perhaps someone had mislaid it. If I could see it I might be able to describe it and see it restored to its rightful owner."

Gamaliel smiled. I bet you would you old fox, he thought. Apparently the queen had talked to the king and Chuza had filled in details to them during the hour break between interviews, where it had been found, and with what other items. But as much as he might wish to, the king would not see it this day, perhaps never. Whether he or any of the royal family ever saw it again would depend on the skill of Agon the jeweler in restoring the false glazing on the one hand, and their lack of familiarity with the pendant's details on the other.

The king lowered his eyes and inspected the tiles on the floor as if they held the key to the mystery of life, or in this case, how best to couch an answer. He had a decision to make. Should he tacitly admit to having colluded with his queen and his steward about the pendant and admit to having a genuine interest in and knowledge about it, or should he let the matter drop? What was it about that pendant that bothered him so? Gamaliel waited. He did not believe the king knew what lay beneath the false ceramic on the bauble. If he did, there might have been no murder in the bath two nights ago.

He glanced at the wall, the perfidious wall, and toyed with the idea that Barak, with his scruples about the royals' level of piety, might be persuaded to assemble a corps of spies from one or more of his wife's acquaintances. He needed to know what these people knew and were not telling him. When he was done with this king he would make a proposition to Barak. He desperately needed to overcome the disadvantage the wall provided those who wished the investigation to sink into the quicksand of lies they'd spread in his path.

Chapter XI

In the previous hour, Agon had hastily removed the paste from the underlying gold. Gamaliel had a quick glance at the inscriptions on its gold rim. It was only a hurried look as he had to rush back to the palace to keep this appointment with the king. But given what little he did manage to decipher, he surmised that if the king knew, odds were the girl would have been elevated into the family circle, not left to defend herself from a deadly, and brutal, attack.

A murder, any murder, he guessed, would not rest easily on the king's conscience. There were rumors that he regretted the beheading of the Baptizer. So, in this latest, could the king have been implicated in some way? Gamaliel could think of reasons why he might have condoned or turned a blind eye to it. If it involved a guest of high station, for example, or someone in the royal family, he might take the position that a servant girl's death did not warrant exposing "one of his own" to scandal. Gamaliel studied his man and waited. Too often powerful men assume as an inherent right of their birth, that they may take advantage of the low born and servants in particular.

"It seems," the king murmured, "that we might have known something of the pendant."

"In spite of what the queen has told us? Are you suggesting she might have had a momentary lapse of memory? It happens frequently. She has so many things on her mind…"

One must provide royalty with a degree of latitude if one wished to move forward with any undertaking which impinges their prerogatives. A lie exposed or a lie excused? Gamaliel did not serve at court but he did possess a glancing familiarity with protocol and precedence. He knew men and knew where power in their hands could sometimes lead them. A necessary excuse for the queen's misspeaking was required.

"Yes, yes, that is the position exactly." The king knew Gamaliel had let him off the hook and he knew Gamaliel knew it. He didn't care. After all, he was the king. "I believe it was worn by the poor servant girl who was killed in the bath. Is that so? Why would anyone want to do that? Such a tragedy."

Foolish man. Why not stop when you have been given an out? Why not quit while you are ahead?

"I do not know, Excellency. It may well have been. I found it in the bath after I had it drained. I also found some coins, a bit of feminine apparel which I also suspect belonged to the dead girl, and a knife."

"A knife? You found the weapon used to kill her? Well, that is a stroke of luck, don't you think? Find the owner and you have the killer."

"I hope so, Majesty. I await a report from the physician who is studying all the evidence and will tell me whether it is or is not the weapon. If so, finding its owner may not prove so easy."

"But it must be. How else would a knife end up in the bath? We do not bathe armed, do we? Of course it is the knife that killed her."

"Point taken. Yes, it is likely, but not yet certain. So, then, I will put to you the questions I posed to your wife, the queen, and your stepdaughter, the princess."

"All of them? That does not seem a very intelligent use of your time, Rabban."

"Perhaps not, but as you have just seen, memories sometime need prodding, do they not? Perhaps your Highness will recall some detail they overlooked or forgot—as just now recalling the owner of the pendant."

"I see. Well, ask your questions, but as you do so I must tell you Rabban that we are not pleased that the royal family has been subjected to this abuse."

"Of course. My apologies. I only do this because the Prefect says I must. I would like to return to the pendant one last time. You say the dead girl wore it. Always or only occasionally?"

"I can't recall ever seeing her without it. I may be wrong in this. I do not, as a rule, pay close attention to servants. The queen, of course might know better."

"Yes, thank you. Another question, please, how did she come into your service? I am led to believe she was not an Israelite. Is that true?"

"That is only partially correct. She is a foreigner, yes, but Hebrew at least in practice. The captivity left many of us in foreign lands never to return, as you know. Some come to the city for the High Holy days as they are doing even now. Most of the Diaspora do not make the effort, alas, and the practice of religion has become, shall we say, varied in extent and commitment." This last observation from one of the least observant Jews in the land, Gamaliel thought. Royalty lived in a world of its own making, clearly.

"Yes, yes, of course, and she came to this court how?"

The king cocked an eye toward the patterned wall and cleared his throat as if waiting for inspiration or perhaps some telepathic signal from across the room and behind it.

"Let me think a moment. Ah yes, she was in my wife's household when she lived with my brother in Caesarea Philippi. When the queen came to me in Tiberias, the girl came as well."

"Yes, I see, but how did she come to the queen in the first place? We have established she is a foreigner. Is it usual for such a person to find a place in a king's or queen's household?"

"Usual? No, I suppose not. If I recall correctly—mind you I am repeating something I only heard but did not personally witness—she was brought into Philip's palace as a favor to a friend. Perhaps an ally in a dispute, perhaps as bond for a debt, I do not know. Then he placed her in the queen's service. I am told he needed someone to keep an eye on her. I don't know why or even why he selected the queen for the duty, but so it was. I never found out and now that both my brother and the girl are dead I rather doubt I'll ever know. Is there anything else?"

Gamaliel mulled over this last speech. He was sure this once, the king spoke the truth. That would be important later, he felt. He sighed and returned his gaze on the king.

"Who is the man Graecus, your Majesty?"

"Who?"

"I am told there is some sort of emissary in the household who calls himself Graecus. As he is a guest in your palace, I would like to know who he is. He is missing, you see."

"I cannot say."

"Cannot, or will not?"

"For your purposes, Rabban, they are the same. Again, is there anything else?"

Gamaliel paused and gathered his courage. What he would say next would not sit well with his king. "Highness, I now speak to you as the Rabban of the Sanhedrin, not the Prefect's agent. I must call you into account. Your actions within this palace, as they have been reported to me, quite candidly I must say, by the servants and staff, are outside the Law. You know the practice of bathing in the pagan style is strictly forbidden. The frescos on the ceiling and walls border on the blasphemous and the practice of men and women sharing the water is also forbidden."

The king's face began to redden and he clutched at the dagger at his side.

"You know all this, yet you continue in this sinful way. Majesty, it is not for your soul only I fear, but as you are our king, your defiance of the Law could bring down the Lord's wrath upon us all. You know our history, you are aware of the things the Lord called down on the Nation in the past when its king proved unfaithful or unworthy."

"Rabban, you do not have leave to speak to your king in such a manner."

"Yet I must. We suffer from the oppression of our overlords from Rome. Is that not enough? Must we also invite the Lord's wrath as well?"

The king began to sputter a reply but Gamaliel held up his hand. "You are to plaster over those pagan images, you are to convert that space into a proper *mikvah,* and you will tell your people they must use it ritually every day."

"You cannot...you do not have the authority to say these things. You do not give orders to the king."

"Yet I have done so, and will again. My duty, Highness, is to keep the nation obedient to the Law—king or servant, slave or free, man or woman. The Lord will not suffer disobedience forever. We will mend our ways or we will be punished, make no mistake about that. And the suffering brought at the hand of the Lord will make the rule of Rome seem like a mother's slap."

"Rabban, this interview is at an end. There will be no more questions of me, the queen, or the princess."

Gamaliel bowed and signaled his compliance. The king left the room red-faced and fuming. Gamaliel twisted the Prefect's ring on his finger and for the first time appreciated the fact that Pilate had saddled him with this task. Whether he solved the murder now or not was of little or no consequence to him anymore. He had a higher calling here—to bring the palace to repentance and into line. The Baptizer had tried and lost his life in the attempt. But the Baptizer was not the Rabban of the Sanhedrin. The palace would bend the knee. Oh, yes, finally he, the Rabban of the Sanhedrin, knew why he'd been called to this place.

Chapter XII

The sun hovered over the roof tops in the Upper City to the west and Gamaliel turned his thoughts toward home and supper. He still had one or two tasks to attend to before he could leave for the day, and then he hoped to find some level of tranquility in familiar surroundings and put the whole gritty business away until the following day. He gestured to Chuzas to follow him outside.

"Steward, have you any news of this Graecus? I will want to speak with him as soon as I possibly can."

Chuzas avoided making full eye contact with him. He fidgeted and plucked at his sleeve. "The king said you were to cease the interviews."

"Is that how you heard it? Let us be clear, Chuzas, the Prefect has authorized me to do what I must to bring this matter to a close. What the king does or does not want may or may not be relevant, but is of no interest to me one way or the other. Do you understand? Recall please, I asked you a question and your reply did not answer the question I posed. Now, I will repeat it and this time you will please respond. Have you any news of Graecus? I wish to know if you have had any luck in unearthing him."

"No, Rabban, there is nothing to report. I feel certain he has gone to ground."

"We shall see about that. Secondly, you misunderstood the kings directive. He said the royal family is no longer to be harassed. Unless you are suggesting this Graecus is also a member of the family, I will speak with him. Are you suggesting that?"

"Am I what?"

"Are you suggesting that Graecus is part of the royal family in some way?"

"No, certainly not." Chuzas eyes darted over Gamaliel's shoulder, a sign he took to indicate the steward had something besides telling the truth in mind.

"No? Very well. Further, as the king only specified himself, the queen, and Princess Salome, to be left at peace, I insist you schedule a session with the man, Menahem, for tomorrow morning as well."

Chuzas stood mouth agape, then collected himself and nodded his assent. Gamaliel did not believe he would get much more from him anytime soon and turned to dismiss him.

"Oh, and one last thing, please send the captain of the guard to me on your way back to the palace."

Chuzas left, shaking his head and muttering. Gamaliel found Barak and motioned for him to sit with him.

"Barak, I need to have a word. You know of the sinful behaviors practiced in the palace?" Barak looked uneasy, glanced over his shoulder at the departing Chuzas, and nodded in agreement. "Good, then you and I must do something about it before the Lord rains down his wrath on all of us."

"Sir, do you truly think that could happen?"

"As we know, the Lord moves in mysterious ways old man, and he has put up with much of late, so I cannot promise you that. Who knows? But you remember the stories you learned as a child, surely, of the exile, of the Judges and the Amorites and the Amelakites sent into the land to punish us for our disobedience?"

"Oh yes!"

"And you remember he sent one judge to redeem us from the oppressors?"

"Gideon?"

"Yes, and today, you will become our Gideon."

"I, Rabban?"

"Yes, well in a way. I will not ask you to raise an army, of course, not in the usual sense. But we must do what is needed to stay the Lord's hand. I wish you to organize the servants, those in close contact with the royal family in particular, but only those you can trust. They will be your army, a silent army doing the Lord's work. I need to know everything your masters do, what they say, with whom they correspond. Do you understand?"

"But dare I do such a thing? What will happen to them if the king finds out?"

"What will he find you doing? Surely in your years of experience serving this king and the one before him, you have noticed that the rich and powerful treat servants as though they were invisible, deaf, or if not deaf, certainly stupid. They speak of any and all things without a thought in the world as to whether their servants can hear and understand."

Barak's worried expression eased and he nodded and grinned.

"You have noticed. Good, then you will know what to do. I will not be asking you or your comrades to do anything out of the ordinary, Barak. I do not want them to change what they do, when they do it, or make any alterations in their routine. Just listen and tell me what you and your fellow servants, slaves, whoever, hear during the course of their duties, understand?"

"Yes." The old man hesitated, then nodded.

"Your wife, her name is…"

"Minna, sir."

"Minna, yes. She will be a great help I am sure. Yes, good. I will see you tomorrow, Barak, and you can give me your first report."

He dismissed Barak and pivoted toward the gate as if to leave.

"Ah, it is the captain of the guard."

That man had entered the courtyard earlier and had stood a respectful eight paces away until Gamaliel finished with Barak. When the old man left, the captain stepped forward and saluted Gamaliel.

"The king's steward says you requested me to attend to you."

"I asked to see you, yes. Do you know the man named Graecus?"

"Yes, sir, he is a guest of the king."

"What else can you tell me about him?"

"Very little. We are not taken into the king's confidence as a rule."

"But what have you heard?"

"He is said to be an envoy sent from up north somewhere to negotiate a trade agreement. I cannot confirm it. I was told by the guards assigned to him that he has lately dropped from sight—probably left the city."

"When did you or one of your men last see him?"

"That would be yesterday. We had guards posted at the entrances to the baths with orders to keep everyone out until you were finished with your inspection."

"When was the watch set?"

"Immediately after the alarm was raised."

"And did you keep everyone out?"

"We did…well, that is not exactly true. The king and queen made a visit to the site of the murder."

"Anyone else?"

"No, sir. Wait, yes, as a matter of fact there was someone else. The king's steward came through once."

"And when was that?"

"The morning before the attendants drained the bath. And the man you seek attempted to enter on two occasions but was turned back."

"Thank you, Captain. That is excellent. I congratulate you on your efficiency. As soon as possible I want you to form a search party and comb the palace and, if necessary, the city for Graecus."

"You do not believe he has fled the city?"

"That, of course, is a possibility, but my instinct tells me that he is still somewhere about. He will not leave—not just yet. I could be mistaken but I do not think so. To flee would constitute a near admission of complicity in the girl's murder, don't you think?"

"Yes…well possibly. There could be other reasons for leaving just now."

"His disappearance immediately after a brutal murder might be nothing more than coincidental, yes, but, as I said, I do not think so. I grant it might be. In any case, seek him out and bring him to me, if and as soon as you can."

"Where shall we begin?"

"Captain, I have no doubts about you or your men. You know more of how one goes about searching a palace than I do or ever shall. I leave that to you. Proceed as you think best. If and when you do find him, bring him to me, in chains if necessary. I would have words with this Greek."

The guard saluted again and left to assemble a party to search for Graecus. Gamaliel, satisfied and very tired, made his way home just as the sun, now large and golden, finished its descent and quite suddenly winked out.

Yom Revi'i

Chapter XIII

The next morning, while still at table finishing his morning meal, Gamaliel received a messenger sent by Chuzas. Menahem, it read, had been called away temporarily. He would, however, make himself available to The Rabban of the Sanhedrin at the eighth hour. Gamaliel told the messenger to wait while he prepared a message of his own. He thought a moment and then dictated a brief report for Pilate. He listed the steps he had taken thus far and the thoughts he had. He did not include his ideas about the pendant. He did request the Prefect's help in locating Graecus. He sent the young man off to the Antonia Fortress and returned to finish his breakfast.

What he must do next occupied his thoughts as he chewed absently on a crust of bread and a slice of hard cheese. There was the business of the pendant, of course. He should visit Agon and mark the jewelry fabricator's progress. He should also confer with Loukas. He had had the corpse for several days now and the girl needed to be interred. She should have been in the ground well before now, but given the exigencies of the situation, he thought he could bend the law a bit. But not for much longer. There were but two days left before Shabbat. Time was running out. But one question still needed an answer before he buried the child. Who was she?

He left his house and headed for the Sheep Gate. He would call on the physician first.

‹›‹›‹›

Loukas occupied a solid stone house outside the city walls beyond the Sheep Gate. It had the high walled court at the back typical of the area except the rear wall had been fashioned by removing a portion of the hillside. The builder had cut into the limestone and dressed it so that it formed a perfectly perpendicular façade that joined the side walls to form a rough square. Gamaliel scratched at the physician's door. A servant of indeterminate sex and uncommon ugliness answered. The aroma of garlic, olives, and herbs enveloped him with the door's opening. Gamaliel asked if the physician were in. The servant nodded and beckoned him to enter. Gamaliel declined.

"Tell him I will join him in his rear court."

He walked along the narrow pathway beside the house and stood by the heavy cedar gate. It had no latch on its outer side. If it were closed, it could only be opened from within. In a moment, it swung open and he stepped into the court. The servant closed, relatched the gate, and disappeared. Loukas stepped into the open and greeted his friend and frequent opponent in debates about the world, the gods, the future, people in general, and the Roman Empire in particular. Loukas had a table and benches set up in the shade of a olive tree of indeterminate age. Loukas gestured for his guest to sit and poured a cup of wine as he did so.

"Greeting, Gamaliel. I have asked Dracos to bring us other refreshment. Do not say no. You cannot refuse me. I have saved this small skin of new wine just for this occasion. It is not of pagan origin, I promise you."

Gamaliel waved off the speech and took a seat on a stone bench carved from the same buff limestone as the house, the walls, the hillsides, and indeed the entire Holy City. There were times when he wished his people would emulate the daring of the Greeks, and color the stones in bright reds and blues. Anything to break the monotony of an endless sea of beige.

"What can you tell me of my murder, Loukas? Have you anything new for me? Time is short. I must see to her burial.

I have stretched the Law enough already. But before Shabbat, surely and I should have arranged for a *Shomer*. It is preferable that *shomrim* be members of her family or friends, but that was not possible."

"It is a law that applies to the Jews. Does it also apply to pagans like this girl?"

"That is the problem. I do not think she is pagan. I am certain she is one of ours. In any case, I cannot take chances. She must be in the ground soon."

"Not a pagan? That is interesting. So, someone in the palace has butchered an Israelite?"

"A very strong image, but wholly an accurate one. I did not say she was an Israelite. Calling her one supposes she is local, or her parents were. I am not so sure of that, but Israelite or not, she is most probably Jewish. What of her? She must by now be…"

"I had some women come in and prepare her in your fashion as a precaution. She has been washed, anointed, and wrapped and is well enough as it happens. You see that semicircular stone set against the rear wall? It rolls to your right and behind it is a cave in the hill where I store things I wish to be protected from changes in temperature. She rests there. Is that sufficient to serve as a tomb for the time being?"

"I must stretch the Law a bit further, then, and accept that is does for now."

"Good that is settled then. You ask about the murder. First I must tell you some news that I assume is connected to it. I had an uninvited visitor two nights ago."

"An uninvited…? How so?"

"Someone climbed my wall over there." He pointed to a spot on the wall where Gamaliel could see the plants at its base had been trampled.

"He entered the house, rummaged through my things."

"What was taken?"

"Strangely, nothing. I do not have much in the way of valuables, but there were coins on the table, and they were not disturbed. I gather he sought something else and so I assumed whatever he was after must have somehow been related to the murder."

"It is interesting that he came here, don't you think? If your break-in relates to our dead girl, he had to know you had brought her here with some of the materials I found on the bottom of the bath. How would he know that, do you suppose?"

"Someone in the palace is not as reliable as one might hope. That palace, like all palaces, is filled morning to night with gossip and tittle-tattle. It would not take a genius to find me out. So you can confidently seek your murderer there."

"You say nothing is missing?"

"Nothing that I can see. More importantly, he did not take the knife."

"So, not the knife. That's interesting."

Loukas put the object in question on the table. "Isn't it. Of course, he may not care one way or another if you identify it. I find that hard to believe, but if there were something else of greater importance among the girl's things and he intended to leave town once he had it in his possession I imagine he would feel free to ignore this knife. It is a very fine piece of workmanship. Egyptian, I think."

"Egyptian? I wondered at that. Was it, in fact, the murder weapon?"

"The girl's throat was slashed, as I said, right to left, by an exceedingly sharp blade. This knife is a dress piece, usually worn for show, not for battle, and not terribly sharp. It may have been used. It may not. It is a noteworthy weapon, as you can see, and could be easily recognized. Why would a killer leave his knife at the scene in the first place and particularly one that could be identified so easily?"

"I take your point. And as your visitor ignored it, I must conclude it likely had no connection to the girl at all. Would he not have taken it, a valuable clue, if it were the weapon that killed the girl? Yet he didn't. It lay in the bottom of the bath with the other things. What do you make of that?"

"I have nothing to offer beyond what I have already said, either the knife was not his, or in any case, he didn't care if you had it."

"I'm inclined to the former or that your intruder had some other purpose in breaking in. One not related to our dead girl. Did you get a look at your visitor?"

"Not I but Draco, my servant, did, but he has not much to offer. Cloudy night, everything in shades of gray. His eyesight is failing."

"Too bad. This servant, I do not recognize him. He is new?"

"I found him begging in the streets a few months ago. As you can see, in his condition he is not likely to be taken on by anyone else. I offered him a place. He is grateful and therefore very loyal. He has a story."

"Indeed?"

"As a child he was prepared, if you take my meaning, to be a catamite."

"That would explain why I could not determine his gender."

"Possibly, but there are other considerations. When he was in his eighth year or so, he is a little vague about that, he was sold to a wealthy merchant from Ephesus. By the time he was in his twenties, when he had matured and lost the beauty and freshness of youth, he was sold again to a local Arab who placed him in his harem, the women's quarters to…well, you know what his duties must have been there."

"I can but imagine."

"He might still be there but for the disease that took him. When the malady you see had disfigured him so horribly took over, he was kicked to the street. When I found him he was nearly dead. His disease, combined with the fact he had no skills beyond those he was raised to perform, left him helpless in a harsh world, and particularly in an uncompromising city like Jerusalem."

"A pitiful story. If I live to my promised three score and ten, I will never understand *saris*. Our Law will not permit the practice of castration even for animals. It is one aspect of your pagan culture which will doubtless forever separate us."

"My pagan culture? You presume, Rabban."

"Do I indeed? Perhaps I am mistaken. Well, at least Draco has you, Loukas. It must be a great comfort for someone with such a terrible past life and present condition to find himself in service at the home of a physician."

"But only for a while, I fear. I have seen this disease before. It is progressive and always fatal. I can give him palliatives but I cannot alter its course. He will not be with me much longer."

Gamaliel studied the physician for a moment pondering this complex unbeliever, if that was what he was. He had always assumed Loukas practiced some form of paganism as his Greek name suggested. He had to admit, however, there seemed to be no evidence of whatever it might be in his home or speech. Did not most pagans keep at least one stone image on the premises? He didn't know, but guessed it must be so. Why else would the Lord have made such a point about graven images if not to point out the practice among the nonbelievers?

Loukas sat silently waiting for Gamaliel to continue.

"We must continue this at another time, Physician. The palace beckons me like the sirens of that epic Jason the Greeks so admire, but my Scylla and Charybdis are of the Prefect's construction."

The Rabban exhaled rather louder than decorum dictated, picked up the knife, secured it in his belt, and bid his host farewell. If he hurried, he would still have time to see Agon before confronting Menahem.

Chapter XIV

Chuzas sat by himself in the courtyard where he and Gamaliel had last spoken the previous evening. In point of fact, he had not yet informed Menahem of the Rabban's request for an interview as he'd been requested. First, he needed to grapple with the problem of the knife. Anyone who knew the various personalities in the court would easily recognize it. Like no other of its kind, it stood out whenever Menahem wore it, which he always did on State occasions and frequently at other, less notable times. There could be no doubt that the knife Gamaliel found in the bath with the other trinkets belonged to Menahem. Therefore, that knowledge would soon be made known to Gamaliel.

Chuzas rubbed his eyes. He had difficulty sleeping since this murder business. It made his mind as muddy as the stream at the bottom of the Kidron Valley after a rain. He forced his mind back into focus. The knife was in the pool. The girl's body was in the pool. The girl's throat was slit. The Greeks would say a logical connection existed between those three facts. He scratched his ear and squinted at the sun which had just cleared the wall to the east. Chuzas had studied the Rabban enough over the past few days to conclude that he did not manage information as others might. Rabbis, or more accurately, Pharisees, it seemed, were not trained in the finer points of Aristotle's disciplines, not that he, Chuzas, had made an exhaustive study of the Greek either. But the question he struggled with came to just this: Would the Rabban make the connection between the facts or would he, Chuzas, find it necessary to point Gamaliel in that direction?

But first he needed to make a decision about Menahem. What would the old man say to Gamaliel? He knew the girl better than anyone in the court. Why he had taken time to befriend this particular servant girl was anyone's guess. If Menahem were younger, Chuzas could easily understand it. After all servant girls, particularly young pretty ones like this one, were always sought out by the men in the palace for their pleasure. Age rarely slowed them down. Many outside the palace argued that the girls were brought to court specifically for pleasure. But Menahem must be near his seventh decade. Usually, that many years would put him beyond suspicion. Only a very few lived that long—well, since Genesis anyway. Even fewer could contemplate undertaking a liaison of that sort. Of course, there were old men like Menahem who still lusted after young girls. Herod, the old king that would be, had been known to pursue young women almost until the day he died. Men's desires did not always wane as their faculties did. He'd heard the girls sent to their rooms laughing at them after they returned from such encounters.

But Menahem, if not by virtue of his advanced age, then by his devotion to the Galilean's teaching certainly would have dismissed any thought of such a tryst. The Galilean! One way or the other, Chuzas thought, he must pry Joanna from that man and his dangerous ideas. Her insistence the rabbi cured her of her delusions and erratic behavior could not be true. Other very fine, indeed notable rabbis had tried and failed. What could this carpenter rabbi have done that they could not? No, it was a trick. As Menahem must have planted these absurd ideas in her head, Menahem must be made to root them out.

He could no longer put it off. He would arrange for Menahem and Gamaliel to meet and he would watch through the lattice and hear everything. Gamaliel could not miss discovering the owner of the knife.

⟨⟩⟨⟩⟨⟩

Agon had raised the shutters at his shop signaling the beginning of his work day when Gamaliel arrived. He greeted the Rabban and invited him in. It was barely past the second hour and there were few customers in the street in search of jewelry. The wealthy, his clients, would not bestir themselves much before the fifth hour and by the sixth, when the sun was at its zenith, they would disappear again until the streets cooled once more. He ushered Gamaliel into a back room and pulled out a stool for his guest.

"Were you successful?"

"As you will see, yes and no, Rabban. I completed the removal of the paste-like false pottery and copied the inscription for you. I should say inscriptions. I do not read but the small bit of Greek I need to conduct my business. For anything else I must go down the street to the scribe who writes and reads for me. Obviously I dared not employ his services for this project. I can't be sure but I think I can see that the writing is in three languages."

"Three? Let me see."

Agon handed over a slip of papyrus that he'd evidently sanded clean and on to which he'd copied the figures exactly as he saw them. Gamaliel picked it up. As Agon's reading skills were in fact limited he could not know where the words in the inscriptions began or where they ended. Consequently, all the letters were strung together and the words, where they could be made out, were out of order. Gamaliel, who could read, had little difficulty sorting them out after a quick inspection.

"The inscriptions are in Greek—you recognized that, I suppose—and repeated in Latin and Aramaic." Gamaliel frowned in concentration. "Now, that is odd. Not in Hebrew. Why do you suppose that is? Why write in Aramaic and not Hebrew?"

Agon could only shrug.

"I think it may be important, but do not know why. Our late king never was an easy person to understand, my friend. Is that why you said yes and no? What about the second task. Were you able to replace the glazing or whatever it was? I do hope you managed. I can work as well if you haven't but…"

"Yes and no? Here, see for yourself." Agon dipped his hand into his apron pocket and produced a pendant which he dropped on the counter beside the papyrus.

"Ah, that is perfect. I am amazed. One could never tell the old false glaze has been removed and replaced. You are a *mitzvah*, Agon. This looks almost like real ceramic."

Agon's grin split his beard into unequal and unlovely halves. He reached into his pouch and withdrew the original gold piece and laid it next to the first one.

"What's this?"

"Recall, I said yes and no. You should have asked me to explain. I tried for hours to figure out how the coating had been done and failed. I knew you wished the pendent restored. I tried but frankly, I have no idea how it could be reproduced. I have seen this thing on pieces from the east—beyond India even, but again, how it is done, I do not know. I could not do as you wished, so instead, I made you a copy."

"I can't tell them apart. This one looks like clay baked and glazed."

"There is a reason it looks like ceramic. It is ceramic. I simply molded a pendant from clay, glazed and painted it and then fired it, a far simpler task than reproducing or repairing the covering on the original."

"That is even better. Now I do not have to worry about it being stolen. I can keep the original in a safe place and dangle the copy if needed." He paused and narrowed his eyes. "Yes this is perfect. I could set a trap with it."

"A trap? To catch what?"

"A thief, perhaps."

"What does the writing say, Rabban?"

Gamaliel reread the inscriptions again, compared them to the papyrus to be sure Agon had copied them faithfully, and shook his head. "Do you know the symbolism of the lion's head in the center?"

"Is for a king I think. Is it a King David's pendant?"

"No, not King David, a later king, much later, but just as important to many. No, I will not tell you today, old friend. You will be safer knowing only what you do already, trust me. And be warned, if someone comes asking questions, you must do two things. First, erase any memories you have of this object and what you have seen, and second, in the event they do not believe you about the first, make sure they know you cannot read. The knowledge this pendant carries is, for now, a dangerous thing to possess, I promise you."

"You will tell me later?"

"When it is safe to do so, yes. But it may be a while yet. We will have to wait and see. Secrets, Agon, secrets in the wrong hands can bring down a kingdom. Unless you are the one plotting to bring them down, it is best not to know any." Gamaliel added the fake pendant to the pouch with the knife and the coins and stood. "I must leave you now or I shall be late. This business gets more interesting even as it becomes more dangerous. I will see to it you receive a substantial reward for your work this day."

He left the shop. He needed to hurry to keep his appointment with Menahem. As he turned into the street that led uphill toward the palace, he caught in the corner of his eye Agon's next customer entering his shop. The identity of the person did not immediately register but he was certain he had seen him before and the name would come to him later.

Chapter XV

Chuzas waited at the entrance to the room set aside for the interviews. He looked agitated.

"Am I late? Have I kept Menahem waiting?"

"No, your Eminence, it is he who is delayed. An unfortunate conflict in schedules."

Gamaliel wondered about that. Whose schedule? Chuzas' or more of the royals who might or might not be lurking behind the latticework? Was it Menahem's, or some other, as yet unannounced, party? It was a question with no answer, but it gnawed at him anyway.

"Very well, we shall wait. Steward, you have heard all of the interviews thus far. Have you formed an opinion on the matter?"

"An opinion? It is not my place."

"No, of course not, yet you heard the king, the queen, and the princess each in turn deny any knowledge of the events occurring before this tragedy, and any substantial knowledge of the girl, and yet you also heard the earlier testimony of the servants and players which contradicted them. Why do you suppose they were so loath to own up to some of it? A scintilla perhaps?"

Chuzas jaw dropped. He stammered something Gamaliel could not make out. One of the royal family must indeed hover somewhere behind the lattice. Good. It is always best to know the breadth of one's adversaries, which in this case, he regretted, included at least one wearer of the purple.

"Sorry, Chuzas, I missed what you were saying."

"I only said that…if their Highnesses denied knowledge of the events, it must be so. It is the others who must be mistaken."

"You think? Extraordinary. Ah, this must be Menahem at last."

A tall man, old but not stooped as many of the elderly are, strode into the room. His manner and carriage were almost regal. If anyone who did not know the king by sight and were required to pick him out of a crowd in which this man also stood, he or she would undoubtedly select Menahem over Antipas. Impressive. He sat easily and gazed unblinking at Gamaliel.

"You are Menahem, companion to the king."

"And you are Gamaliel, Rabban to the Sanhedrin."

"So we know each other."

"Yes, it would seem so."

"As a point of reference, can you tell me how you came to be here?"

"Here? The king and his entourage always travel from Tiberias to Jerusalem on High Holy days. They did this time and so, here I am."

"You misunderstand me. I am aware that the king prefers the relative laxity of his new city on the Sea of Galilee to the holiness of David's. No, what I am asking is, how you came to be in the king's entourage in the first place?"

"With respect, Rabban, is your knowing that pertinent to your investigation?"

"Let's just say it might be. Indulge me in this. There are aspects of the situation, I find, that appear to transcend a simple murder of a servant girl." Gamaliel thought he saw a shadow cross the old man's face. "You know something of these matters I believe."

"If you believe I know more of these matters than I let on, you are mistaken, Rabban,"

"Perhaps, but I think not. Very well, we will return to this line later. What can you tell me about the dead girl?"

"Why would you think I knew anything about her?"

"Menahem, I have trained myself to read people like some men read books. I turn your pages, scroll through your content, and I see things. You are an interesting read, if I may say so. I cannot quite make you out, but something is there. You know of this girl, of that I am certain, not merely guessing."

"Do you indeed?"

Menahem's gaze shifted away from Gamaliel. He turned his head and stared at a spot on the far wall, probably contemplating who sat behind it listening. Gamaliel started. He had seen that profile before, and very recently, but where? Menahem twisted back and nodded.

"You have read me correctly. I know something of the victim. She did not have many friends and seemed so lost and unhappy, I took pity on her. It is an old man's prerogative. We have so little else to offer, you see. Most servant girls are here because they have been sold into service, have been acquired from a grateful petitioner, or simply taken from the streets and offered a better life. Many would argue that point, but there it is. They are resigned to their fate and most make the best of it. This girl was different. She came to us when the king married the present queen. How she came to be in the queen's household is a mystery that the child either could not, or would not confide. But clearly she did not belong, or so I thought."

"I see." Did he? What was it about this stately old man than puzzled him? "Tell me this, then, did the girl have a name. Everyone I've asked thus far denies knowing her or maintains her name was Cappo, which seems unlikely"

"Why unlikely? It is the sort of name a servant would have."

"It struck me as odd. That is all. She did not fit my notion of a palace servant, but how would I know, you might ask. Well, for one, the facts of her murder suggest she was not, but I will let that pass for now. Can you help me?"

"You have a difficult puzzle to unravel, Rabban,"

"I do and I could use some help."

"Her name was Alexandra."

"An odd name for a Jewish servant girl, isn't it?"

"Perhaps. I thought at first she might have come from Egypt. That would have explained the name. But then, Antipas' grandmother, once removed, you could say, was also named Alexandra so, who knows?"

"But you liked Egypt. Did she come from there?"

"No. She said she didn't, but she refused to confide where she did come from."

"Beside the name, was there anything else to suggest Egypt?"

The old man hesitated and looked hard at Gamaliel. "Are you reading me again, Rabban?"

"I am. Sorry, it is what I do. Tell me about Egypt."

"Why would you suppose I know anything about that country?"

"No reason, really. But you were hesitant to talk about your early life, how you came to be the king's companion. I thought I made a connection. Tell me if I'm wrong."

Menaham allowed a ghost of a smile to cross his face. It disappeared quickly "I came to the king, not this one, but his father first. He had conquered Nabataea and its capital, Petra. I was traveling through there when he found me. He brought me to this land and placed me in his household."

"Placed you. Forgive me, but you are obviously older than our king, yet you are described as his companion. Am I missing something?"

"You are aware of the late king's obsession with plots against him, I am sure. Anyone living in the land will know of it. The king, then, also worried about his sons. Two he had executed for their involvement in a plot to overthrow him."

"Yes, Alexander and Aristobulus."

"Just so. I was seventeen when he brought me into his house. Antipas was but ten. The king wished to protect him. My duty was to provide that protection as his constant companion."

"Protect him from assassination?"

"From that, certainly, but more importantly, from those who might seduce him into becoming part of a plot like the one that ended in his half brothers' deaths. King Herod could be cruel, and often acted unbalanced, but killing his offspring went down hard with him. He did not want to repeat that act again if he could help it."

This was a side of the man Gamaliel had never considered. Unbalanced? He'd put that down as an understatement.

"So, you were in Petra and the king found you there. You were traveling through or…?"

"I had been traveling, yes. I needed a place, he offered me one. That is all there is to it."

"I see." Clearly no more of the old man's past would be forthcoming and as so much time had passed since he'd arrived at court—nearly fifty years—it would be a waste of time to pursue it any further. Still, it would be nice to know. He placed the reproduced pendant on the table.

"That is the girl's."

"You know it then?"

"Yes. She wore it always. It hung about her neck on a leather thong. How did you come by it?"

"I found it in the bath with this." He reached into his belt and pulled out the knife which he laid on the table beside the pendant.

"In all your moving about the court, have you ever seen this rather wonderful knife?"

"Yes, of course I have. It is mine."

Chapter XVI

Menahem confesses. The knife is his! Gamaliel sat back in his chair and waited for what must come next. Could it really be this easy? He felt a flicker of hope. If this is where it ends, he thought, he'd soon be back with his scrolls, his books, and his students. He thought he heard a gasp from somewhere behind the intricately worked wall. Chuzas? Or one of the royal family?

"Where did you find it? I have searched and searched since it went missing." Menahem's eyes were without guile.

Gamaliel extended the knife toward the old man who reached out his right hand to take it. Gamaliel pulled it back.

"I found it in the bath with the pendant and a thong which still had a knot where it had been secured, but cut through further along its length. There were other items in the bath as well on the day after the girl was found in it with her throat slit. I supposed this knife did the slitting."

Menahem sat back. He slumped as if the wind had been knocked from him. If he didn't know better, Gamaliel would have said the old man shrank a half cubit in stature before his eyes.

"That will make me your primary suspect, I believe."

"Indeed, my only suspect. Have you anything to say to me?"

"What is there to say? I was not at the baths that night. I did not murder the girl. What possible reason would I have to do so?"

"Why would you kill an innocent girl? I can think of several reasons. She resisted your advances. You grew angry and something inside of you snapped and in a rage, you drew your knife and killed her."

"I never attend the revelries at the bath. You may ask anyone."

"This would have occurred after the revelries, as you call them, were over. Later, perhaps you went to the baths because you heard she was there and…" Gamaliel raised his eyebrows marginally.

"But I did not."

"Then you must explain how your knife—this knife—ended up in the baths where a servant girl, a child almost, had her throat cut and—" Gamaliel stopped. And what else? Menahem was an old man, seventyish. Had he the capacity or the strength to do to the girl what had been done?

"That knife has been in my possession for over fifty years, Rabban. I have worn it as ceremonial weapon at occasions many times. Everyone in this palace and hundreds of others know it, recognize it, and have commented on it. If I did as you say, kill the girl, what sort of fool would I be to use this knife, and even if I were to do so, would I be such a fool as to leave such an obvious thing behind?"

"An old fool, Menahem. Can you explain how it came to be at the scene? If not you then who?"

"I will say this and no more. That knife went missing the morning *after* the girl was found. As you can see, I am neither strong nor vital. Vital, do you follow my meaning? I do not know if that has a bearing, but you should know it."

"Yes, I see." Gamaliel stared at the man as if to squeeze something more from him. Nothing emerged. "Well, if you can't add anything more, and in light of your relationship to the king and your years, consider yourself under house arrest. I must consult with my expert on both the veracity of your story and the certainty this knife can be certified as the weapon used in the crime. In the meantime, you are not to leave the palace and will be in the company of a palace guard at all times."

"As you say, Rabban. But I must tell you, you have not solved this mystery."

"I have not?"

"You have not." Menahem stood and strode from the room. He did not do so with the same confident aplomb he had on entering. Gamaliel didn't blame him.

Chuzas popped up at his side as the door slammed shut behind Menahem.

"You are to be congratulated, Rabban. You are finished here. The king will be very disappointed in his friend. He might even ban him from the court, though I don't see how the old man will survive if he does. Certainly he will be shamed and lose his place."

"You are under the impression that the punishment to be meted out by the king for murder will be banishment or shaming?"

"But she was nothing more than a servant. Servants die all the time and in circumstances worse than these." Chuzas seemed quite relaxed, even happy at the outcome. Strange.

"I hate to disappoint you, Steward, but we are not done here."

"Not done? But—"

"You will attend me here tomorrow. By then I hope they will have found the Greek and I will be able to talk to him. In the meantime, I want a list of everyone who had access to Menahem's quarters and who might possibly have taken his knife."

"You don't believe his story."

"Don't I? No, not at the moment, but as he would be tried for murder if he is guilty, I must be sure there is not the slightest doubt about it. The king will be eager to exonerate him, of course. However, if he is to be stoned or turned over to Pilate for crucifixion, we must be absolutely sure."

"Crucifixion? Surely not. He is an old man and...I don't understand."

"No, that is true enough. You do not understand. Listen to me then, this crime was committed in the king's palace during High Holy Days. The potential scandal surrounding the king and his family dictates he must be punished publicly and severely. It cannot be ignored, do you see? Flogging at the very least. A lashing of more than ten would likely kill him, so we must be absolutely certain of his involvement before we act. I do not want the blood of an innocent man on my hands."

"But, all this for a mere servant girl?"

"Yes, even for a servant girl. A life is a life irrespective of station. It is what the Law teaches. You would be wise to remember that. Tomorrow morning, Steward, with the list as I asked."

The usually florid Chuzas left the room looking, Gamaliel thought, rather paler than when he'd entered. He sat a moment rehearsing in his mind all that Menahem had said. An idea, a flicker of something…Important? Something had surfaced when the knife came up but it had slipped away from him. What had he missed? Something about the girl…something Menahem had said, or not said, yes that was it, not said. He had side-stepped on some important detail and Gamaliel had let it go when the knife…What was it?

〈〉〈〉〈〉

Gamaliel did not sleep well that night. Normally he would read for an hour before seeking his bed. He'd a special lamp made for him by the potter. Instead of a single wick spout, he'd had the man create one with four. He learned from trial and error how much oil to place in the lamp so that all four wicks sputtered and went out in exactly one hour. He would then say his prayers and fall into bed. Normally he would drop off within moments, but not this night. Like naughty children, too many thoughts careened about in his brain bumping against each other, laughing at his attempts to corral them, robbing him of sleep. Images of Menahem, his best suspect, his only suspect, floated in and out among them.

Was he truly the one who'd slashed the girl's throat in such a brutal manner? There was enough evidence to turn him over to Pilate. If he were to do so, the inquiry would come to an end and he could return to his old life. He would be free. So, why hesitate? Gamaliel was a righteous man and the motive that would have driven the old man to such a terrible deed eluded him. Why would an old man do such a thing? If he did it, why use such an obvious weapon? As he said, he wasn't a stupid man.

And there was the girl and her mysterious medallion. What more should he know about the girl? Would it be pertinent? Who was the man called Graecus and where had he disappeared to? And why? There were just too many whys.

The questions bedeviled him and he tossed and turned in his bed into the depths of the night and only then drifted off into a fitful sleep. In the morning he would tackle these questions, if he could stay awake long enough.

Yom Chamishi

Chapter XVII

Gamaliel had developed his daily routines over a lifetime. A restless night or not, he rose at dawn and settled in to his morning devotions. This day his time with the Lord was noticeably shorter than usual and if asked about it later he would probably admit he had no idea what he had said or thought beyond the prayers he intoned without thinking every day. He had his breakfast and then sat at his desk to compose a brief report for the Prefect. Whether Pilate would read it he did not know and secretly hoped he would not. He indicated that significant progress had been made and that he had a strong suspect but left deliberately vague any mention of who he might be. He felt no need to bring up Menahem as he was disinclined to settle guilt on the old man yet. His agitated night had convinced him he needed to dig more before serving up the old man to Pilate on a platter. He dispatched a messenger to the Antonia Fortress and left for the palace.

Chuzas and Barak waited for him in their usual place just outside the entrance to the bath. The water had been replaced and the fires relit. In a few hours the bath would be warm and inviting. He thought that if he were not the Rabban and not an observant Jew, and if he had not specifically instructed the king to cease and desist, he would be sorely tempted to shed his garments and luxuriate in that steaming water himself. A small part of his mind leafed through the laws governing the practice, searching for a loophole, an exception, so to speak, that would allow him to rebuild his own *mikvah* along the lines of this pool, without the frescos of course. Would a little heat be such a sin?

"Rabban." Chuzas seemed eager to get on with it; he must have had difficulty sleeping as well. "I have notified the Guard. They await your orders to arrest Menahem. Shall I call them?"

"Excuse me—arrest Menahem? No, you are ahead of yourself, Steward. I am not prepared to arrest anyone just now. You were charged to produce a list of names for me first. Do you have it?"

"Yes, but I can see no purpose for it now. The knife, it is his, and the—"

"In good time. Menahem is not going anywhere and as I told you before, we must be absolutely sure of our man. Have you considered the possibility he may have had an accomplice, for example.?"

"But he might flee. An accomplice?"

"He is an old man. Would he have the strength to draw a knife across the throat of a struggling girl alone? And then, if he were to flee, where would he go? He is old. He has no friends in the city. He has lived most of his life as the companion to the king. What could he do?"

Chuzas did not look happy. It seemed he was at least as anxious for a return to normalcy as Gamaliel, more so, in fact. "A few more days, Steward, then we will tidy up this mess and you and I can resume our lives. Find me Graecus and also, I'll have that list now."

Chuzas handed over a wax tablet, the sort merchants use to calculate their sales. The list seemed unnaturally short.

"These are all who have access to the apartments occupied by the royal family and their retainers? What of the servants, the guards, yourself?"

"I didn't think that you wanted all…I mean, weren't you interested in the suspicious ones. Surely you do not suspect the king or the queen to have entered the man's rooms and taken the knife. Sir, there is no point to this inquiry."

"Whether you deem it useful or not, Steward, it is what you were charged to do. What you have just told me is that if the knife was in fact stolen as Menahem claims, practically anyone could have done it. That assumes, of course, he told us the truth. Leave me now, but stay where I can find you. I wish to have a word with Barak in private. And the Greek. Where is the Greek?"

A chastened and annoyed Chuzas scuttled into the palace.

"He did not like being chastised in front of me, Rabban. You will hear of it from the king, I think."

"The steward's chronic annoyance is of no interest to me, nor is the threat of another reprimand by the king. I am here, reluctantly, at the behest of the Prefect. I have his authority to do what I must to clear up this tragedy and I will do it. Now, what have your sources in the household to tell me?"

"Ah…the princess and her mother, the queen, are crowing. They do not like Menahem and are happy to hear he will soon be in disgrace. The steward, by the way, shares their feelings."

"Why is that? Aside from the possibility that old man murdered the girl, he seems harmless enough. Now there is a statement some Greek tragedian could weave into a play, I think."

"If you say so, sir. The problem for Chuzas is connected to his wife."

"His wife? How so?"

"It is said she communicates with the Nazarene."

"You mean the rabbi who is causing so much discomfort in the Temple?"

"I wouldn't know about that, but as Menahem is also a follower, they say Chuzas believes his wife's straying is due to his influence."

"Ah ha, but is that likely?" Barak's eyebrows waggled. "Very well, go on then, what else?"

"The queen and the princess are happy at his downfall because he was a supporter of the Prophet."

"The Prophet?"

"Yes, John they call the Baptizer."

"There are questions about his being a true prophet, Barak."

"Are there? Everyone I know believed him to be. It is why so many flock to hear Menahem's rabbi."

"I take it that Menahem did not approve of the Baptizer's fate."

"He did not, and attempted to dissuade the king from beheading him, but the king had given his word, you see. I think he still broods over it even now."

"The king broods, or Menahem?"

"Both, but the king surely."

"He thought the Baptizer was a prophet?"

"I do not know about that. I think he might have. He has not been the same since that day and his relationship with the queen is strained because of it. That is what the chamber attendants say."

"And as to Menahem?"

"The king was very upset at what you have discovered. He sets great store by Menahem. He would have complained to the Prefect but since he heard that you hesitate arresting his friend, he is happy enough for the moment. His cup bearer tells me he offered Menahem the means to flee to the palace in Tiberias."

"Did he indeed? And?"

"Oh yes he did, but Menahem refused. The cup bearer heard him say he had no intention of fleeing from a crime he did not commit."

"What do the household think?"

"We find it hard to believe Menahem killed that girl. He was the only person of note to take any interest in her at all. She was different, you know, not like a servant, really. Her presence in the house has always been a mystery to us."

"Just how was she different?"

"In every way, I should say. I know that sounds like I'm avoiding your question, but I know no other way to put it. She spoke like a person of high station, you know? Most servants, men or women, speak the language of the streets. This girl sounded as much a princess as our Salome."

"Did she? How else was she different?"

"Well for one thing, she could read. I caught sight of her one day in the garden. She had a letter or something very much like one in her hand and she was reading it. When she finished she began to cry."

"Crying, you say. Do you know why?"

"I can only suppose it had something to do with what she read in her letter."

"And her name was Alexandra?"

"Was it? We called her Cappo. I don't know why. I think she must have told us that when she came. Everyone called her Cappo."

"And yet Menahem insists her name was Alexandra. Strange. You have monitored the guards' search for the Greek? Have they had any success?"

"I do not think so. Their search has been confined to the west end of the palace. I don't know and it's not my place to say, but if I were looking for someone in the palace, I would be poking around in the basements. They are like a warren or those caves men used to live in, and there are all sorts of places to hide. Also there is food to eat, wine to drink, and under the right circumstances, it could be very comfortable, particularly if one had an accomplice."

"You think that's possible?" Barak shrugged his shoulders and held his hands away from his sides, palms up. "See if you can find out for me, old man. Someone will know if he does. Where is his servant, he must have traveled with at least one. Where is he?"

"He remains in the palace with nothing much to do. He visits, chats, casts the stones with the other men."

"If you can, follow him if he slips away. If the Greek is sequestered in the basement, the servant will surely know and will be in contact with him."

"I will or one of us will. Most everyone knows I am assigned to you and so will be wary if I come too close, but there is a man in the kitchen who visits the basement from time to time. He will be less noticeable if the Greek's servant is to be followed."

"Very good. See to it. Now, Barak, it is time for us to do some searching of our own."

"For the Greek?"

"No, the guards will do that."

"What are we looking for then?"

"Answers, Barak, answers."

Chapter XVIII

"Barak, which name shall we use when we interrogate the other servants do you think, Alexandra or Cappo?"

"They will know her as Cappo. If you ask after Alexandra, you will only get a blank stare."

"Will I? I wonder. What are the chances she confided to one of the other servants? Girls are given to sharing confidences with friends. At least that is what I have been told."

"You may be right, but how will we know?"

"Wait and see. Perhaps if we drop the name in casually. Are we there yet?"

"Around this last corner. The servants will be coming and going during the day. We would have better luck at night when things are less demanding."

"Maybe, but I want to catch them unawares. I want to limit the cross talk. And we will not be interviewing anyone right away. I asked Chuzas to put the girl's things together in a safe place. He tells me they are in the care of someone named Nathan."

"They were. No more. Nathan is superstitious. Because the girl was murdered and, he assumed her not to be a believer, he feared the goods could be possessed by the spirits of death. It is fortunate he is so convinced because he is also a thief and otherwise would have taken the lot and sold it all by now."

"That is monstrous, but fortunate for us. Understand this, Barak, the forces of darkness may lurk in the hearts of men but not, I assure you, in their clothing. Besides, the girl may not have been observant, but I am quite certain she was of the faith. So, who has the goods now?"

"Minna, my wife, has them hidden in our quarters."

"Excellent. Take me to Minna, then."

Minna met them at the entryway of the quarters they shared with their widowed daughter and an old woman who would be called a hag by the younger members of the king's staff, but definitely not to her face. She had, Gamaliel decided, the most terrifying expression he'd ever encountered. He prepared himself to be verbally attacked. It did not happen. When the old lady spoke, it was with the softest voice he'd experience in years, marred only by the ragged gutturals that are the inevitable marks of age. Her relationship to Barak went into aunts and cousins of some degrees of separation that Gamaliel did not try to sort out. He would overlook the fierceness of her face.

"You have the dead girl's things, your husband tells me."

"I do. I cannot guarantee they are all here. The others, the young people, you know, picked through them as soon as they heard the news of her death. It is what we do, I am sorry to say, but servants have little and receive less, so property left by the dead is considered communal. The king's steward came with a palace guard and demanded the things be returned, but I do not think everything found its way back home."

"Well, let's have a look at what did come back." Minna bent and retrieved a small bundle from under the couch where the old lady sat staring balefully at the proceedings. No wonder Barak said they were in a safe place. Who would dare face up to this old lioness? Minna opened the bundle and spread the contents on the floor at their feet.

"Is there anything in particular you are looking for?"

Gamaliel scratched absently at his beard. "Barak, you said you saw her once in the court reading a letter. Is it in with her things?"

Barak spread the pathetic residue of the poor girl's life across the floor. A worn leather pouch, more like a large wallet, fell free from a bundle that Gamaliel recognized as the scraps of cotton fabric that matched the one he had retrieved from the bath.

"Let me see that leather thing there." Barak handed him the folder. In it were letters, as he'd hoped. He sorted through them. None were dated that he could see, and judging by their condition, none were recent. They had been folded and refolded repeatedly so that the brittle papyrus had cracked along several of the folds and threatened to fall apart. But they were inscribed on papyrus. The correspondent could not have been poor. They bore no dates. He inspected the seals and judging from the condition of the wax and the wear at the folds, he arranged them in what he guessed were the order the girl had received them. He sat and began to read.

"That Cappo, she were a beautiful girl," the old crone said, oblivious of the fact that she was interrupting the Rabban of the Sanhedrin. Minna tried to shush her. The old lady only raised her bushy eyebrows and offered a toothless grin. Gamaliel nodded his head in agreement and continued reading, first one missive, and then the next, one by one in order.

"What do they say, Rabban? Is there a clue to her killer in them?"

"They are not easily read. All I can gather is, not directly. It is what they do not say about her that is interesting, I think. There is no indication here to whom she may have been connected and, of course, we have only this side of the correspondence to go by, the letters she received. The language is so circumspect as to be nearly incomprehensible to a stranger who might intercept it and attempt to read it. I have to suppose that was done on purpose. The letters will require much more time and study before they give up their secrets. If we possessed the letters she wrote it might help, but of course we don't."

"You believe she wrote letters?"

"So it would seem. The person, persons to be precise, who sent her these—all but the last were by the same hand—seem to be responding to questions she put in previous letters. I confess at this moment I cannot deduce the questions from the answers."

"But the last is different?"

"Yes. I believe it is the one you saw her reading in the court and which produced her tears."

"It is a sad letter, then?"

"So it would seem. It tells her that someone—her father? Who knows? Apparently someone she knew intimately died or at least there is a death of some sort reported. I will need some hours to squeeze the sense from it—from all of them. They are oblique in their discourse. Almost a cipher. How odd. If I have it correct, it appears that she is told she must be careful and wait for someone else to fetch her back to her home now."

"Who will be doing that?"

"I cannot say. The letters are very carefully constructed to make sense to only the recipient. The writing is obtuse, to say the least. I believe they were written by someone, a parent or a relative perhaps, who feared they might fall into the wrong hands. That in itself is interesting, don't you think?"

Barak looked puzzled. This whole situation seemed beyond his comprehension. "If you say so, sir."

"I do say so. I will take these letters with me. I will study them for their secrets. It is what I am trained to do. Usually I plumb Holy Writ for meaning, but these documents surely will respond in the same way."

Minna and Barak exchanged glances. He shrugged. They were in the presence of the Rabban after all. If he said he could pry secrets from dry papyrus, he could.

"So, what else do we have of interest?"

"I cannot say. Clothes and some trinkets, a pair of sandals, very worn down at the heels, a scrap of cloth…" Barak pushed the bits and pieces around turning them over and separating them in turn.

"What is that?"

"What?"

"There is a small case under that scarf. I assume it is a scarf or another headdress."

Barak pushed the flimsy piece of cloth aside and lifted the case. It appeared to be covered with the same sort of ceramic as the pendant.

"I'll have that please." Gamaliel said. He took it from Barak and pried open the lid. "I am surprised the other servants did not take this as well, or that it was returned when the steward required the things to be given back." He pulled out a small object. "Well, well, well, do you know what this is, Barak?"

"No, sir."

"It is a seal. The sort used to seal letters and documents. Only people of a certain stature own or have use for such things. Indeed, they are the only ones who need them. It suggests what?"

"Sir?"

"If it wasn't obvious before, it is certain now. This girl was no ordinary servant. It confirms something I guessed at before."

"Before?"

"Yes. There is the matter of the pendant you recall." Barak frowned. He obviously did not recall anything. "Never mind. It seems we now know who she wasn't. We must set out to find out who she was. When, or maybe it's if, we do we will be closer to discovering her killer."

"It's not Menahem then?"

"I didn't say that. I have a feeling, an intuition, perhaps. In the past I always denied such a thing was of any use when dealing with a problem. Nevertheless, while I am sure he has a murky past, I have my doubts about his guilt. But if his past happens to have crossed with the girl's, he may, indeed, turn out to be the one we seek."

Chapter XIX

"Shall we visit Menahem now, sir? He'll be in his rooms this time of day."

"Not just yet, Barak. I need some time to reread these letters and I want to have someone look at this box and seal."

"I see. Will you be needing me anymore?"

"No, not until later this afternoon. Come to me after the noon meal in the room we use to interview. Oh, and one other thing. Have the captain of the palace guard come by then, too please."

"Sir."

Gamaliel made his way to the room assigned to him for his interviews. He pulled his chair up to a table, sat, and spread the letters out on its surface. In the next hour he read each multiple times, sometimes shifting his gaze from one to the other. Finally, at the start of the second hour, he shook his head and frowned. Deciphering the letters would need some time—a lot of time. He scooped them up and left the palace. He headed back to Agon the jewelry fabricator.

◇◇◇

Chuzas, who had been spying behind the lattice work, watched him leave and then made his way to the king's apartment to make his report. He didn't know it but his were not the only eyes locked on the Rabban. The second observer frowned and considered his options. Had he done enough or should he linger on? His commission was to retrieve the pendant only. Anything beyond that was left to his discretion. He had failed in the primary mission but doing the girl in accomplished the same thing, didn't it? He couldn't be sure what his employer would say about that, but guessed it would not be pleasant. He wanted that bauble, whatever it was, and if he did not return with it before the news of the girl's death reached Caesarea, there would be trouble.

But the death of an insignificant servant girl would not likely reach all the way to the north anytime soon, if at all. If, however, the authorities in Jerusalem discovered that she was anything but insignificant, well, that could change things in a hurry. This meddling rabbi might very well be successful in discovering the truth. And he'd failed to find that pendant at the physician's house. So, now he had had to consider which of the only two courses he should follow. He could leave and hope to collect the bounty without the medallion in hand and before the rest of the news arrived. If he did and if he were paid, he'd be free at last to live where he wished and how he wished. He could head to Ephesus or some other distant venue and start over. Or he could wait for another chance. They said the rabbi carried it in a purse on his belt. If he were to kill him, take the thing, and then leave, he would be in the clear on all accounts. What was one more death? With that thought, decision actually, in mind, his course at the moment was set. He would wait for the right moment and seize the thing and then be gone.

He cared little which of the two brothers were to play Cain in this latest version of Genesis and would then challenge a new Caesar. The grandfather couldn't prevail, so how did they imagine they would succeed where he failed? Perhaps they had more powerful gods on their side, but he doubted it. For reasons his uncomplicated mind could not grasp, they seemed to believe they needed the pendant to secure the throne and were willing to pay dearly to get it.

He would watch the old Jew and when the time was right would strike like a snake.

<>◇<>

Agon had a customer when Gamaliel burst through his door. The poor man fell back at the sight of the Rabban. He stuttered an apology but Gamaliel stopped him.

"Stay, finish your business. I will wait for the goldsmith, please."

He took a seat in the corner of the shop and pulled the girl's box from the pouch at his belt. Agon completed his sale. The other potential customers had bolted at the sight of Gamaliel. He turned to the Rabban.

"You would do me a great favor, Rabban, if you would confine your visits to early morning or late in the day when my shop is usually empty. Have you any idea how many sales I may have lost when you come barging in here like that?"

"Really? Why? I had no idea. I am sorry, Agon, but the exigencies of the situation do not…never mind. I'm sorry. Now take a look at this box and its contents and tell me what you think."

He handed the box to the jeweler who turned it over, held it close to his eye, and ran a finger over its surface. He inspected the clasp and then opened the box. He removed the seal and placed it on the counter without also inspecting it and turned his attention instead to its interior. Satisfied nothing more would be learned from the box, he picked up the seal and scrutinized it with the same care. Finally he returned the seal to its container, closed and re-engaged the clasp and replaced it on the counter.

"So, am I to tell you what you have already deduced, or is this a mystery to you? I doubt it, but I give you the choice."

"I wish an independent appraisal. I hope you will confirm what I suspect. The covering is familiar, is it not?"

"Yes, of course, it is the same material as the pendant. I suspect they were both disguised by the same artist and at the same time and presumably for the same reason. Will you tell me what this is all about now?"

Gamaliel held up his hand. "Patience, my friend. What do you make of the seal?"

"It belongs to a very important person. I would wager it is the property of someone close to, or a member of royalty. Have I got it right?"

"I think so, yes. Male or female?"

"Ah, that is hard to guess as the box is covered. If there were a name on it, we should have to remove it. Shall we?"

"I don't know. I was hoping to extract this object's identity without having to do so. Give me your best guess."

"It is unusual for a woman to have a seal this heavy. I know because I have made them for the wives of some of this city's more prosperous men. I would say this is a man's seal."

"And yet we find it in the possession of a young girl. How is that possible?"

"A gift from her father, or an uncle. Possibly she stole it. Who can say?"

"Suppose there was some urgency. Say, he knew something dire might happen. There is no time to run to his Agon to make an appropriate seal, so he gives her this one as he packs her off to wherever she was going."

"May I know where?"

"I cannot be sure but I think to the court of the late Philip, Tetrarch of Gaulanitis and half brother to our king."

"Ah. And then she arrives in this city, or in the palace, I should say, in the company of Queen Herodias and her daughter, the princess, yes?"

"Very good. Yes, it would seem so. Now the box."

"As I said, there is not much I can learn from the exterior. I can tell you that some writing on the inside has been removed some time ago. And there is a design, perhaps a name on the surface. I must remove the covering to tell you which, but I warn you, I cannot reproduce this box as I did the pendant."

"There will be no need. It seems I am the only one who cares about the box enough to want to discover its secrets. Peel away the cover."

Agon worked with the studied hands of a master craftsman. Gamaliel had to hold his tongue, frustrated at the time he took. Finally the exposed surface of the lid appeared.

"There you are, Rabban, it is writing, as you can see. I cannot read it. Tell me what it says."

Gamaliel narrowed his eyes and read the inscription. He looked up to the ceiling for a moment and then back down again.

"I might have guessed." He said, more to himself than to the jeweler. He ran his finger across the surface, his mind turning over possibilities and probabilities. "Agon, when you were in the service of Rome, you spent time in the north. Do I remember that correctly?"

"Ah, yes. I was in a cohort of one of the *auxillae*. As you know, the troops composed of volunteers not having Roman citizenship are not as selective of their membership as the Italian Legions. Even a suspect Jew was welcome if he were willing to die for the emperor and fight on Shabbat. And then there were those other Jews who had been forced by Tiberius to leave Rome and into the military assigned to Sardinia. A very strange man, our emperor."

"Strange barely covers it. And I take it you were not sent to Sardinia but were you willing?"

"Willing to take his money and my chances? I was. I served in Cilicia for a time, also Cappadocia, Galatia, and Iconium. I would have been to Bithynia except for the leg."

"You were wounded?"

"On the road between Caesarea and Tarsus, some bandits attacked a caravan. You know cohorts of legionnaires are regularly rotated out to secure the roads. A band of brigands surprised some travelers on the road. There were only four of us on post at the time and we drove them off but not before one almost hacked my leg from my body. It was Shabbat, I think. Do you suppose the Lord punished me because I did not keep Shabbat?"

"I think I am supposed to say yes, but I will not. The Lord, in my view, does not punish folks who act in the face of limited choices. How he feels about those with many and who still stray, is another matter."

"That is reassuring—if you are right. Either way, I cannot do anything about it now."

"So, you were wounded and then retired."

"Released as in 'of no more use' without pension or compassion, more like, yes."

"But you landed on your feet, so to speak. Now, what can you tell me about Cappadocia?"

Chapter XX

"Cappadocia? What is there to tell? It is a very strange place, Rabban. Stranger even than this land. Archelaus, one of Herod's spawn, I think, but maybe not, was its king for a while, but no more. His position depended on Rome's willingness to have him serve as a client king. As long as he behaved and paid his taxes, he sat on his throne. But like so many men enthralled with power, he took it into his head to seize more of it or maybe it was territory he sought. I can't remember which, but for his overreaching, the emperor had him arrested and put on a boat to Brundisium."

"He has a successor?"

"A Pretender, you mean. What king doesn't? There were many, but none that were given his place. The sons of his daughter Glaphyra were the noisiest. There were others but it makes no difference now. Caesar declared it a province and appointed a governor."

"I see. These sons of Glaphyra, they were by her marriage to Alexander. Is that right?"

"I never could unravel the lines in the royal families. I suppose they were, if you say so. Plotting and conspiring seems to be the chief occupation of those born into royalty and sorting out the who and why of them is beyond my poor abilities."

"Yes. How many sons were there?"

"Of Princess Glaphyra? I have no idea. Two or three, I think. I can tell you this, there is talk recently of rebellion in Caesarea.

That would be the Caesarea in Cappadocia, not the one from which Pilate governs or the late Philip did. There is not much in the line of originality when it comes to naming either cities or princes. Of course, there is always talk of rebellion in the capitals of kingdoms."

"How do you know this about Cappadocia?"

"I made many acquaintances in that area when I served and some of my old comrades from the cohort stop by from time to time with news. I am as current as any, I think."

Gamaliel scratched his chin and studied the jeweler. "Would the captain of the palace guard be one such acquaintance?"

"Oh yes. He drops by regularly. The cohort was disbanded a year or two after I received my release. Geris was luckier than I. He received severance pay and as it happened, he had family in Tiberias. When he traveled there after the cohort's abolition he heard the king wanted to add numbers to his guard. He was taken on, because of his military training."

"That was who I saw yesterday entering this shop after I left."

"Yes, it was."

"You didn't say anything about the pendant to him?"

"Oh, no, I daren't. You said not to speak of it and I didn't. I think he'd be very interested, though."

"Yes, I suspect he would. Under no circumstance are you to even hint at it to him, you understand? Not a hint, not a word, a wink, or a nudge. There is always entirely too much gossip in the palace. It would only take one person to say something and the whole entourage would have it by nightfall"

"No sir, nor a peep from me."

"Good. It is exceedingly important that no one know of this matter. You said you knew Tarsus?"

"Not well, but yes, a bit."

"I have a student who comes from there."

"Is that so? It is a very nice city. Sits on the river it does. Boats come there to clean their bottoms in the fresh water, they say. The creatures that attack the planks in the salt sea cannot live in the fresh water so a week or two in Tarsus will kill them and then they sometimes haul the boat ashore and scrape the remains away. They say Cleopatra's barge sailed in there with Antony. Quite an excitement, to hear it told. Her and him and the little boy they say was bred from Emperor Julius"

"Indeed? It must have been quite a sight."

"What is his name, your student?"

"Saul. His family manufactures tents, among other things."

"I could know of them, possibly, if they made leather ones. A good leather tent is a necessity for a soldier. Not so much in these parts but for those heading to Gaul of Britannia where it snows and rains more than here, a good leather tent is worth having even if it makes your pack heavier."

"I don't know about leather. Handling hides and animal parts is an occupation requiring special permits from the priests and Saul strikes me as singularly rigorous in his faith. Agon, we will talk more, but now I must return to the palace to continue my probing. Remember, speak of this to no one, you hear?"

But Gamaliel did not go directly to the palace. The sun was still not yet directly overhead and he estimated he had another hour before he needed to return. Instead he took the street that led to the Sheep Gate and to the physician. He didn't need to talk to Loukas as much as he wanted seclusion and a quiet place where he could think.

Once again he indicated to the servant, Draco, he wished to enter by the courtyard gate, and once again he entered that area and marveled at the way Loukas had carved it from the adjoining hillside. Loukas met him as he stepped through the gate.

"Welcome again, Rabban, you do me honor."

"I honor you? How is that possible?"

"Tell me, sir, how many people that you believe to be outside your faith have you willingly visited in the past year and then of that number, how many more than twice?"

"Oh, I see. I must be truthful, Physician, as much as I enjoy your occasional company, and please do not repeat that, I am here to relieve my aching brain."

"Is your pain real or rhetorical? If the former I have a powder that will help. If the latter, how can I serve you."

"Speak to me about anything but this tiresome murder, political conniving, and Roman rule, rulers, and the Empire. I am weary of the whole business."

"Very well, I am happy to oblige. I will bring refreshment. You sit."

He left to give Draco his order and returned and sat across from Gamaliel. A hint of a smile crossed his lips.

"You wish conversation not related to the investigation or anything even peripherally attached to it?"

"I do."

"Very well, we will attend to your area of expertise. Tell me, Rabban in the Holy Book there is a passage that puzzles me, to wit.

And in those days there were the giants on the earth, and again afterwards, when the sons of Elohim had come in unto the daughters of men, and they bore children by them. These were the heroes, who of old were men of renown.

"Can you tell me how I am to understand that passage?"

"You have read Genesis, the first of Moses' books? How so?"

"I read Greek and consider myself a man of the world. In Alexandria, in the Greek version of The Book. I have had sheets copied out and at my disposal from time to time."

"You have read from the Septuagint?"

"If that is its name, yes. I suffer from a curious spirit that makes me thirsty for knowledge. I read and I ask questions. I believe it is the only path to truth."

"The Law is the way and the truth."

"And the life, for you, yes, I know. But for me, truth devolves from inquiry. I ask about this particular passage because, as you know, those who subscribe, however reluctantly, to a pantheon, read this passage and see something familiar. You speak of giants and mighty men of old. They speak of the Titans. You speak of the sons of your *Elohim*, and the offspring of their union with women. They speak of gods, goddesses, and demigods. In Persia they might say angels. Can you tell me the difference? And if not a difference, how do I reconcile your insistence on one true and indivisible Creator with this passage?"

"Loukas, you are toying with me, I think. The reading of this passage is never clear, but becomes less so if you assume nothing precedes or follows it. But if you continue reading to the end you will find the whole of it blends together and reveals a Creator, *Adonai,* as you say, and a story to follow. In it, then, the reference to sons can be seen as a reflection of an indwelling spirit he bestows on his human creation, his sons and daughters in the broadest sense. And do we not say of one who has accomplished much beyond what we took to be that man's abilities or capacities, that he is a giant?"

"I think you are stretching the point, Rabban. I do not fault you for that. Most of what the pagan priests insist in the story of Zeus or Jupiter, take your pick, is enormously more fanciful than this. But I think both Hebrew and pagan would benefit from an acknowledgement that there are some things in heaven and earth that cannot be reconciled to our understanding and it is just possible that this passage is a reflection of that commonality. That would include our holy books, logical systems, and the mundane as well. Wouldn't you agree?"

"I might be tempted to, Loukas, but I cannot. I feel much better for having had a problem set before me that I may or may not solve and whether I do or do not is of marginal consequence. Shall we have some wine to wash this down? And, thank you for reminding me why I am not a pagan."

"You are most welcome."

Chapter XXI

Chuzas found the queen in her quarters. He had orders to keep her and the king informed of every move Gamaliel made. She knew that while the Rabban did not hold that John the Baptizer was a true prophet, he did agree with the holy man's opinion of her marriage to the king. She also knew that she could not eliminate his disapprobation like she had John's. Gamaliel's presence in the palace stood as both a threat to her position and a great personal affront. She also knew the king's weaknesses. Would the Rabban persuade the king to put her aside? Everyone knew the guilt brought on by John's beheading still weighed on him.

"What have you for me, Steward?"

"There is not much to tell. The Rabban pokes and probes but gets no closer to the truth. He has spoken with all the servants and searches for the man called the Greek, but with no success. That also raises a question I would put to him but seek your opinion first, Highness."

"What question is that?"

"Is it not possible that this man has not fled, but lies dead somewhere himself?"

"Is that possible?"

"I know the captain of the guard has searched the palace and not found him."

"Then he has fled, surely."

"I think not. I took the liberty of inspecting his rooms and all his baggage is still in place as is his servant whom I have questioned carefully though he pretends not to fully understand. I find his behavior suspicious to say the least."

"It is critical we get this righteous meddler out of the palace. Chuzas, I charge you to see to it. I thought you said you had done so, I thought you said that the Rabban had a suspect. What has happened?"

"I do not know. The knife found in the bath belonged to Menahem. He admitted it was his. Yet the Rabban hesitates. He asks why Menahem knew the girl's name when no one, including your Majesty, would admit to it."

"She is Cappo, that is all, a servant thrust on me by Philip for reasons I do not know. He gave me orders to keep her safe. Well, he is no longer my husband nor is he alive to enforce them so I have no obligation to care for her any more. Now she is dead as well and good riddance to them both."

If Chuzas was shocked by her position regarding King Philip's death, he did not show it. "Menahem says her name was Alexandra."

"What! That cannot be. The only girl of that age with that name is…but it cannot be. Do not repeat this to anyone, Chuzas, do you hear? To no one."

"Yes Majesty, but I cannot say to whom or if the Rabban will broadcast it."

"We must bring this nonsense to a close. If you value your position, you will see to it, Steward. Do you take my meaning?"

"Yes Majesty. But how?"

"Insist that Menahem is our villain. If the Rabban will not move on him, I will have the palace guard bind him and deliver him to Pilate myself. Make sure that meddling rabbi knows that."

"I caution your Majesty to consider the consequences of such a move."

"What consequences can there be? The man is a murderer. Explain to me what consequences there can be."

"With respect, your position with the Sanhedrin is shaky because of…"

A scowling queen turned on the trembling steward. "Because of what?"

Chuzas swallowed, took a breath and ventured into an area he'd have rather not gone. "Your marriage for one and the Baptizer's unfortunate end for another. The Prefect needs a compliant Sanhedrin more than he needs your good will. I am sorry, Majesty, but he will not take it well if you interfere with the work of an official of the Sanhedrin, and its Rabban at that." He braced for the blow he felt sure would soon turn his cheek a bright red. It didn't come.

After a long moment, the queen turned to leave the room. "Steward you will send a courier to Pilate with this message. Say, 'The Queen sends her greetings to his Excellency, the Prefect, and wishes to inform him of the fact that the murder weapon has been found, its owner identified, and yet the Rabban of the Sanhedrin has scruples.' Say also, 'The Queen has every confidence in the Prefect's judgment but wonders why this murder investigation has not been brought to an end and the palace allowed to return to normal.'"

"Shall I also name Menahem?"

"Well, why not?" The queen stalked from the room leaving a relieved Chuzas behind.

<>< ><>

Gamaliel took the cup Loukas offered and sighed. He could soon get used to this life. A cup of wine in the back court with a friend however distant he might be from the Faith.

"Are you now sufficiently unburdened to discuss your crime, Rabban? If so, I have a small piece of news for you."

"News? Good news, I hope, I could use some good news."

"Draco, on reflection, tells me the intruder, who may or may not have come here as a result of the murder, wore boots."

"Boots? Like a soldier? Those kinds of boots? Tiberius' presumed successor, Germanicus' son Caligula, wore boots as a child. 'Little Boots' the soldiers called him. I gather the name stuck. So, what sort of boots?"

"Draco did not specify, but if they were evident in the failing light and to weak eyes, they must have been more than the short sort worn by camel drovers and sea captains."

"Just so, but of what significance is this?"

"Well. I did not promise significance, only a potential clue, and one might ask, who wears boots in Jerusalem?"

"The hills currently teem with pilgrims from all over the world. Anyone of them could have slipped over your wall."

"But would they not have taken what they could. Nothing, you recall, is missing."

"That's true and leads us nowhere but, I am glad for any information even if, in the end it isn't particularly helpful. Thank Draco for me." Gamaliel sipped his wine. "One day, Physician, I would like to have at my disposal a supply of ice from the mountain tops. They say that Caesar has it brought to him by runners so that he can cool his bath or his wine. I would like to taste wine in the summer that has been chilled."

"When I lived across the Middle Sea near the mountains where the weather brings ice and snow in the winter months, I had that experience. I found it delightful but do not think it worth the cost to make it happen here. Of course if you are Caesar, the cost is of no concern. In winter you can always put your casks outside. That would chill the wine."

"But I do not want it chilled in the winter. I want it chilled in the summer when it is hot."

"Of course. Alas, life is not fair, Rabban."

"Indeed. Speaking of evidence, do you know the circumstances surrounding the death of the Baptizer?"

"I think you have made a giant leap in your rhetoric, Rabban. What has chilling wine to do with the beheading of one of your prophets, and what has that to do with evidence in this case?"

"There is a continuing debate over John's place in the ranks of the prophets. I am one that does not subscribe to the notion he qualifies to join the company of Isaiah, but the people in the streets do so we let it stand. The connection, Loukas is this— Princess Salome caught the attention of the king. I would say he lusted after her but the queen stood in the way of anything ever coming of such incestuous thoughts. Nevertheless, he bade her dance for him. She refused at first, but he promised her anything if she would do it. Legend has it she danced with seven veils which she shed one at a time."

"Seven? One of your peoples' magic numbers."

"Not just my people and not magic. An important number, yes, but please, no magic, my friend. What do you mean my people?"

"You are captive to certain numbers, Rabban. Everybody knows that. Seven, twelve, forty—forty days, forty years, seven years of plenty, seven years of famine, seven demons—not six, not eight, seven…Jews are fascinated with these numbers and increments dependent on them. You really should study Euclid, Rabban, you would find him fascinating."

"Do not get me started on numerology or mathematics either just now. I have enough pagan interference as it is. So, the princess is alleged to have had seven veils and seven only. That is to say when the seventh hit the floor she was, as you might say, *gymnós*. The king was enchanted with her performance—"

"And her appearance no doubt. I have seen the princess."

"Yes, well he breached numerous laws regarding gazing on the nakedness of another by the time she'd finished. At any rate, and at her mother's urging, the princess requested the head of the Baptizer on a silver tray as her reward."

"And of course the king delivered it."

"Not right away. Befuddled as he was, he offered her alternatives. To be fair, he never thought such a request would be made and as he was one who accepted the Baptizer as a prophet, he feared killing him could bring disaster to both him and his court. But a king's word is his bond—sometimes—and in the end he complied."

"Fascinating. All this has to do with your case exactly how?"

"The veils, Physician. The solution to my case, as you call it, dances before me like the princess. I am hampered from seeing her, that is to say to see my solution, by the veils. They obscure and each time one has dropped to the floor, there is another beneath it."

"The imagery is alluring, I must say. So how close to sighting flesh are you?"

"Please, that is not the direction I intended to take, but I must admit you are right. She is very alluring in a 'soon to go to fat way.' You see my problem. I am not a logician like the Greeks you so admire. I am a plodder. I read the Law, I interpret and dispute it. We look at it this way and then that. Can it mean this or something else? What does the Lord want of us, you see? There is never a need for me to dissect a problem like this one. The vision I seek eludes me in the madness of the dance and swirls of silk."

"How very poetic. You may be a plodder but you have promise. Alas, I can't help you any more than I have. If you were to place before me all that you deduced thus far, I might be able to offer an insight or two."

"Yes, that is so. Let me think on that. Now I must return to the palace and grab at one or two of those veils…don't even say it! I will return soon."

Chapter XXII

Gamaliel arrived at the palace gates just as a messenger dashed by. "Pardon, sir," the youth muttered and scurried down the street in the direction of the Antonia Fortress. Barak emerged from the same gate and waved frantically at Gamaliel.

"Sir, there is trouble, I fear."

"What sort of trouble? I have only been away a few hours. What could have happened in such a short time?"

"We have spoken of it before—you know how our rulers assume servants are both deaf and blind—

"Yes, I remember."

"One of the queen's maids passed along the news that she has sent a message to Pilate and told him you have identified the killer but refuse to act."

"But I don't have the killer. I only have a suspect. There is a vast difference. Moreover, I have serious doubts about this suspect and I need a firmer case before I would make any move against him. Does Chuzas know about this message?"

"He drafted it."

"Ah, now that is interesting. He didn't try to dissuade the queen from sending it?"

"No. If the person who overheard the exchange remembers correctly, she said he only urged her not to have Menahem arrested on the spot by the king's own guards. She appeared ready to call them out and have the old man led to the Prefect in chains."

"There are days when I really regret I am forbidden to swear an oath. This is one of those days. Very well, we will deal with the queen's foolishness when we must. I had hoped to have a word with Menahem this afternoon, but I will meet with the steward first. Shabbat will be soon upon us. If we do not finish this up in two days, this investigation will have to be put over until Yom Rishon. Find the steward and tell him I require his presence immediately. I will be in the room assigned to us."

Barak hurried off in search of Chuzas. Gamaliel retired to the room which had become as familiar to him by now as one in his own home. He wondered if any ears and eyes lurked behind that punctuated wall. Did he care? One advantage in knowing you are being watched and overheard was you can easily transmit misinformation likely be viewed as credible than you can if you tried the same thing face to face. The disadvantage: you had to be very careful how you dispensed the truth. He was turning these thoughts over in his mind while he waited for the steward.

A woman entered and glanced nervously around and then approached him. "Rabban," she said with a voice so soft he almost did not hear her.

"I am the Rabban. What is it you want, woman?"

"Forgive me for coming. I have heard you believe Menahem is the man who has killed the girl they call Cappo."

"That is true, as far as it goes. He is the most likely at the moment. There is the matter of his knife, you see. You have something to tell me about Menahem?"

"He is not your killer, sir. I know him and I know he could not have done this awful thing."

"I see. You know this how? Who has spoken to you of this matter? It is not a thing to be noised about in the women's quarters."

"I am not from the women's quarters, Excellency. I should explain. It is my husband who has told me these things."

"Your husband? Who may that be?"

"I am Joanna, the wife of Chuzas."

"Ah! And you know we do not have the right man how?"

"I know Menahem because he it was who led me to the rabbi."

"The rabbi? What rabbi would that be? Woman, the streets of this city teem with rabbis, would be rabbis, discredited rabbis, and pagans who pass themselves off as rabbis."

"I speak of the man Yeshua ben Yosef."

"Ah, I see, that rabbi. Yes your husband mentioned him. And Menahem is a follower, too?"

"Yes."

"And he led you to him?"

"We…I had a great need and Menahem, he found the rabbi and the rabbi healed me, so yes, I suppose you could say he led me to him."

"And what is it about this carpenter-rabbi that makes him so appealing to you? Beyond the healing, of course. It was a serious illness?"

"Yes…you could say so. I was…well it is done now, thank the Lord."

"And you admire him for what he has done for you. That is only natural. But this man has no followers of note that I am aware of, no people of substance deem him any more than a rabble rouser like his cousin, and he teaches without authority. What is it that attracts the wife of the king's steward to join his odd flock of men and women?"

"When he speaks about the Lord, it is different. It is as though he knows him personally. He speaks of mercy—"

"And do you believe it is the place of women to think much on those topics."

"I know it is written, *It would be better to see the Torah burned, than to hear its words upon the lips of a woman,* but I don't understand why that must be so."

"Where is that written, woman?"

"I do not know, sir. I am but a woman and not permitted to learn scripture. But it is often repeated to me by my husband when we, or rather when I, venture to speak about my love of the Lord."

"But you wish to know more of our Creator, is that it?"

"Yes."

"And this rabbi of yours encourages you to learn?"

"He does."

"Does he teach the Law, Torah, Moses?"

A vertical line appeared on Joanna's forehead. "Sometimes, yes, but mostly he quotes from the Isaiah scroll."

"Ah, so it is like that. Yes, I see." Gamaliel did not agree with some of the teachings of his own mentor Hillel particularly those concerning women, and he had his doubts about this untutored rabbi from the north with his emphasis on Isaiah and the Coming Age. He'd neither heard nor seen the man and cared nothing about him. But as he gazed at the earnest face before him, he understood that a willing heart is honored by the Lord irrespective of the breast in which it beat.

"I do not begrudge you the opportunity, child, but as you know, women are assumed to have *binah*, intuition of the spirit. Therefore you are exempt from some of the Commandments. That is why you may not be counted in a *minyan* and why, among other things, when you read Torah, it does not count as a reading in the community."

"Yes I understand. It is a thing some women find burdensome, but not I."

"No? Good. Then, do you know why it is the ordinary people and not the scholars, the leaders in the city, who seek your rabbi out? Why are so many from the countryside where regard for the Law is otherwise so lax?"

"You mean the Galilee. I can only guess, sir. He speaks to them in ways they understand. He talks of sowing and reaping, of lost sheep, unfruitful vines, and of catching fish. He knows about landowners and what it must be like for a man to stand fearful yet forced to wait in the market square, hoping for the chance to earn the day's wages he needs to buy bread to feed his family that evening. The people of the city—David's city—are many generations from tending flocks or pruning branches from vines. In the city we buy and sell the fruits of other men's labor."

"Just so, but we meet at the Temple, we read the same Torah."

"We do, but with respect, Rabban, it is not the same in practice. When we go to offer a grain sacrifice, we buy a measure of wheat in the market along the way and take it to the Priest to place on the Altar. But a farmer takes his measure of wheat from stores he has grown himself and brings it to sacrifice. If he has had a bad harvest, his sacrifice is greater than ours, you see? In the same way that we buy and sell the fruits of another's labor, so also do we sacrifice their fruits, not ours. The farmer, the shepherd, the vintner, all sacrifice from their substance. Our sacrifice is perfunctory, theirs is real."

Gamaliel's eyebrows which had begun to climb his forehead, now dropped down to near normal.

"I see. As I said, *binah.* And now you have a problem, woman. Your husband does not approve of your love of this rabbi. You walk on the thin edge of disobedience when he wishes you to cease and you do not obey him."

"I know that. It is a great worry for me but that is not why I came to you. It is something more…I know my husband blames Menahem for the problem. You see, that is why he did what he did. He is angry at the king's companion."

"What did he do?"

"It is only a suspicion. You found a knife in the bath, it is said."

"I did."

"It was Menahem's?"

"It was."

"Oh dear. I am not certain. It was something he said and…" She sighed and looked away, her eyes troubled. There was something she did not wish to tell him and he suspected it was important. But for her to do so she would have to betray her husband. He could not ask her to do that. Could she know that Chuzas' had drafted the damning letter to Pilate? That must be it.

"So you believe because he held Menahem responsible for your straying from him in this business of the rabbi he hoped to see Menahem discredited?"

"I fear it, yes. But I don't know for sure and I don't want to…I just wanted to say…"

"Enough. I will keep what you have said in mind. In the meantime you have a problem to solve with respect to your rabbi. Your course is to do one of two things. You must yield to your husband," Joanna's face fell, "or, you must persuade him to join you in following this man."

"Which?"

"I cannot say, but am of the opinion he will reap a greater benefit if you bring him to your rabbi than if you yield to his position. But I cannot tell you how to proceed or predict which will be the end of it. Now you must be off before your husband finds you here and thinks wrongly of the reason why."

Chuzas would arrive soon and he did not want him to know his wife had provided him with information. It led no closer to the killer but it might help explain away one inconsistency that continued to gnaw at him.

Chapter XXIII

As it happened, it wasn't the steward who entered next, but a grim captain of the palace guard who marched into the room with two equally stone-faced men. Surprised, Gamaliel started to rise from his chair. He had planned to have a word with the captain, but hadn't asked to see him just then. He assumed the arrival signaled something else, some new turn in events.

"Captain, have you come to tell me you have found Graecus?"

"No sir, sorry. I am sent to collect you and hand you over to a small unit of Roman soldiers who are waiting at the palace gate. The Prefect, it seems requires your immediate presence. And to be sure you comply, he has sent legionnaires. They will escort you to the Antonia Fortress."

"Will they now? My, my, that was quick. The queen's message must have touched a nerve or the Prefect is in her debt. Or… what else must be on his mind that he would yield to a queen for whom he has little or no respect?" The captain shrugged and looked embarrassed. What did he think of Gamaliel's frequent disregard for the exalted position of the royal family? What did any of them think? "Very well, Captain, lead on."

The captain of the guard led Gamaliel to the palace's outer gate where several bored legionnaires, resplendent in dress leather armor, slouched against the palace wall, their short swords drawn. Gamaliel greeted them and gestured toward the Antonia Fortress.

"Lead on, my good men," he said and fell into step between them. The group made its way through the crowd of sweaty pedestrians, pilgrims, not to mention the cut-purses who make a point of attending the High Holy days and risk certain death or dismemberment in search of easy money. It took some shoving on the part of the soldiers to clear their way through the crowd. Gamaliel heard low voices muttering, "It's the Rabban, he has been taken prisoner. What has happened?" He guessed by nightfall the rumor would have spread throughout the city that he'd been arrested, tried, and was even then on his way to Golgotha to hang on a cross outside the city's walls. He waved to the crowd hoping they would understand that he was not in trouble, only responding to a summons. In truth he didn't know if that were true or even if he would return from the interview. Pontius Pilate, though he'd been on station just a little over a year, had already acquired a reputation for harshness and insensitivity in his treatment of the people over whom he ruled. Gamaliel could only guess at what the Prefect might have in store for him. But it did not take a scholar to assume it was nothing good.

As he walked along with his grim faced escorts, a sinking feeling grew deep down somewhere in the pit of his stomach. He wished he'd never been caught up in this business. Why hadn't the Prefect asked the High Priest to do his dirty work? He, the High Priest, would have jumped at the chance to curry favor with the Prefect and would have been an infinitely more pliable agent.

The Antonia Fortress rose up from the great plateau formed by the Temple Mount to the south and the Temple itself. Built by Herod the First and named for his late friend, Marc Antony, it was the station for the small contingent of legionnaires in the city and Pilate's headquarters when he visited the city. There had been rumors he had eyes on the king's palace and would soon require Antipas to resume his residence in Jerusalem in his own, smaller palace near the Hulda Gates.

Pilate waited for him at the entrance in full dress armor but with neither helmet or armament. The Rabban took the latter as a good sign. Pilate tapped his foot as Gamaliel and the soldiers mounted the steps. Without waiting for a greeting, Pilate lashed out.

"Please explain to me, Rabbi, why I must be put in the position of seeming to bow to the whims of the Queen of the Galilee and Perea? Is it true you have found the man who murdered the servant girl and yet you refuse to turn him over to me?"

"Your pardon, Excellency, I can only answer yes and no, I have identified a suspect, yes. What little evidence we have gathered so far points to him as the killer. And yes, I have not as yet decided to turn him over to be punished. I wish it were as simple as our beloved queen would have it, but it is not. So no, as the Rabban of the Sanhedrin, I cannot condone the arrest and confinement of an innocent man. More than yourself, Prefect, I wish to end this business, but at this juncture I cannot."

"You have scruples then, Rabbi?"

"More than scruples—serious doubts. There are discontinuities, and questions that tantalize but do not have answers, not to mention an as yet unsubstantiated bit of evidence suggesting the man in question may well be the victim of a prevarication on the part of a *pseudo martyreo* close to the matter which, if true, will require other actions. It is one of our Ten Laws Moses brought to us."

"A false witness or simply a liar?"

"There is a difference?"

"You people have far too many dogmas for my taste, Rabban." Gamaliel nearly retorted that the Romans had far too few, but thought better of it and bit his tongue. Pilate looked quizzically at him and continued. "Tell me of the…what did you call them? Discontinuities? I require examples. And before you do that, can you give me a good reason why I should not clap you in a cell and drag the suspect in myself."

"A reason? Several, I believe. First the facts of the case as we presently know them. The girl was raped and killed in the bath and her throat slashed. Her body appears to have been discovered within moments of her death. Later, at the scene, that is to say in the emptied bath, I found, a knife, some coins, a cut leather thong, a pendant, presumably fastened at one time by the thong and around the girl's neck, a scrap of clothing, her headdress, and the fact, determined later, that she may have drowned before or as a result of having had her throat cut."

"And the questions?"

"If she was dead already from drowning, why cut her throat? What is the significance of the coins, if any? What kind of murderer leaves his knife behind at the scene, particularly one so easily identified? Who was the girl? What about the headdress? And, finally, what is the significance of the pendant."

"That's all?"

"You are being ironic. Well, it's all I have just now, but it's a start. There are other questions attendant on these, but these will do for now. No doubt the queen has written you that the man we have identified as the possible killer is Menahem, the king's long time companion and foster brother."

"She has. And I take it you do not believe he is."

"I didn't say that. I only said I have serious doubts. You ask for examples. Take this one confusing bit, this *discontinuity*, if you will: the knife that turned up in the bath, the alleged murder weapon, was found at the opposite end of the pool. How, if the knife accidently slipped from the killer's hand, did it end up ten cubits away?"

"The body drifted?"

"Possibly. Not likely, though. Her lungs were filled with water. She sank, the physician said, and there is no current in a bath as there would be in a stream. But I concede she might have moved. Then, and staying with the knife once more, it is Menahem's. It is a ceremonial blade he often wears. It is of foreign design, Egyptian if I am any judge, and unique in its appearance and design. Everyone in the palace had seen it and knows it. What sort of killer would use such a knife, one that everyone could readily identify as his should it be connected in some way with the murder? You see?"

"Perhaps it was a crime of passion and impulse. You did say the girl had been forced. Are you sure it was by force? She was nothing more than a servant girl. Do you really consider it as a rape? Perhaps in your law it is, certainly not in the Roman way of such things."

"Her headdress at the scene suggests she was not there for any immoral purpose."

"How's that?"

"A modest woman, servant or royal, must cover her head. To undo one's locks in public signals the woman is loose and available. She was wearing her covering—"

"That is not a particularly compelling bit of evidence, Rabban. She could have removed it on arrival. There are myriad possibilities to explain the thing. In any case, if her master desired her, he has the right to take her. No consent is required or sought."

"No? Well, under our Law, which is still *the* law in Judea, it would be. Under normal circumstances, that is. I do not know if life in the palace can ever be thought of as normal, but that is a matter to consider some other time. And, as it is beginning to look as if the girl was not a servant, there may be a need to apply a different standard."

"Not a servant? What or who then?"

"I cannot say yet. I am pursuing that line now, or was before you pulled me away. She could read and write, Prefect. She had in her possession an elaborate seal and letters. She was seen by another servant, the man Barak you assigned me, to be reading them in one of the palace courts and crying over its contents. I have since attempted to read those epistles. They are confusing in content but seem to contain answers to questions which she must have posed to her correspondent. *Ergo*, she also writes. Then I must account for the pendant she always wore. It turns out not to be what it seemed at first and further may have some important significance—"

"Important? In what way, Rabbi? Please do not try my patience anymore."

"I do not wish to but at the same time, am not prepared to say. If I am wrong, it may only create more trouble and I am sure you do not want that. So, before I bring anyone before you for the crime, I must know who the girl was and how she fits into the larger picture. If I can uncover the answers to those questions, I will have the motive and the motive, I guarantee, will lead to her killer."

"All this is very fine, Rabban, but I want this matter closed and now. You have enough evidence to convict the man Menahem. Please understand this, whether he is, or is not the killer is of no importance to me whatsoever. Let us have him and be done with this business. You said you wished to be shed of this duty. Be so and send me Menahem."

"Excellency, you are right, I wish to be finished and return to my life. But I cannot send this man to trial just now. You gave me eight days to unravel this snarl, let me have them."

"And if I don't?"

Gamaliel sighed. Why did he always find himself at odds with important people? The queen, the High Priest, and now Pilate?

"If you do, Prefect, I will stand as his advocate in court, and I will see him acquitted."

"How? What is it you think will exonerate him?"

"Three things, Excellency—he is old, he is impotent, and he is right handed."

Chapter XXIV

Gamaliel did not return to the palace at once as he'd intended. Instead he wandered unthinking toward the western wall and out through one of its gates near the old quarry, long since abandoned by the stone cutters. At one end, people of substance had had tombs cut into the rock face. A mound, a low hill in fact, of unquarried stone, said to be fractured in too many places to be of use for construction formed the other end. Between the two a garden of sorts had been planted, Gamaliel did not know by whom. The Romans had established their place of execution on the hill. Golgotha they called it—the place of the skull. Gamaliel shuddered at the sight. There were no naked bodies hanging on crosses today. He realized that there might have been had Pilate not yielded to his stubborn refusal to hand over Menahem. It was a near thing, if one took into account the acknowledged temper and reputation of the Prefect.

He turned away at the thought.

Without realizing how he'd managed to circle the northern edge of the city, he found himself at Loukas' doorstep once again. He looked up when it swung open to reveal the grotesque features of the servant, Draco.

"Is your master in?"

The servant mouthed something akin to a positive acknowledgement and, without asking, closed the door and proceeded to the back gate to admit Gamaliel into the rear court. The physician met him and offered a bench. Gamaliel sat heavily and exhaled.

"You look like you have just escaped death at the hands of the Scythian hoards, Rabban. Where have you been?"

"Close enough. I have narrowly missed a very bad outing with the Prefect. He lost his temper at the end of our interview. I think if he'd worn his sword, my head would even now be rolling across the Temple Mount."

"Well, that is an exciting picture to conjure. Not one I would enjoy, of course, but ah…very graphic, very Roman. What did you do or say to the Great Man to incur such a reaction, or do I really want to know?"

"Exciting for you, not for me. You remember our last conversation about the difficulty I am experiencing with sorting through the business of the dead girl?"

"Your wonderful seven veils? Vividly. By the way, I saw the princess in the entourage of the king when he made his symbolic visit to the Temple this morning. I must tell you, all I could think of was your image. She is very beautiful. One can only wonder—"

"Thank you for that. I was not trying to stimulate your licentious Greek imagination, only attempting to answer your question. You can be very trying sometimes."

"First, I am Hellenized, that is to say Greek only by inclination, Rabban. Secondly, trying is a perception only."

"Both are distinctions without a difference as far as I am concerned. I meant the business of the murder and the problems I have in connecting the evidence to the probable killer, not to the princess in whatever state of undress you imagine her. Anyway, the Prefect wishes to close the case. We had, he said, enough evidence to arrest Menahem. I should add that it did not matter to him if the man was innocent or guilty. He just wanted it over and was angry I refused to go along."

"And so the Righteous Man, that would be you of course, said that he would not convict an innocent man and would bring his own considerable power to bear to prevent that from happening."

"You know me too well, Loukas."

"Everyone does, Gamaliel. It is the thing they love most about you. It mollifies all the other things they find disagreeable. You are a lucky man that way."

"Things they find disagreeable? About me? How is that?"

"Rabban, you interpret the Law of Moses for them. People, if you haven't noticed, do not want the Law to be interpreted for them. They prefer to interpret it as they will. There is far more freedom for them in that approach. Allowances can more easily be made for their bad behavior. A god of one's own imagining is far more comfortable than one imposed from outside and over which one cannot exercise any control. You bring that sort of divinity into sharp and unyielding focus. People would rather you didn't, would rather you left them to their own devices. And the fact that many of your students are also abroad intruding into their lives in much the same way with opinions, reminders, and chastisements does not help your reputation very much either."

"But the Law is the Law. If we abandon it, we turn our backs on the Lord, deny our history, forfeit our future, and invite retribution."

"Come now. Think for a moment on what you just said. Is it possible to punish the people of Israel any more than they have been already? Think of the suffering the ordinary folk in this occupied country must daily endure. What could be worse than this Roman oppression?"

"It is terrible, I know, but—"

"Do you...do you know truly? Your problem, the problem more appropriately, of the rich and well off, if I may say so, is that their wealth and position insulate them from the consequences of their actions. You do not worry where your next meal will come from or if you can feed your family. Will enough be left of your harvest to pay your taxes? Those are not your concerns. Your difficulties with Roman rule are almost wholly cerebral. The poor and dwellers on the margins of society have a very different sense of outrage, I assure you. "

"I know, I know, you are correct. They are suffering, we are not and it is certainly an easy enough ditch to fall into. Alas, I think it has always been so and will remain so. Human nature is distressingly predictable."

"Again, spoken like a philosopher, not the Rabban of the Sanhedrin."

"Yes, yes, and that said, I do understand and I am sympathetic." Was he really? At his level so much was taken for granted. What was it the steward's wife had said…*He speaks to them in ways they can understand.* What had she meant by that exactly?

"So you say and I am sure you believe it. Consider this, haven't the Pharisees, in their zeal to define the Lord so closely, become nothing more than spiritual scolds, only telling people what he doesn't want rather than what he does? To many of us it seems that the men you train in the Law have managed to divide the faithful into two quite distinct and, I may say unequal, camps."

"Come, come, Loukas. Nothing is that simple."

"But it is. You have reduced the Lord's people into the Righteous and the Sinners. There seems to be no middle ground. Suppose one wished to speak the Lord's name, he is a blasphemer. He unties a knot on Shabbat, he is a sinner. This city, with its Temple and Pharisaic hierarchy, has become the citadel of the Righteous. The rest of the country, Galileans, the country folk all the way to the Gaza, indeed those camped without the walls at this moment, are Sinners, scorned by your minions even as they collect their sacrifices and taxes. You see? Your minute rendering of the Law binds the people tighter than they say the dead are in Egypt."

"Without the time and study required, that is an easy thing for you to say, Loukas, but at this juncture it is beside the point. Where we stand at any moment in history has nothing to do with the Lord's expectations of us in eternity. The Law is timeless. Rejecting it in whole or part can only lead to sorrow. That path, as I said, can only carry us to disaster as a Nation and a race."

"Then you had better hope the Lord has a more generous opinion of his creation than you do, my friend. But this is not why you are here, is it? I'm sorry to have distracted you with this ranting. You see I visited the Temple today and witnessed your people at work."

Gamaliel shook his head, suppressing his anger. Criticism of his life's work from a non-believer did not sit well at the moment.

"Not all my people, I fear. Do not apologize, Loukas. Even if what you say makes me angry, you still have a genius for diversion and that is what I need most when I am pressed about as I am this day. We must debate the Law some other time, however."

"Of course. You know I am always ready. So, you defied the Prefect and he turned red in the face and threatened you. How did you manage to make him homicidal and more importantly, how did you manage to avoid a trip to Golgotha or wherever Roman justice is currently being meted out?"

"Still Golgotha. I visited that place on my way over here. Very frightening. Well, as you suggested earlier, I told him if he tried Menahem for the girl's murder, I would defend the poor man in court and I would win the day."

"Did you indeed? As the definitive arbiter of the Law, I assume you would. So you believe the man is innocent?"

"Actually, I am sure he is. But whether he is innocent or guilty is not at issue, only that he is not convictable. If I am to finish this business, it must be that the guilty man is found or, failing that—a not unlikely outcome—at least an innocent will not be sacrificed on the altar of political expediency."

"Well said. Now you are thinking like a Greek. Of course you realize what that will mean to your long term prospects? Greeks are thinkers. Romans are doers. Guess which of the two rules the world."

"Please, Loukas, I have had a difficult day. Do not make it worse by labeling me a Greek, particularly after having castigated me for being Jewish."

"Sorry. It was meant as a compliment. Clearly the problems of guilt and innocence in the death of the girl are complex. Tell me, have we also not a clash of cultures here? The Roman sees no reason to be finicky about who shall pay the price for the death of so insignificant a victim as a servant girl. You hold that a life, any life, is as equally precious as any other."

"That is part of it, certainly. The rest seems to be largely political in nature. Symbolic steps made to please or delude the populace. A chance to report a positive outcome to his overseer, that sort of thing."

"Then you must provide your angry Roman with a viable political reason for accepting what you are doing. Can you?"

Gamaliel turned that thought over in his mind for a while. Could he? Should he? Was playing the game an honest approach and if he did, would he not be as devious and self-serving as the men who opposed him?

"I think I can, yes. Thank you, Loukas. You have just triggered the beginning of the solution, I think."

"You will play at politics then?"

"Not play, no. The solution is, unless I miss my guess, political in fact. I cannot be sure, but I think so. Listen."

Gamaliel carefully laid out the clues for him. To his annoyance, Loukas insisted on labeling them his *veils*.

"First, there is the fact she was drowned before or as a result of her throat being cut. Why cut her throat and then drown her? One or the other should be sufficient. If rape were the motive, why kill her at all. If she was only a servant, is it likely she would be in position to complain or seek a response? Then there are the coins, what do they signify if anything? Do they lead anywhere even if they are not directly related to the death? They had to come from somewhere, and they nag at me. What are they trying to prod out of my mind? There is the pendant which was not what it seemed. Was it the thing the killer really wanted, and if so, why not take it and run, why violate the girl? There is the knife, the too obvious knife—"

"Too obvious? Oh, you mean it was one everyone would or could quickly recognize."

"Yes and...wait, that's right. So why...? Ah! The steward, who saw it the very morning I pulled it from the bath failed to say something? He looked at it and said...what did he say? 'Is that the knife the killer used?' Something like that, yes. Why did he say that when he, of all people should have...I must go.

This Chuzas needs to be queried again. This time I think I will ask the captain of the guard to stand behind me when I do it."

"But you haven't finished your list. Stay. I must know."

"Very well, but for a moment only. Next, the girl could read. She received letters and apparently she wrote some as well. How did she post them? Do servant girls even post letters? Do they even read? I think not. Again, why does Menahem know her real name when no one else seems to, and where is Graecus? Goodbye, Physician, you have been very helpful."

Chapter XXV

Chuzas did not appear overly anxious at the presence of the captain of the guard, probably because he considered his position superior to Geris. Gamaliel bade him to sit.

"Steward, were you aware that I spent some time with your wife earlier in the day?" Chuzas looked at him quizzically and shook his head.

"No? We had a fascinating conversation about her rabbi, the man of whom you and I once spoke and about whom you worried."

"She said nothing about your meeting to me. I hope you were not offended. Since she has fallen in with that lot of…well, since she heard about that man, she's not been the same. I will see to it she will not disturb you again and I am sorry."

"Do not apologize. Is it true she experienced some sort of cure at the hands of that rabbi?"

"She believes many things, but what is true is less clear to her. She was ill and she recovered. People do, you know."

"I see. And this illness, what form did it take?"

"She was…They say she was possessed, but you know how people talk. She had difficulties and suffered from feelings of being persecuted, a not uncommon ailment with some women, I have observed."

"Have you, indeed. Possessed, you say? How so?"

"It was all in her imaginings, Rabban. She is fine now but insists it is due to the rabbi's intervention. Nonsense, of course."

"Of course, that is often the case, but the important fact is, she believes she was cured. If true, I would think you would be happy in that. Do you know what I suggested to her?"

"No, how could I?"

"Exactly, how could you. I suggested that if this man is all she believes him to be, she should urge you to join her in her admiration of him. You recall when the two of us spoke earlier, you described a problem and I, I regret to say, did not treat it with the consideration it deserved. By your account I naturally assumed she was, to put it nicely, resisting your position as head of the house. I told you to rein her in or words to that effect. I see now that I should have listened more closely. The problem is not of a recalcitrant wife, but rather a threatened husband. You do not like to hear the teachings of this rabbi coming from the mouth of your wife."

"Sir, it is only that she is a woman and you know the saying, 'I would rather see the Torah—'"

"I know it and it is wrong when used that way. Women have a place in the Law that is different than men. They have *binah,* among other things, and understand intuitively what must be hammered into the heads of the likes of you. Go with her in this."

"But this rabbi, they say he is a trouble maker and does not teach the Torah as it is to be known. Do you think he is a good rabbi?"

"Good? No, probably not. He is untutored. He has not studied with anyone as nearly as I can determine, certainly not with me nor any one of my contemporaries. He does not speak with authority—"

"Yes, there you see, I wish to protect us from—"

"Let me finish, Steward. As I said he is not a rabbi whom I would recognize or endorse in the schools and synagogues. At the same time, he, and his teaching, is probably no worse than a hundred like him who walk the roads of this land proclaiming what they believe to be the mind of the Lord. And I understand he has one strong characteristic to recommend him, he speaks to people in ways they can easily understand. That is a gift. I suggest you take it."

"I still think that my wife is wrong and should be brought back to her senses."

"It appears she has been, if your description of her illness is accurate. So, you would be well advised to put aside those feelings. They have already led you to do a thing unworthy of the king's steward and it could put you in jeopardy with the authorities, that is to say the king and Pilate were I to report it."

The captain of the guard shuffled his feet.

"Unworthy act? I don't know what you mean? I did something to compromise the king? I don't understand."

"No? Tell me again about who has access to the royal apartments."

"Well, the servants are there at the times they are required and—"

"You can come and go at will, is that right?"

"Me? Of course, and even Geris here, but—"

"Yes, Geris. Captain, I will not require your immediate presence anymore. Perhaps you would linger in the hallway in case I need to call you later. Thank you." The guard frowned but left. In the silence that followed, Gamaliel stared at the steward.

"It is my duty to see to it that all the things that must be done to keep the palace running smoothly are done," Chuzas stammered.

"So you could easily have entered the rooms of Menahem at any time he was not there and left and no one would have noticed or cared."

"Yes, but I don't see why that is important."

"Don't you? Explain to me something else then. Do you remember the morning I had the bath drained? You came into the area and you looked at some items I had placed on the rim of the pool. You said, 'Is that the weapon used to murder the girl?' Do you recall that?"

"Did I?" Chuzas frowned as if lost in thought. "Perhaps I did. I do not remember. Is it important?"

"Important? Oh yes, whether you recall the day or not, I do. You looked straight at that knife and asked if it were the weapon used to kill the girl. I did not think too much of it at the time because it seemed a very normal question. In fact, it had crossed my mind as well. But there is a problem, Chuzas. One that could lead to serious consequences for you, do you understand?"

"Rabban, I am at a loss."

"Are you? I could recall the captain of the guard, you know." Gamaliel nodded toward the door. He studied the little round man he found so difficult to like and who sat fidgeting on the edge of his stool, eyes darting from the door, to the latticed wall, and back to Gamaliel. So someone lurked behind the screen listening to them. If so what would he or she make of this? Gamaliel did not want to share what he knew of Chuzas' duplicity with whoever lurked there and how he intended to use him because of it.

"Shall I set for you a parable, Chuzas?"

"Rabban, I..."

"Listen, once there was a rich landowner who had two servants. To one he gave charge over ten hectares of land, to the other twenty, and said to them, 'Cultivate my land and bring to me the fruits that are mine.' When the first man saw that the other had been given charge over twenty hectares to his meager ten, he was envious. 'Why,' he said to himself, 'has my lord given this man twenty hectares and I but ten?' Over time this envy ate at him so that he made up his mind to act against the other man. To do so, he sought to discredit him by telling the merchants in the village this, 'The man who has charge over twenty hectares of my master's land has cheated you in the weights of his wheat and barley he sold to you.' The merchants were astounded and reported this to the landowner who called in the man with the twenty and would punish him. But the man said, 'I have not cheated these people, my lord. See here are my scales and here are the measures of wheat and of barley I sold to the merchants. Weigh them and see.' And he showed him his scales and the land owner ordered the measures reweighed and the weights were true. 'Who told you that the weights were false?' he asked of the merchants, and they pointed to the man with the ten hectares.

When the land owner saw what the first man had done he was extremely wroth and....What do you suppose he did to that unfaithful servant, Steward?"

"Sir, I do not know."

"Venture a guess. What would that land owner have done? Finish the parable for me."

"I suppose, in the parable, he would have beat the envious servant and cast him out."

"Yes, that is the end of the parable. Do you hear and understand?"

"Sir?"

"Chuzas, everyone in the palace needs only to glance at the knife to know it belongs to Menahem. You did not become the king's steward because you were stupid. Do not pretend to be so now."

Chuzas had begun to perspire halfway through the telling of the parable. Now he squirmed on his stool like a naughty schoolboy caught out by his teacher.

"What will you do, Rabban?"

Gamaliel frowned and lowered his voice so that only Chuzas could hear him and even that with difficulty.

"As I said, Chuzas, you are not stupid. You behaved as if you were this one time because you thought someone had interfered with your place in your own house. But in doing so, you wasted my time. It has resulted in me being called out by the Prefect. It has deflected me from finding the girl's killer, and caused irreparable damage to the reputation of an honest man. What do you think I should do? Shall I speak to the king...to the Prefect? It could go hard with you, Chuzas."

The steward seemed to have shrunk to a third his size. "Sir, is there no mercy?"

"Indeed, there is. I believe the Lord is merciful and I shall be also, but from me this mercy must be earned. I will extract from you three promises. Promises made here in the sure knowledge the Lord will hear them. Agreed?"

"Yes."

"You will put aside your envy of Menahem and follow your wife to this country rabbi. You will put your entire effort in helping me solve this mystery without resorting to reporting to the royal family behind my back. And you will reform, repent, and return to the Lord. Do you understand me?"

"Yes, thank you. It will be all right now?"

"That, of course, is in your hands. The business of the knife is in mine. You must make it all right, Steward."

He watched as Chuzas, evidently relieved, slipped out of the room. Was he relieved because he had been shown mercy or because he no longer carried the guilt of his deed around or...there was one last possibility, of course. He knew he'd be caught in the ruse sooner or later and...If I were a killer, Gamaliel thought, what better way of avoiding suspicion than to be found out as one who planted evidence? Once exposed, who would think to look further or deeper? Of course the same could be said for old Menahem. Once cleared of guilt, who would dare reopen the case against him? But he told Pilate he couldn't because Menahem was old and impotent and right handed. Was he? If you weren't sure why the girl was killed, did any of that even matter?

Gamaliel's head began to ache.

Chapter XXVI

It had been a day Gamaliel hoped he'd never have to repeat. If he had his wish, he would never allow himself to be tangled up in this sort of thing again—ever. Murder and political intrigue, jealousy and deceit, betrayal…he smiled at the irony. If he were not so engrossed in this business, he would be reading the scriptures. And the history of Israel's kings and heroes were mostly about intrigue, jealousy, deceit, and betrayal. It is the continuing human condition, endless conflict between good and evil, between the Lord and the forces that oppose him. Is it any wonder he seemed so angry so much of the time. Still, as he reflected on his day, he came close to regretting that he'd not accepted Pilate's offer to throw Menahem to the dogs. With his only suspect, however poor, off his list, where could he turn now? The probable removal of a guilty Menahem left him with no other choice but to start all over again. He left the palace after charging Barak to tell the steward he wished to interview the captain of the guard and Menahem the next day. He made his way home.

He trudged the width of the quarter and turned in to his house in time for his evening meal. He could only toy with his supper. He'd had it served early. He'd even skipped his prayers and *mikvah*. This business was slowly eroding away his routines, the things that defined him, things he'd forever held sacrosanct. He felt as if some new Gamaliel was replacing the old one, pushing him aside and introducing someone he did not recognize, someone who did not fit comfortably in his skin.

He knew he needed to find a quiet place away from this sewer of royal plotting and scheming and sort the whole thing out, starting at the beginning, starting with a dead girl lying on the bottom of the bath, her throat cut, raped, and cast off like the carcass of a sacrificed lamb. Who was she? He secluded himself in his private room where he ordinarily pursued his studies apart from his students. He contemplated the physician's remark that he had begun to think like a Greek. It was not a comfortable thought, but on reflection he believed it might be correct and further, that it might also be necessary if he was to ever sort through this basket of entrails.

He sat at a small wooden table and lit his reading lamp. The scent of olive oil mixed with just a pinch of incense filled the room. The incense had been his late wife's idea. He had objected at first—thought it unseemly. He'd heard of the houses in the city that were said to offer travelers the delights of the flesh. They were known for mixing incense in their lamp oil. But in the end, he became used to it and had to admit however reluctantly, the ambience it created relaxed him. Tonight he desperately needed relaxing. When he was a young man and newly married, he recalled, he had a more immediate method of finding relaxation and release. But he was older now and more importantly, his wife was dead these two years. So now it had to be the incense or nothing. Of course he could always remarry. He would think about that some other time. He had grown sons to consider. He poured a cup of new wine and set it close at hand. The lamp flickered and brightened as all four wicks of his marvelous reading lamp flared and settled into steady burning.

One by one he placed each of the items he had collected over the last few days on the table in front of him. First the headdress which he smoothed flat. In spite of its overnight soaking in the bath, it still retained the faint scent of nard and cinnamon. If he were skilled in the use of hair oils, he could have positively identified the scrap of cloth as belonging to the girl. Next he spread out the bit of clothing he'd at first referred to as a loin cloth even though it was shaped and sewn. He had to admit he knew little or nothing about the garments women wore beneath their robes, nor did he wish to. Where would the mystery be then? Next to the rumpled bit of linen he placed the coins he'd recovered, carefully lining them up in a neat row their obverse side up. They glittered dully in the lamp light, the faces of emperors and kings stared off into the dark in dull bas relief. Next to them he placed the pendants, the replica and the original that now glittered faintly in the lamp light. Agon had done a marvel with the false one. He dropped the thong next to them which he also rearranged so as to juxtapose its cut ends. At the far end of the table he placed Menahem's knife. In a second row away from him on the table, he put the box and its seal next to the girl's letters.

Somewhere mixed in this pitiful collection of odds and ends, information, and guesswork he hoped to uncover both motive and killer. He closed his eyes. He wanted to sleep. To sleep a dreamless sleep and erase the awful images, blood, the ragged gash across the poor girl's throat. Alas, not now. As much as he detested the Prefect and the task he'd been set, he owed justice to this poor anonymous girl. She'd been brought to the court for a reason and serving clearly wasn't it. So what was?

Not on the table, but etched in his mind, were the facts of the girl's death. Alexandra, or Cappo, had been raped, held underwater and either drowned and then had her throat cut, or drowned as a result of having her throat cut. He would probably never know the truth of that. All this done, it seemed, by someone who used his "dirty hand" to do it. If he was going to rape her, why kill her as well? To prevent her from identifying her assailant? Probably, but…If the rape was not the primary purpose of his attack, it had to be something else. What else was there? The pendent. He picked up the gold original and stared at it.

"It must be you," he muttered, "but if so why hadn't he taken it? Ah, unless you slipped from his fingers at the same moment Barak entered the bath on his rounds."

His view of the items on the table blurred and swam before him. They beckoned to him and seemed to say. "Look at me, no look at me. I am the answer to the question you have not asked." He rubbed his eyes to bring them back into focus. He thought of the physician's notion of veils and absently counted the items on the table. Seven? More than seven. His dancer, he thought irreverently, would be a bit more heavily clad than the princess. He shook his head to lose both the thought and the image it evoked. He needed to act, to do something.

If he could reconstruct the crime, at least in his mind, if he could arrange all the items in the right order perhaps something would emerge, a hint, a peek at the way of things. There had to be a chronology—first this happened and then that. In his mind's eye he pictured the bath and the girl. Torches barely lighting the space, steam rising from the water, and debris from the revelries scattered about. Coins in the water, carelessly discarded clothing, wine and food and those suggestive murals. What possessed that child to go there? Was she one of the revelers playing with the others but who stayed behind for some reason? Of the little he'd learned about the girl, it seemed unlikely she would be one of them, much less to have lingered. But she did go to the bath and once there was savagely despoiled and murdered. Why? Because someone persuaded her to. What sort of news or person could entice this young woman to leave the safety of her bed in the middle of the night and go to the king's bath?

Perhaps it was not so much a who, but a what? *What* lured to her death? He closed his eyes and tried to remember everything he could about the girl. What was he missing?

A letter!

Of course. She went because she believed there was a new letter. The night of her murder someone must have brought the promise of good news, a reversal of fortunes, perhaps another letter. It would not fail to bring her out.

Chapter XXVII

If one ignored the pendant, the thing that set the girl apart from the servants and others who shared her station were the letters. Except for the privileged few, most women could not read or write and those who could, did not do so with regularity or facility. Yet Barak said he'd seen her weep over one letter which he took to be the most recent. To read and to weep! It obviously contained bad news. As she had undoubtedly been receiving the letters in secret, a request to meet discreetly and late at night in just such an out of the way place as the bath, would not have seemed unusual to her. Even if it had, the thought of a new missive would quickly dispel any hesitation she might have felt. It had to have been the promise of news that lured her to her death. The beginning of the end, he thought, will be found somewhere in the letters. Then all he would need to do is determine who gave her the message that sent her to the bath and her death.

Gamaliel scooped up the stack of letters and spread them across the table, moving the other items out of the way. He'd read them before with superficial success. Now, he would read them again, this time slowly. He, of all people in the country should be able to tease the truth from them. He'd spent his adult years studying Torah, inspecting documents, hundreds of them from around the empire. Some written in Greek, some in Hebrew, some in Aramaic and some in languages so old and arcane he could barely fathom their source much less their content. He'd been trained to discriminate between various versions of the same text. He could scan a scroll or sheet of papyrus, leaf through a bound volume and tell by the way the characters were formed, by the word usage and idioms it contained, sometimes even by the ink, the writing surface, or any of a dozen reference points, when and often by whom a particular piece had been crafted. He felt sure these letters, although not separated so much in time, still had meanings and information he could and would dig out.

They were all in Greek. They were idiomatic but not in the vernacular Greek spoken in Jerusalem. These letters had been composed elsewhere by a different Greek speaker. The language was not literary, that is to say not Homeric, but neither was it street patois. Obviously, the writer had had the advantage of a formal education of some sort. Also, there were Latin words and expressions scattered throughout the text. Gamaliel could read Latin, though not with proficiency, and he would never admit that he did. In a world ruled by arrogant Latin speakers, he found it to his advantage to feign ignorance of their tongue. Let them come to his level and speak Greek like everyone else.

All the observations regarding language and style applied strictly to the earlier letters. The letter he considered to have been the last—the one wept over—he felt sure had been composed by a different author. Where the older ones seemed wordy even erudite and included references to many topics, the last seemed terse, painfully blunt, and had a finality about it, as if to say there would be no more missives sent. But the syntax seemed as vague and the idioms as difficult to interpret as the earlier ones. He read.

Dear one, the girl obviously. *The one of whom you love...* did it translate, the one you love or the one who loves you?...*has gone to his relatives...* visiting, travelling?...relatives, male...his brothers, fathers? He's joined his fathers...he died. Someone close to the girl, someone she had been corresponding with probably, someone, *whom you love,* has died. Could it also read killed? Yes, possibly. Whether it meant killed or died depended on the placement in the sentence, the context, the case. *Your relatives* plural, male and alive...brothers, cousins? *Your* meaning the loved one's…brothers? Her uncles? Yes, definitely uncles. Regrets and so on.

Who in the empire had been assassinated recently or died suddenly and perhaps mysteriously at the hands of his brother or close male relatives? He sat back and regretted that he considered the intrigues of the powerful and ambitious of insufficient interest for him to follow. Did he dare ask the Prefect? Of all the people currently in the city, the one person who most likely could answer that question was Pontius Pilate. Not just yet, maybe later. The Prefect could be intimidating to say the least and he'd had more than enough contact with the man lately. He'd try the physician first. A man not quite as well informed as the Prefect, but more so than Gamaliel, and a far safer interview to conduct than one with Pilate.

He slid the last letter aside and then read the others in order. They were not in code but it was patently apparent that the writer did not want anyone who might by chance come across the letters and read them to grasp the contents. They were filled with circumlocutions and vague references to places and events that the girl must know and share with the writer, but only someone equally familiar with the two of them, or who had also shared the experiences, would know what they referred to. Very clever.

You will recall the pergola where I yoked you with the riddle… Did what? One yokes an ox or a team of oxen. A riddle? A mystery…something covert or hidden? He draped something mysterious…no, hidden, no, a thing which hid something else, around her neck. It had to be the pendant. The writer wanted her to remember the place where he, must be a man, placed the pendant around her neck. Why remember the place? It must have some significance, perhaps it symbolized something greater. The same reference that he'd read in the last letter followed, a mention of the relatives. The cousins, brothers, uncles, definitely masculine, so not women. The next bit read, *Remember your mother's mother*. Odd way to refer to a grandmother, if that is what it meant. Or if it came from a pagan household it could refer to something altogether different, to Hera or Gaia, or any of a pantheon of goddesses. Gamaliel shuddered. Idolatry always made him anxious. He knew the Lord had no patience with idols; they were proscribed by the Commandments. And as he was the Rabban, the rabbis' rabbi, he would have even less patience with him should he be caught spending too much time in their contemplation.

Was the Greek usage consistent with a pagan writer? Possibly, but he thought not. The physician knew the Hebrew Scriptures but he was an exception…or was he? Another mystery for another day. This letter writer cited bits and pieces from the book of Judges. An interesting and puzzling book to cite.

He poured over the letters finding they raised far more questions than they answered. He did arrive at one or two conclusions. They dealt with the girl's identity. The queen had reported she'd been placed in her household by her first husband, the late Herod Philip. But he had since passed on to his reward, a dubious one, Gamaliel thought. He had admonished the queen to "keep an eye on her." This girl, young woman, must have been the daughter of an important acquaintance. But what king will take in a friend's daughter, place her with his queen, and not tell her what or who she was? A man to whom he owed a debt? Possible but…no…family. The most likely explanation would be that Cappo must somehow be connected to him by blood. She must have been one of the myriad multigenerational offspring of the late Herod. That knowledge would help, but not much. Offspring from his multiple marriages and liaisons plus his children's similar behavior had resulted in an array of princes, princesses, kings, queens, and those who were neither one or the other but had ambitions in that direction.

Gamaliel read on until his wonderful lamp began to sputter. He lit another and stretched out on a low couch to continue his reading.

His servant found him the next morning asleep on the couch, the letters scattered across the floor where they had fallen from his hands when he had finally drifted off to sleep.

Yom Shishi

Chapter XXVIII

The palace seemed unnaturally quiet when Gamaliel entered it at midmorning. Earlier he'd sent a messenger to the Prefect informing him that the evidence against Menahem had collapsed and the investigation had recently taken a new and politically dangerous turn. He didn't know what he meant by that exactly, but he assumed the combination of the words *politically* and *dangerous* would get Pilate's attention and hold him at bay for a few days. Barak met Gamaliel at the entrance to the room he now thought of as the Interview Room. Barak waggled his eyebrows and glanced toward the wall. Gamaliel nodded his understanding. It seemed he had a monitor again. Who could it be this time?

"Is the steward here?"

"He said he would attend you soon. There has been an incident in the cellars."

"An incident? What sort of incident would that be, Barak?"

The steward bustled in and interrupted any answer Barak might have given.

"Rabban, your pardon, but I fear there has been another death."

"Murder?"

"No, yes, no…I can't say. It's suspicious. A man is dead."

<>·<>·<>

The cellars of this palace—like those Herod had built elsewhere—on the shores of the Great Salt Sea at Masada, the

Herodium to the south, and Machaerus across the Jordan—had been designed by him to hold stores for extended periods of time. He'd lived in a chronic state of agitation, fearing possible plots against him, attempts on his life, his kingdom, and his family. To secure his body and court, he constructed his palaces like forts and his forts like palaces and all with storage space for enough food and water to sustain him and his followers for prolonged periods of time, even a siege by his enemies if necessary. But in Jerusalem under Antipas, less than half the space in the warren-like arrangement of connecting cellars did in fact hold material of that sort. Still, the goods and their amounts were substantial. Some served the current residency and the rest were the supplies needed for an extended stay or another later stay should the king suddenly force an unscheduled return.

All these goods were stacked close to the entry to the kitchens and servant's work areas. Another cellar farther along had been designated as a place to store miscellaneous items and things no longer pleasing or useful to either the queen or her daughter. It was in this area that the crumpled body of a kitchen worker had been found with the back of his head crushed. Scattered next to him were the shards of a large clay pot along with the metal clasps, fasteners, and rivets it once held. The pot appeared to have fallen off the shelf above him which, Gamaliel noted, extended the width of the room. It contained rows of similar earthenware jars along its length with the one solitary gap where the shattered jar must have once been placed.

"An accident do you suppose?" he asked.

"It would seem so but…we may never know."

"No? Did this poor man reach up to secure this jar only to have it slip and fall on him? And who is this man? What reason had he for being in the basement in the first place?"

"According to his master, he was sent for wine. It is kept in the large stone urns over against the opposite wall. He had no business in this area. His duties are simply to aid the cooks and cup bearers. His master said that he would go to the stores every morning and bring up whatever the cooks needed. He also had the duty to replenish the wine skins and urns from those great stone jars."

"If that is so, what was he doing over here in this storage area?"

Chuzas held out his hands and shrugged. "I cannot say. Perhaps he thought to help himself to something among the queen's things."

"A pot full of fasteners? I think that unlikely. Let us try something else, he was drawn over here because he saw, or thought he saw something suspicious or out of place. He accidently bumps into the shelf and the pot drops on him."

"Suspicious? Like what?"

"I can't say, Steward, but it might have been anything or nothing, another servant pilfering, rats, a shadow, who knows? And there is also the real possibility that the jar did not fall on his head by accident."

The steward's face blanched and he began to sweat in spite of the mildewed chill afforded by the cellars. "If that is the case, you may have another murder to contend with, Rabban." Chuzas' eyes darted here and there, beginning panic, as if this new murder threatened to upset his household in ways the other didn't.

"It will be my responsibility only to the extent that it can be shown to be connected to the death of the girl, Chuzas."

"But surely, it must."

"I don't see why it must, but I concede that it most likely does.

"I see. Yes, well, what should we do?"

"For the time being, leave him exactly where he is." He turned to the old man, "Barak, run fetch the physician, Loukas, and bring him here. Tell him it is urgent and that he should come at once. You remember where he lives?"

Barak nodded and hurried off. Chuzas found a rough measure of sacking and covered the body. He sent away the servants who had originally come in response to the cries of the person who'd discovered the body, and stayed to gawk—alternatively at the dead man, and at the famous Gamaliel.

"What would have caused that jar to fall in such a way as to kill this man?"

"Sir?"

"Sorry, Chuzas, I am thinking out loud, but as you are here, tell me, if this is an accident, why would he have tried to steal something of so little value?"

"He must not have known the contents and assumed the jar must have value. Why else would it be stored in the king's cellars?"

Gamaliel reached up to the shelf and attempted to dislodge another, similar jar. It took considerable strength to move it a finger's breadth.

"Even if he were trying to steal this jar, and had begun the process, he would have quickly learned that it would not be an easy task. Further, given the difficulty in moving these jars, I would expect that if it started to slip he would have easily stepped aside."

"So?"

"So, I don't know. We will await the arrival of the physician and hear what he has to say, but I am almost sure he will conclude this man's death was not an accident. If that is the outcome, then we will indeed have to consider this another murder."

"But, can you establish a connection to the dead girl?"

"Chuzas, I cannot even say it is a murder at this time, much less one connected to any other. Wait and see."

While he waited for Loukas to join them, Gamaliel paced the area. He didn't know what he thought he'd find but he searched anyway. That the area received a number of visitors each day seemed apparent and not just in the area where the food and consumables were kept. He saw traces, here and there, of visits to other parts of the cellar.

The physician arrived, greeted Gamaliel, and bent over the body. He turned the man's damaged head to one side and stood.

"Congratulations, Rabban, you have another murder to reconcile for your master."

"How can you tell?'

"The man's head has been struck by a blunt instrument like a club or the heavy end of a sword, the hilt, maybe."

"But what about the earthen pot?"

"Undoubtedly dragged off the shelf and allowed to shatter to create the illusion of an accident."

"I do not need this additional distraction."

"Yet here it is."

Chapter XXIX

Too many things were piling up around him. He hoped the physician could help him if it meant only listening to him while he talked. The two men, polar opposites, as Loukas might have described them, sat on the bench in the atrium just outside the bath. "Sometimes," Gamaliel said, "just hearing the words in your own mouth can prompt a new thought. What do you think? This is the spot where this uncomfortable journey began."

"I remember it so. So, Rabban, has your mysterious woman been dancing for you? Are there any new revelations you wish to tell me?"

"I wish you would erase that shameless image from your mind and our conversations. It is unseemly."

Loukas smiled and cocked his head to one side. "I will, if you refrain from pontificating about your Law. Tell me what you have turned up, or would it be down? Sorry. Proceed."

Gamaliel tilted his head back and closed his eyes. He let the late afternoon sun turn his world behind his eyelids red. After the damp of the basement, the warmth felt therapeutic. He cleared his throat and began. He told Loukas about the letters and what he surmised about the girl from their content. He said he felt sure the girl had been drawn into the bath with the promise of yet another letter. He told him of the evidence regarding Menahem's knife and the role Chuzas played in that debacle. And he told him what he thought must have happened the night of the murder. He turned to his friend and saw the frown on his face.

"What?"

"I follow you as far as you seem to want to go. Something puzzles me, and has from the very beginning. Why was that girl raped and murdered? If, as you speculate, the object was to obtain the pendant, why kill her? As far as anyone knew, she did not warrant a second look. With the pendant gone, she had nothing."

"The man was a brute, I suppose. Is there another reason to rape the girl?"

Loukas shrugged. It was a question without an answer.

"Wait, perhaps, Physician, there is. Rape in our Law is a heinous crime. Chastity is held in high esteem. If a man, for example, discovers his bride is not a virgin on the wedding night, he may ask for and will receive an annulment, no questions asked and…What was your question again?"

"I asked—"

"Yes, yes, I know what you said. Listen, suppose for a moment this girl represented a powerful family, which she must have, judging by the inscription on the pendant. She is a member of or close to someone with power or maybe only potential power, a threat either way to certain parties. Then suppose there were forces allied to prevent her family from assuming that power or, if they got it instead, intended that there be no successor from their rival?"

"Sorry, I am not following you."

"No one would marry her if she was impure, don't you see?"

"Impure? Surely if a woman is forcibly deprived of her virginity, she can't be thought of as *impure*."

"Perhaps not for you. For us, it is a fact, like it or not. We can debate the justice of that position some other time. It is not critical in the high thin air of royalty always, but it can be. The point is, the man did not need to kill her. But having said that, I should point out that when he raped her, she became damaged goods, and unlikely to marry and therefore not likely to bear a son or daughter. Supporters of her family's claims, if they were to find her offspring years later, would have had a legitimate pretender to put forward, you see? But as she was murdered in the bargain, the whole thing is now academic. Thank you, Physician, you have been most helpful."

"I have no idea what you are talking about, but you are most welcome."

"I will tell you later. Now, tell me, why was the man killed in the cellars?"

"The stock answer would be either he saw something or he knew something that might reveal the girl's killer to you. He, the killer that is, dared not take a chance of him talking either to you or someone else and so, removed him from the list of people you might have eventually interviewed."

"It's possible. Or he may have seen something, but did not know what it was but the killer could not be sure. If we could find out the thing or event he witnessed we would have the key to unlock this business." Gamaliel twisted in his seat to face the entryway to the bath. "I am not a trained observer, Loukas, but I would swear there was evidence of other sandals scuffling through those cellars."

"Is that so unusual? Men and women must wander in and out of the area all the time. Didn't you have the guards search the palace? The marks may have been made by the searchers moving about here and there in that place."

Gamaliel deflated. Of course, why hadn't he thought of that immediately? "You are right, of course. But…"

"But?"

"But they were sandals, not the sort of foot coverings the guards wear."

"I see. No, I don't but then it is not my place or responsibility to, is it? Moving forward, it is my humble opinion there is one very important question you should now address, Rabban."

"And that is?"

"How or through whom did this woman receive and send her letters."

"Yes, and I think I know. I will need to confirm it, but only when I think it is safe to do so."

"Safe?"

"There is more at stake here than meets the eye and the possession of certain information, with the wrong person knowing you have it, can be dangerous. If I confront the individual, others will soon learn of it. There is no privacy in this palace as far as I can tell, and he could be harmed, even killed. If I am right, that person's life is in jeopardy if it were to come out that he knew or could reveal that important bit to me. I want him alive. For the time being all I need is the probability to proceed."

"Who?"

"Not yet. I trust you, Loukas, but I do not wish to burden you. Your house has been violated once already and I do not think your man Draco is up to resisting someone with murder in his heart. Have you had any more midnight visitors?"

"No, but Draco seems to think he recognized the boots."

"He knows who wore them?"

"In a manner of speaking. He thinks he recognizes the style and the people who wear them. It is not the same thing, alas, but for what it is worth, the boots are the sort worn in places like Armenia and Cappadocia, maybe Syria or Phrygia. In the north at any rate, not Greece."

"Not?"

"No self-respecting Greek would wear such things."

"And why would a Greek not wear them?"

"I do not have this firsthand, understand, but they are the sort of footwear Persians are partial to, therefore shunned by patriotic Greeks who still have issues as regards that race."

"Ah! A very thin sort of argument, if I may say so, Loukas, but north you say. That is helpful. Yes that would fit. Now if we could just find this wearer of boots."

"North is important?"

"It is. The worst of it is with all these people in for the Feast and camped everywhere, our murderer could operate from within or even outside of the palace if he had a sure means of entry. Unless the former, he could be anywhere."

They sat in silence for a moment each lost in his own thoughts. Gamaliel watched the sun begin to sink in the west and stirred.

"I have let the time slip by me, I am afraid, and I must leave you. The Shabbat begins in two hours and I must be settled.

You should too. I know you are not a believer, but Jerusalem will be shut up tight as a drumhead when the Shabbat begins. You had best be safely home."

The two stood and left the garden. Gamaliel to his home to make sure the meals for the next day were cooked and set aside, and the large Shabbat lamp filled with oil and set alight. From this evening to the next he would do no work, which meant all items still arrayed across the table in his study would be covered with a linen cloth and banished from his thoughts. He would be occupied exclusively with prayers and thanksgivings, and the contemplation of Holy Writ. He might venture out to the Temple, but no further.

The physician, he knew, would leave the city through the Sheep Gate and make his way through the throngs of pilgrims camping on the hillsides and in the shadow of the wall. He would wend his way home and share none of his friend's Shabbat discipline. He would enjoy a cooked meal and he would work. He allowed himself to be a God Fearer, a practicing skeptic, but definitely not a follower of the god of the Jews. On the whole, he felt, it was a far more convenient place for this odd friend to be, but he still wished he were in the fold, so to speak. He cared for him that much.

‹›‹›‹›

Gamaliel found his way home and through the portico of his house with time to spare. He made sure the servants had laid out his meals for the next twenty-four hours. He had time to spread the sheet of fair linen over his collection of odds and ends gleaned from the palace, his evidence, and sat down for the last hot meal he would have until sunset the next day. He managed to put aside his frustration at not being able to pursue his inquires further. The Law of Moses was the Law Absolute and he, of all people should know it. He managed to read and pray a bit before the lamp dimmed. When his wife was alive and there were children and family in the house, there would have been psalm singing and retelling of the stories and the mighty deeds of the judges and kings. The children never tired of hearing the stories of David and Solomon, Gideon and Sampson—well, not Sampson in their early years, of course. Gamaliel usually skipped the story of David's involvement with Bathsheba and her husband, Uriah the Hittite.

This night he sat alone with his thoughts. When the lamp finally sputtered out he went to bed. He slept very well, a fact that surprised him when he woke in the morning.

Shabbat

Chapter XXX

Shabbat. The Shofars on the temple mount announced dawn and Gamaliel rose and contemplated a day filled only with holy things. No Pilate, no palace, and no death. He lingered over his breakfast of cold beans and lamb and devoted the rest of the morning to quiet contemplation. It was not an easy task. He had to force his mind to stay focused on spiritual thoughts and Shabbat's requirement he pray and wait upon the Lord. He managed, but with great difficulty. Never in the past had he dealt with so large a distraction as the girl's murder. Not since he left home as a young man and took up his studies. And then to compound the problem, he had a murder occupy him and at the same time the Prefect, the king, and the queen were angry with him, all within the short span of only a few days. It had to be a first for him, for any Rabban. If it weren't for the inherent danger in this odd set of circumstances, he thought it might have made a good story line for one of those Greek comedies Loukas fancied. He could only guess at that. He'd never seen one of the scandalous performances by either a Greek or a Roman imitator, but he'd heard about them. He put thoughts of masks and scatological playmaking aside and forced his thoughts back into an appropriate spiritual rut.

At the sixth hour he ate some bread and cheese and drank a cup of water for his midday meal. He threw a cloak across his shoulders and made his way through throngs of people on their way to and from the Temple. His usual Shabbat routine, once on the Mount, consisted of a stroll along Solomon's porches. He enjoyed listening to the speakers, mostly rabbis from the city, but during High Holy Days, many others from across the length and breadth of Israel appeared. In addition there would usually be a few Zealots drumming up rebellion, but carefully. They knew there would also be soldiers, Temple guards, and spies planted in the crowd eager to turn them in for a reward. And finally there were those men blessed with minds that had deserted them before their time and who would rant on about issues long since decided, or of incomprehensible dimensions, and occasionally would reveal visions of startling originality.

Because this particular Feast would not end for another three days, there were more than the usual number of men vying for attention scattered along the porches. Some had attracted sizable crowds, some fewer. He strolled along and paused at them in turn, listening and occasionally disputing with the rabbi on a minor point. He identified many of his former students in the crowds doing the same and he listened to their arguments as well, dispassionately, like a teacher. When he resumed their tuition in the next few days, he would point out to one or the other where they had done well, where they might have made a stronger case. He was in his element and the exhilaration he felt blotted out the business of the murders.

One rabbi, he noticed, had collected a larger crowd than the others. He wandered over and listened. The man's disciples were among those who had gathered around the unusually tall man. They, however, had their backs to their teacher and were engaged in murmured conversations with a few spectators. They offered what Gamaliel could only assume were answers, explanations, or possibly an exegesis of the speaker's points. This did not strike him as usual, although he had seen it done once or twice before but usually with a well-known rabbi, not like this unknown.

As with all the speakers on the porches, a certain group of young men gathered to heckle or harass the rabbis. This tall rabbi had attracted some of them as well. When he paused, one of the young men smirked at his companions and asked, "Tell me teacher, which of the commandments given us by Moses is the greatest?" It was a transparent attempt to trap someone they took to be no more than an itinerant country rabbi. To the young fool's apparent dismay, the rabbi quoted the Summary of the Law. The answer any student used to discourse would have made, of course. That should have ended it but the youth would not be put off. Having made a fool of himself once with a question any thirteen year old could have answered correctly, he pressed on. Whether he sought to regain some measure of dignity or was just stupid, Gamaliel could not say, but with the supercilious expression common to men of his age plastered across his face he asked, again, "Well, then who is my neighbor?"

Gamaliel waited for the sharp words of dismissal he expected, words that he would have used had he been it that rabbi's sandals. But none came. Instead the speaker fixed the boy with a sad look and set him a parable, one about a man traveling to Jericho and beset by robbers, beaten and left for dead. Righteous types would not help him, but passed on the opposite side of the road. Finally, he related, a Samaritan, the most despised of all their neighbors, stopped and gave aid and that well beyond anything needed or expected. When the image had been sufficiently drawn, he asked the boy which of the travelers was the man's neighbor. Very neat.

Gamaliel turned to a man he took to be one of the disciples and asked the identity of this quick witted rabbi. "Yeshua ben Yosef, a man from the Galilee," he said. So this was the hair in the High Priest's soup. He shook his head. He turned back to Yeshua ben Yosef and thought, give that man to me for a year and I could really make something of him. So many of Gamaliel's own students were mere imitators of their betters. The number of original thoughts they expressed could be numbered by using their fingers. Some of them would only require one hand. This man had potential.

He left the crowd and made his way to the Temple itself. The second part of his Shabbat routine involved stopping to visit the priest's vestry. Whether he would find the High Priest in or not, he could not say. He hoped not. Another rant from Caiaphas did not fit into his idea of a pleasant Shabbat. He was in luck. Only a few older men on the roster whose names had come up for this day loitered about with Ehud, the High Priest's clerk.

"Ehud, Greetings in the Name. I take it that the High Priest is not about?"

"No, Rabban, he is finished for the day."

"Yes, well when you see him, tell him I have at last witnessed the rabbi he is so worried about and can find no fault with him."

"That is true? But I thought…I mean we sent…I will tell him."

"Yes, do that." He turned to leave and then paused. "Ehud, tell me, why did your parents give you such a name? Are you left-handed as the judge in the Book?"

Ehud blushed. "They were told by one of the elders that the judge would be found somewhere in the line of our ancestors. They hoped it would strengthen me, I suppose."

"Indeed? Well, let's hope they were correct."

Ehud, the left-handed judge. Loukas insisted the killer had been left handed. Had he been? Did it matter? If it mattered, how did it matter? Gamaliel caught himself in this speculation when he realized that he'd failed in his determination not to let the business at the palace interfere with his Shabbat. But he also realized that the preoccupations of the previous days could not be held at bay forever. He muttered a prayer of atonement and made his way home to await the end of Shabbat so he could recommence his investigation with a clear conscience.

Yom Rishon

Chapter XXXI

Rishon arrived, or more accurately, the previous evening Shabbat concluded and Gamaliel resumed his work on the palace murders. But for his brief lapse at the Temple, he had succeeded, more or less, in maintaining the discipline that he would not entertain any thoughts about either of the two murders. And he had assiduously stuck to his decision with the one exception when he'd encountered Ehud. However, he knew from past experiences that when he struggled with problems whose solutions did not quickly come, a clean break from any attempt to solve them would often result in useful insights hours or days later when he reopened the "book of his mind." Shabbat especially seemed to turn over answers to questions on the First Day that he could not have thought of on the Sixth. With that hope in mind, he removed the cloth covering the several items still on his study table. He pulled up a stool, sat, and stared at them intently, willing them to speak to him.

He lifted Menahem's ornate knife and gripped it first in his left and then his right hand, imagining a killer wielding it or one like it, and slashing at a throat. His eye fell on the leather thong. He picked it up and arranged it so that the cut ends were clasped in his fist and the loop closed. He placed the knife against the opposite side and tried to cut the leather. He couldn't. The strip was either too tough or the knife too dull. If he wanted to slice through this thong he would need a far sharper blade or would have to slash at it with considerable force. But either way, probably not with this knife. Years of disuse had rendered it useless for anything more than slicing through fruit and opening letters. Yet another pass for Menahem who'd had no reason to use it as it had been designed anyway. How sharp must the knife be?

He put both items down and stared at them empty eyed and unfocused. A vision of the girl's face swam into view, her eyes wide and pleading. Her face and part of her torso, probably, under water. A knife swings toward her neck. To cut her throat or...? Is it held in the attacker's left hand? No, not left, right. The killer makes a loop of the leather thong...his hand tries to cut through...is cutting the thong. She is drowning. With her head submerged, what would she do? What instinctive act would having one's head held under water produce?

She'd try to lift it to the surface for air. Of course.

He leapt to his feet. He knew why and also how the woman had been killed. He paced around the table in a circle, once twice, and once again. Stupid, stupid, stupid. There had been no need. If only he'd had more time, had kept the loop to the other side of her neck. But that was about the time Barak had entered the corridor leading to the baths and he had to hurry... and the girl had died as a result. That had to be it.

What next?

The coins. What was it about those coins that had eluded him? They were not the prize the killer sought, obviously. Probably they were the means men used to lure servant girls to dive into the bath, laughing and splashing about, diving under the water's surface to retrieve them, their tunics plastered to their bodies. That may have been the reason for the coins to be in the bath but that wasn't the reason they called to him. They were tarnished but still glittered on the rough table's surface. There was something else about those coins he was supposed to see. He spread them out and studied them again. He pushed them about with his finger, turned them over, made mental notes of their denominations. Nothing out of the ordinary, just coins, some quite old and worn. They had images embossed on them, a bearded Herod, some emperors—Augustus, Julius Caesar, and this latest one, Tiberius. A madman by all accounts. All of the coins had a profile, nobly carved on them. The Law forbade the worship of graven images and this was just such a one, surely. What were these doing in a nominally Jewish household? Nominally said it all. The Roman Senate had declared Augustus a god and to be worshiped. Why not emboss his profile on a coin? Sadly, more people worshiped gold and silver and with greater enthusiasm than they did the Lord.

One coin especially caught his eye, a Roman coin well over a half century old. He held it up to the light…something. The image on this one? A good likeness of a Caesar, if you allowed for the fact that coins were stamped or cast and likenesses were more a function of approximation than reality. But there was no mistaking this one. Then he had it, knew its importance. It seemed unlikely but if he remembered the rumors correctly, the boy, the queen's son…he would have been just a boy then, well a young man, but still, a long time ago.

Menahem. That man keeps intruding into this business at every turn and there seemed no end to it. Always it came back to Menahem.

Next, the pendant. He'd dismissed the headdress and undergarment as related but not importantly so and had discarded them for the moment. The fact the girl's clothing had been removed was obvious. Now the two pendants—the original cleaned and waiting to be connected to the rest of the story, and its duplicate, Agon's masterpiece. Side by side on the table. It had belonged to the girl. She wore it always. Someone wanted it badly enough to kill her for it. The inscription linked her to the line of Herod. How? Was she a child born in a misalliance and tucked away in Philip's household to remove her from any claims she or others might make on the royals? The letters suggested something better, bigger. How did she come by the thing? She wasn't indicated in the inscription, certainly, so…Someone gave it to her, clearly, and that someone had kept in touch with her over the last year or so. The likelihood that she was an off-line child did resonate with the rest of the facts. Which of the sons, grandsons, and by now greatgrandsons who shared a Herodian origin did she connect to? The House of Herod was not very creative when it came to introducing new names to its sons and daughters. Which one spawned this girl?

And finally, where was Graecus? Who and where was he and, more importantly, why had he gone into hiding? If he had been only some sort of low level envoy, how had he come to be a guest in the palace? If he were something larger and more important, then who or what?

Gamaliel resumed his pacing as he attempted to weave these threads together. He stopped abruptly and stuffed the false pendant, the seal and its box, Menahem's knife, and the letters in his tunic and headed for the door. He needed to go to the palace. He needed to talk to the captain of the guard. He needed to press Menahem about why he and he alone knew the girl's name.

He needed to set a trap.

Chapter XXXII

Barak and Chuzas loitered in the corridor and each, like bright school children, seemed eager to tell him something. Before either could speak, however, Gamaliel greeted them and waved them into the interview room.

They both began to speak. "Sir," they said.

"Wait, I will hear you out in a moment. Right now I need to know certain things and I have important commissions for each of you. Chuzas, there is the matter of a second interview with Menahem."

Chuzas tilted his head in the direction of the lattice. "We have friends in high places who are interested in what you will do today, Rabban. They wish to know if you have a lead into the death of the dead kitchen servant and other things."

"Very well, Chuzas, I understand. And there are some things I would like to be known as well, if you follow me. Find out for me how letters are received into the palace, how they are distributed, and who has that responsibility. If there is such a person or persons, I wish to speak to them immediately. Also, I want to know if it is possible to receive one any other way. That last part is important."

"I can answer that now. Letters are received at the gate. If they are for the king, the messenger waits to be dismissed or if there is a reply, to carry it back. Dispatches which come by any other means—"

"Thank you, but you must tell me all this later, after you have explored the possibilities of alternate deliveries. Now, Barak, I want you to make queries about the dead kitchen worker, how often he went into the cellars, who else might also have visited them with him or went there separately and finally, when did the guards search the area for Graecus." He turned back to Chuzas. "As to the question about the dead servant found there, you may report that I do have some thoughts about that." Did he? That would depend on what Barak discovered. "Anything else, Chuzas?"

"Menahem wishes to speak with you in private." He rolled his eyes once again toward the screen.

"And I him. Make arrangements for that to happen in some appropriate place. I understand he sometimes suffers a phobia about enclosed spaces. Perhaps in the courtyard or garden would be a better spot for an interview." He did not acknowledge Chuzas' suppressed smile. "Barak, you were about to tell me something as well. What is it?"

"The captain of the guard says he has a report for you about Graecus."

"Does he indeed? He has found him at last?"

"I think not, Excellency. The reverse I believe."

"Well, let us have his bad news then, send him in." Barak left to find the captain, Chuzas to arrange the meeting with Menahem and to discover if there were alternate ways to receive messages. He knew there must be. What palace did not have its intrigue and conspiracies that required clandestine communications, messages secreted in and out, plots hatched and quashed?

Gamaliel seated himself and with exaggerated gestures, withdrew the pseudo-pendant from within his tunic and placed it on the table beside him. Then he sat back and closed his eyes, or nearly so. He left a narrow gap between his lids which allowed him to watch the shadows behind the elaborately decorated wall to his right. He waited. Something moved. Something? More like someone had shifted his or her position back in its dim recesses. Did whoever lurked there see the pendant or did his bench become too hard for sitting and he had to shift his weight? These thoughts were interrupted by footsteps in the corridor and the subsequent entry of the captain of the guard.

"Greetings to you, Captain. I intended to seek you out and here you are. Have you any news for me?"

"Sorry, none good I'm afraid, Excellency. We have traced the movements of the dead man though."

"Have you? That is useful, I should think. Did you discover anything out of the ordinary? Anything that could shed some light on his murder?"

"No, sir, sorry, but all we know now is pretty much what we knew before, other than when he went into the cellars. I don't know if that is helpful or not."

"Probably not, but you never know, do you. You are Geris, is that right?"

"Some call me by that name."

Some call me by that name? What kind of answer is that? His name is or it is not Geris. Why not a simple yes or no? "Are you called by any other?"

The captain shuffled his feet and averted his eyes.

"You were once in an Auxilla Cohort, is that so? Stationed in the north?"

"Yes I was. It has been years since." He sniffed and ran his forearm across his nose. "Long time ago."

"Yes, I suppose it must. You joined the palace guards in Tiberias, I hear. Is that so?"

"Yes."

At the start of the interview Gamaliel had not had his guard up, willing to take the captain at his word. After his evasion regarding his name, Gamaliel wondered. He switched to his *vetting a new student mode* and listened for evasions and half truths if there were to be any. In the back of his mind he wished that once, just once, he could deal with someone from this palace and not think of them as suspect. Well, there was Barak, of course, one innocent lamb among a pack of wolves .

"You served with the goldsmith, Agon, is that right?"

"Agon? Oh yes. A fine soldier and companion. After he fell to a bandit's axe on the Tarsus road, I feared he'd not recover."

"The wound was very bad?"

"Oh, yes. I felt certain he'd end as a crippled beggar. We all did."

"So you have not seen him lately?"

"Seen Agon?" The captain scratched his ear where it rubbed against his helmet, deep in thought. "No…wait, yes. From time to time I drop by his shop to catch up, you could say."

Gamaliel sat back and studied the man before him. He wondered what the captain would do when he visited Agon the next time now that he'd admitted knowing the goldsmith. Would he be bolder in seeking news to share with the other guards and servants, or would he be more circumspect for fear that Gamaliel could identify the source and perhaps have something to say to the king about it?

"I am curious about your search of the cellars. You did search them?"

"Thoroughly, Excellency."

"Do sit down, Geris."

"I am used to standing, sir."

"As you will."

Gamaliel shifted in his chair and toyed briefly with the pendant. Geris made a show of not noticing it.

"So, you or your men searched the length and breadth of the cellars and found nothing? No sign of anyone, no evidence of, say, food crumbs, a sleeping pallet—nothing like that?"

"No, none."

"Thank you then, for your efficiency. I am sorry. I interrupted. You meant to tell me something. I understand you do have some news for me."

"Yes, Rabban, I have. My men, on their own, mind you, have scoured the city and the hillsides outside the walls. They tell me the man, Graecus, has joined up with some of the foreign pilgrims in the Kidron Valley."

"Has he indeed? That is excellent news. Can you fetch him to us, Geris?"

"I'm afraid not. It seems the pilgrims are leaving the city now, as you know, and he has slipped away with them."

"That is most regrettable. You're sure?"

"Yes, Excellency."

"If he is the girl's killer, we will not be reporting any success to the Prefect. If not, well, we will soon know one way or another. So, we press on. With no motive or connection between him and the girl, it would be a stretch to link him to her murder, don't you think? Anyway, if he's been outside the walls all this time we will not be able to connect him to the kitchen worker's death either. Well, thank you for trying, my son. And I will report your efficiency to the king when I see him next."

"I do my duty. But thank you." The captain, who might or might not be named Geris, turned on his heel and left.

"Barak, you heard. Tell me what you think."

"It is not my place to question so eminent a person as the captain of the palace guard, but…"

"Yes? I think he shades the truth, Barak. Why does he do that, do you suppose?"

"Sir, I…"

"Never mind. Let us wander to the kitchens and see if there is any news of the dead man beyond what we have been told. You can tell me what you think of our captain on the way."

He scooped up the pendant from the table, tucked it back in his tunic, and led Barak out the door. A glance in the direction of the lattice work failed to produce a shadow or even a hint of movement. Perhaps his watcher had fallen asleep. Perhaps he didn't exist at all. The complexity that pierced wall created had shifted his investigation from difficult to nearly impossible.

Once in the corridors and out of earshot of a possible eavesdropper, he turned to the old man. "Yes?"

"I have had reports…you understand, from the servants, who cannot be identified, naturally."

"Naturally."

"One is about the dead man. He sometimes met with one of the women servants in the cellars for...immoral purposes, you understand, and the woman in question said he told her that he'd seen and knew something. She said he thought it would be worth some money, but he did not tell her what it was he knew or saw."

"Do you think the captain told the truth about his search?"

"Not entirely. Some of the servants said parts of the cellars were searched, but they were not sure they all were."

"Not all? It seems I was right, then. The captain is adept at lying. Why, Barak, do you suppose he said he had done a search if he hadn't?"

"Sir? Perhaps he did not know his guards slacked off when they had a chance."

"Yes, that is one possibility. Then he would not be the liar I thought. Possibly some of the cellars are inaccessible either for searching or hiding. We will have to sort that out later. Now, I must have my midday meal and afterwards I will speak with Menahem."

Chapter XXXIII

But Menahem would have to wait. When Gamaliel gained the street he found a messenger from the High Priest accompanied by four Temple guards waiting for him. His day seemed to be filled with armed men. He found himself escorted to Caiaphas' house which, mercifully, was a short distance south of the palace. He thought to protest. As mighty a position as the High Priest occupied, his was at least its equal in the larger scheme of things. But, he realized in the long run, broadcasting his personal pique in the Sanhedrin would only reveal another crack in the Nation's leadership, one which Rome would gladly exploit. Better to live under the Lord's Law, if only at the sufferance of Rome, than bow one's neck to *Lex Romana* or whatever version of it their conquerors decided to impose.

Once in Caiaphas' rooms, he waited for the High Priest to work himself up into a state of sufficient irascibility. Everyone knew Gamaliel could best Caiaphas in any argument or disputation. The only way the High Priest could possibly prevail in such a confrontation was to shout the Rabban down. That took a certain level of anger. Thus the delay. Gamaliel asked for and received a cup of water to drink. The water in the city had always been suspect unless drawn from the well that gave David access to the city. He knew this water came from that well, now covered and linked to the pool of Siloam inside the walls by Hezekiah's tunnel, built by that ingenious leader seven centuries earlier. Surely, he thought, if we could accomplish such a feat then, we can find the leadership to cast off this Roman burden now. But he could think of no one in the Nation who fit that bill. Certainly not the High Priest.

As if this thought had summoned him, Caiaphas appeared in the doorway and bore down on Gamaliel like a Greek trireme in full attack mode. Gamaliel could almost see the wake he left behind.

"High Priest, you wished to speak with me? I take it is a matter of some urgency or you would not have dragged me away from the task assigned to me by the Prefect himself."

"You are the Rabban. You are the one who can say yea or nay to this upstart. Even your students report he is a blasphemer yet you report you find no fault in him."

"I assume we are back to discussing the rabbi, Yeshua ben Yosef. Blasphemy is not so easy to define, High Priest. If he speaks the Name, yes he blasphemes. That is the Law. But too many of our rabbis confuse sin with blasphemy. I would be careful how you throw that word around."

"Do not lecture me. I am not one of your students. Is it not enough that he consorts with the lowest sinners, tax gatherers, and the unclean? He does not observe Shabbat. His own people boast that Shabbat is made for the man, not the man for Shabbat. What does that mean except blasphemy?" Gamaliel opened his mouth to speak, but Caiaphas waved him off. "He healed a man of lameness two days ago—on Shabbat! He claims he can forgive sins. You tell me, what does that signify to you? Does he put himself on a plane with the Lord? What are we to do? Please do not tell me to wait and see. And another thing," Caiaphas had slipped from his carefully prepared remarks. There is a downside to pumping up one's anger and that is it often takes over and diverts you from your intended path, verbal or otherwise.

"You had the man in your hands. You had a murderer and you let him go. If you had done as our queen asked, this murder nonsense would be done and over by now and we could concentrate on more important things."

"Like your annoying rabbi?"

"Precisely."

"Is there anything else, High Priest?"

"What? No, I need answers from you and now."

"Answers? Is it correct to assume your early remarks were aimed at the Galilean and the latter referred to Menahem?"

"What? Of course the man who claims to speak to the Lord directly and the…of course."

"Answers, then. Here are a few that may or may not address your concerns, if I understand them. First, if we were to arrest and punish everyone who breaches Shabbat, half of Galilee would be in prison by nightfall. A condition, by the way, they would share with their king, the queen, and the princess, not to mention at least four members of the Sanhedrin that I know of. Are you sure you want to do that?'

"Don't be absurd. Of course not, but this man is passing himself off as a rabbi and he has no training, no learning. He cites no authority."

"Do we license rabbis now? I didn't know. Where is it written one must study with Gamaliel, or with Shammai, or anyone else for all that, before one may teach? As regards the request by the queen to turn over Menahem, the king's long time companion, to Pilate for disposition of punishment, there was no firm evidence then, none at all now, to convict him of anything more serious than befriending a servant girl. The Prefect would have been perfectly amenable to meting out some penalty, even knowing the man's innocence. For him a quick political gesture endorsed by me was all he ever wanted. The question of guilt had nothing to do with it, you see?"

"But…. I have been reliably told you found a knife in the bath the day after they found the dead girl and it has been positively identified as having belonged to Menahem. Is that not evidence enough?"

"As far as that goes, you are correct, a knife was found and it did belong to Menahem, but it was not the murder weapon. It was placed in the bath after the deed had been done by someone wishing to implicate an innocent man, in this case Menahem. That man has been found out and has been dealt with. Since then there has been a second murder and if I do not soon return to my investigations there may well be a third."

"Pilate wished you to turn this man over and you did not do it. It could have been a poor decision on your part. We continue to exist as a Nation at the sufferance of Rome. Should it be necessary to preserve the Nation would it not be better to sacrifice one man, even an innocent one?"

"I cannot believe you, as High Priest, would ever condone the spilling of innocent blood simply for political expediency."

"No? Even so, we have an obligation to those who will follow us, to the future."

"I must go. Time passes and my killer grows desperate."

"Desperate? He will have fled the city by now, surely."

"No, I believe he's still here and getting more agitated by the hour. He wants something he knows I have and he will stop at nothing to get it. Perhaps I should leave it in your hands for safe keeping."

"My hands? Certainly not. Are you mad? He might try to attack me. What is it he wants that is so dangerous?"

"Oh, I have no doubt he would attack you or anyone else for the bauble, for that is what it is. He has already killed for it twice. And, as he is not a believer, he will show no respect for either the High Priest, the Rabban of the Sanhedrin, or the Law. Sad but true. We allow too many people of questionable backgrounds into our city to share our hospitality, don't you think?"

When Caiaphas stopped sputtering and calmed down a bit, Gamaliel sat and looked him in the eye.

"High Priest, I know how much you wish to rein in this rag-tag gang of reformers and their rabbi. But under our Law, we can do nothing more than prefer charges, try him in the Sanhedrin, and perhaps flog some sense into or exile him and the rest of them, maybe a little of both. If we do, however, I am sure it will accomplish nothing. As soon as this rabbi is gone another will take his place and another after that. Let him be.

At some point he will say or do something serious enough so that even his closest followers will not be able to defend him. Then you may act."

"But—"

"Trust me on this, my old colleague. We have had what? Ten generations of men, who would be, indeed some were even declared to be, Messiah. They come and they go. Only we, the Sanhedrin, the backbone of the Nation, only we endure. We must continue to do so or all is lost—the city, the Temple, everything. Do not spend what little currency we have on this man. Not yet."

Gamaliel rose and left Caiaphas pondering and alone. Enough of that for now. He knew his killer lurked somewhere in the shadows and he would have him. He hurried to the palace where Barak awaited him.

Chapter XXXIV

"Excellency," the old man began.

"*Ha Shem*, Barak, you have news for me? Is something amiss? You look worried."

Barak's face looked like a map of the wilderness, lines criss-crossing it like so many goat paths. Something, it appeared, had him agitated.

"No, no, I thought you would be here earlier and when you didn't show up, I wondered. Then, one of the men who provide the kitchen with garum said he thought he'd seen you in the street near the Temple and you had been arrested by the High Priest or someone from the Temple. He said—"

"Nothing to concern you. The High Priest is in a state over one of the local rabbis and wanted me to confront and suppress him."

"I imagine I can guess who. Well, you see the news of your arrest, only it wasn't, of course, gave me cause to worry, Excellency, that you might not return I mean. At any rate, there is no news to report today. Chuzas says he has not yet arranged to have Menahem made available for you yet again. I am not sure why that is so and the guards have given up their search for Graecus, of course—"

"Of course."

"Sir? Oh, I see, yes, and the queen is reported to be very angry at you for failing to turn Menahem over to the Prefect. They say she has since informed the High Priest about what you did, or rather did not do."

"I thought as much. Rest easy, Caiaphas and I have had that conversation as well. The queen's anger can't be helped. I suspect she has reasons we can only guess at. It can't be easy married to this king and to have a daughter like the Princess Salome. Now, I have a question for you and I must ask it out here where it is not likely we'll be overheard."

"Yes, Excellency?"

"I am curious about all that intricate lattice work in the room assigned to us to conduct our interviews. How is it arranged?"

"How? I don't understand."

"As you well know, people who wish to listen to us can sit behind it without being seen. What was the purpose of placing it there and how has it been used in the past? I assume you will know as you were in the old king's service before this one."

"Oh, I see. It was built by the old king, as you suspected. He prided himself on his ingenuity, you know. He would stand behind the screen to spy on people who were scheduled to come before him. He thought they might reveal things in their conversations while they waited for him. He thought he could gain an advantage in any negotiations that might follow. That sort of thing."

"Did it work?"

"At first, I think so. You would have to ask the steward to be sure, but there are no secrets in palaces and soon everyone knew about the trick and were careful about what passed their lips in that room. I do not think the Romans ever knew. Whatever we might have felt about our king, we would never betray him to Caesar's people."

"I see. That is very commendable. Is there anything else?"

"The room also was used to hold small receptions and the like, with food and drink and sometimes entertainment. It would depend on who he met and how important they were or he thought they were."

"I see. How does one enter the spaces?"

"Oh, well there are only two that can be used. The space to the left opens directly from the royal apartments. The king, the queen, or the princess can slip in and out without anyone knowing. The screens are set on the two side walls. The ones with the entrances to the corridors are decorative only, you know, to make all the walls match. There the fretwork is set directly on the stone behind so there is no hiding space behind them. Of course the depth of the arch in the middle of each would show you that."

"And the screens on the right?"

"It is a similar space as to the left but the only entrance is from the basement, not the rooms behind the wall."

"Really? Tell me again. How were these hiding places to be used?"

"As I said, the first Herod would like to watch his guests before he greeted them. If there were to be refreshments or entertainment, the servers or performers would approach through the basement to the other staircase and emerge through the center archway, which has or had a working door. Herod did not want the servants to be crowding the corridors, you see."

"That's all?"

"No, actually, the more important use fell to the palace guards. King Herod feared for his life and he nearly always had armed guards in the space that led to the basement in case something untoward happened. They could rush in and protect him."

"So, the guards would know?'

"That was back in the old king's time, Rabban. I do not know about these new ones. I suppose they would. They must be acquainted with the palace and its points of access to do their job."

"Yes, of course they would. How about the other door? Is the door set in the left wall operable?"

"I do not know. I believe it serves only as a decorative item to complete the symmetry with the other walls. But that may have been changed since. Shall I try it?"

"No, I don't think that will be necessary just now, but that would mean, if the king or whoever sat behind the left-hand screen wished to enter the room, he would have to exit back through the royal area and come around to the far entrance."

"Yes."

"And the people called to serve the guests or the guards would enter through the door to the right."

"Yes."

"That is interesting. We must go to that most fascinating room and have a look at those wonderful hiding holes."

"I'm not so sure that is a good idea. Suppose the king or the queen is seated in one?"

"We will pass on the left-handed area for now. It is not the one that interests me. I want to inspect the one to the right."

Barak looked doubtful. "I don't think anyone has looked in there for forty years."

"I think you may be wrong. But if that is true, then we shall be the first to do so in four decades."

Nothing had changed since their last visit to the room. Gamaliel, instead of taking his place at the table, stepped close to the wall and inspected its construction. It had been painted vermillion originally, but either age or the composition of the paint had darkened the hue to a deep ox blood. He peered through one of the spaces and realized that the inner surface of the lattice had been covered with a gauzy material that further prevented anyone from being seen as long as no light was allowed in the space. As nearly as he could tell, the walls behind were painted the same color and had faded as well, but not as much. Apparently the sun's rays that poured through the glazed slits in the ceiling had some effect on the fading.

He made his way slowly around the room chatting with Barak and making sure that if anyone sat behind the screens they could hear him and know of his intention to open at least one door. He might have imagined it, but he thought he heard footsteps, the scrape of a shod foot against a gritty stone floor, to the right. He paused and then, with effort, pulled open the door that accessed the right hand area. As he expected, it was empty. He glanced at, but did not step close to, the stone steps that led down into the cellars. He had what he needed. Now it came down to selecting the proper time. The longer he waited, the more desperate his man would become and the greater the likelihood he would make a mistake.

And the guards knew about the space. He smiled. He would have his man after all.

Chapter XXXV

Loukas would have blamed the *Moirai*, those Greek entities who determined the shape, length, and end to the thread of life. Pilate would have called down the Fates, but Gamaliel simply assumed the Lord had a plan. However or whoever would now shoulder the blame, the Lord, some goddesses, or just the workings of one man going about his business, his attempt to talk with Menahem was met with yet another delay. Chuzas bustled in to join him in the interview room just as he completed his survey of the lattice work.

"Chuzas, have you made the arrangements for me to—"

"Rabban, excuse me, but I have an urgent message—"

"Another? Can't it wait?"

"Sorry, no. I have been charged to find you and tell you to make yourself available to speak with the king."

"The king? I thought he did not intend to ever speak with me again. As I recall he was very firm about that. What is so urgent that the king must speak with me now?"

"It appears he has relented. He does indeed want to speak to you. I believe he wishes to thank you for something."

"Thank me, whatever for?"

"It is not for me to say. He will attend you shortly, he said."

As quickly as he'd come, Chuzas disappeared in the direction of the royal apartments. Gamaliel took his seat and waited. He could not imagine what the king had to say to him, and gratitude seemed the last thing he'd expect. Would wonders never cease?

First, a show of patent animosity and now an olive branch? He rose when the king swept into the room. Except for Chuzas hovering at his heels he was alone, no retinue. Interesting.

"Follow me, Rabban," he said and motioned towards the corridor. Gamaliel guessed the king did not wish to be overheard either. Who else skulked behind that screen? Did the king fear the queen might be lurking there? It must be difficult, living in a palace where no one could be trusted, even with a casual conversation.

"You wished to speak to me, Majesty?"

Once in the corridor and well out of earshot of the room and its spider's web of a wall, the king stopped.

"I wish to thank you, Rabban, for resisting the pressure applied on the queen's part to turn Menahem over to Pilate."

Menahem again. At every turn this man popped up like a poor relation at meal time. If he didn't know better, Gamaliel would have sworn the key to the mystery lay at the feet of that old man. In fact, he wasn't sure it didn't.

"There was no cause to turn him over."

"No. So I have been told. But even if Chuzas hadn't told me the knife you found in the bath had not been used to do the deed, I would not have let him go. Guilty or not."

"You would defy the Prefect?"

"I would. He is powerful and has the emperor at his back, but he cannot depose a king and would not try. Not for Menahem."

"You are close to Menahem, then."

"He has been my confidant and friend for nearly five decades, Rabban. That is a long time and yes, we are close. Growing up in the house of the king, my father, could never be deemed normal, if you follow me. The first Herod had many interests, many enemies, and many wives. Two of my brothers and one stepmother and her mother as well, he put to death as you know. He told me about it at the time, how he had them strangled while he watched. He wanted to make very clear to me what happened to those who plotted against him. I had never thought to do so, and after hearing the story from his lips, never thought to in the future either, you can be sure."

"I am guessing, of course, but Menahem served as a stabilizing presence in your life?"

"You could say that."

"Who is he, or where did he come from? And how did he come to be a foster brother, if that is what he was…is?"

"Who is he? I am not sure. He is very discreet about his origins. Certainly he never confided in me. He did say at one time it would not be healthy for me to know. There were rumors, of course. There always are. The only one I credit has him the son of a Roman woman my father knew when he spent time in Caesar's court. That would be about the time he petitioned the Emperor Julius to support his bid to become king of Israel. Menahem has those western features, you see."

"Yes, that is true."

"He arrived when I was in my fifth year. He must have been in his seventeenth at the time and he was much older than I but now, as we both age, I think I have caught up and then passed him. When he speaks about things of the world, he sounds like he is the younger."

"The queen also contacted the High Priest about turning him over to Pilate. What is it about Menahem that so annoys the queen?"

"Ah…" The king let his gaze wander over an unusually designed silk tapestry hanging on the wall. "The queen has a very determined personality. She does not like to share with anyone. Menahem is a gentle soul and she resents the fact that I listen to him. She would prefer I only seek advice from her. She also knows that Menahem counseled me not to put aside Phasaelis to marry her."

"And the business with the holy man, John?"

At the mention of the Baptizer's name, the king blanched. "It was a mistake, Rabban. You must tell the Sanhedrin, the leaders, I did not mean to put the Nation in jeopardy over that man. He annoyed me and spoke untruths about the marriage. I asked the leadership and they all said there were precedents for my union with…well, we had our disagreements. But, as to the beheading, I had foolishly given my word in public and I could not back away. Trust me, I never dreamed the child would ask for such a terrible prize, that she would be so bloodthirsty, or more to the point, let her mother rule her in it."

"But she did. No doubt, little will come of it, Majesty. The people in the streets believe him to have been a prophet, but those of us who know the Book remain unconvinced as to that. You may rest easy."

"Hearing you say that is a great relief for me." The king started to leave and then stopped. "Tell me, how are your investigations proceeding?"

"Well, I think. Can you help in one last thing?"

"Certainly, if it is in my power to do so."

"I do not require power, Majesty, only an answer. Who is the man Graecus?"

"A king, Rabban, has many favors expected of him and in return, receives many. I cannot always keep the 'books', you could say, straight. At any rate, this man came to me with a paper from an old ally who wished me to help him in a transaction of some sort. To be honest I cannot remember what I did or received from him but I agreed to help. I have not had a further interview with the man since and they tell me he has left the city anyway."

"I see. So, you do not know him personally?"

"No, but I am persuaded he is who he claims to be, if that is what you are after."

"Thank you. That is a great help."

"Is it? Well, well. How so?"

"You have shown me another corridor that seems to lead nowhere and one, therefore, I do not need walk down and so I can direct my search elsewhere."

"I am not sure I follow you, but no matter. Do you know who killed the girl?"

"I hope so. It is not easy. But in any event, I cannot say at the moment. There are a few loose ends to tie together and then all will be revealed. I must catch him first."

"You think you can?'

"Again, I hope. Failing that, I will identify him and let the Prefect's men bring him in."

"I will leave you to it then. A word of caution, Rabban."

"Yes?"

"The walls have ears." He cocked his head back in the direction of the interview room. "Be careful what you say, if you do not want the queen and her spies to hear it."

"Thank you, Majesty. I will bear that in mind."

The king squinted at Gamaliel for a moment and then a trace of a smile crossed his lips. "But you knew that already, didn't you?"

It was Gamaliel's turn to smile. "Oh, one last question, Majesty, if I may."

"As long as you refrain from taking me to task for my poor observance, certainly."

"The Prefect heard rumors that one of your brother's children might be in the city and in pursuit of questionable ends."

"Who would that be?"

"The son of Alexander by Glaphyra, Archelaus."

"That is not possible."

"With respect, Majesty, why not possible?"

"Because he is dead these last seven months."

"Ah, then it couldn't have been him."

"Pardon?"

"It takes a turn, Majesty, thank you. Dead seven months, of course."

Chapter XXXVI

Gamaliel indicated that Chuzas should follow him and return to the room.

"What do you make of that, Steward?"

"Of what?"

"Pilate seemed certain this Archelaus had come to Jerusalem for some possibly nefarious purpose and the king declares him dead for over a half year. How can the vaunted Roman information gathering network have been so wrong?"

"There are many things our overlords do not know, sir, and there is the time-honored practice in this country for dispensing wrong information to them. I am sure others must do it as well."

"Yes. That may be so. Now, to the business at hand."

When they arrived at the room, they paced the length and breadth of it. He spoke to Chuzas in a low voice, opening doors, motioning toward the steps that led to the cellars, the ceiling and the opposite wall ostensibly used by the royals. Then he waved the steward back out into the corridor. There, still speaking to him in a low voice he spent the next half hour explaining to him what he wanted him to do, how and what to say to the captain of the guard, and when to say it. He spent half again that much time reassuring him that no risk would accrue to him, and finally running through it all once more so there could be no slip-up. When he felt confident Chuzas knew his assignments and when he was to execute them, he sent him off to perform his routine duties.

"I will want you again before I leave, Steward," he said in parting and proceeded to the garden where Menahem at last waited for him.

The old man stood at the arrival of the Rabban. Gamaliel wondered how long it had taken him to adapt to the expectation of others that he rise in the presence of those deemed superior in rank or position. It couldn't have been easy for one brought up being deferred to by princes and generals and not the other way round. Humbling oneself, Gamaliel had read, strengthened a man's character. If that were true, this man's character must have the strength of Sampson by now. Or had some "Delilah" got to his spirit and shorn him of it by now. He looked into the old man's eyes, noted the flinty stare he returned, and guessed she hadn't.

"*Ha Shem*," he said and gestured for Menahem to be seated. "Your queen does not like you very much, it seems, Menahem."

"So it has been reported. It is a thing we share, Rabban. She is not easy in your presence as well."

"*Not easy* does not do her feeling toward me justice—hostile more like. It comes with the title, I think. Many people are leery of me and with cause, I am told, for what I represent."

"And that would be?"

"The Law can be an uncomfortable companion, Prince, and its interpreter even more so. Never mind, you and I have lived long enough to know that popularity is fleeting and no guarantee of either happiness or security. Look here, I have brought you your knife. You may need it—for ceremonial purposes only I hope. Still, this is the palace of a Herod and—"

"You are being cynical."

"Realistic, I think. At any rate, I now know that it was not used in the murder by you or anyone else."

"You are sure of that?" The old man took the knife from him and turned it over in his hand. "Are you positive you would not like to keep it?"

"I? Do you wish to gift me with this beautiful piece of the knife maker's art? Or are you offering it to me to keep until such time as you are certain you are vindicated?"

"I am an old man. How much longer I will be around to wear it is highly problematical. You look like a man who would appreciate it. It is very old, you know."

"I guessed as much, old and of foreign design. You brought it with you, I assume."

"Brought it with me? Yes I did." Menahem narrowed his eyes as if he were trying to see into Gamaliel's mind.

"No, you keep it. I have no use for a dagger of that quality and origin. Now, there is a question or two I must ask you."

The old man laid the knife down on the bench between the two of them and waited.

"Why is it that you, and apparently you alone, knew the dead girl's real name?"

"Did I?"

It was Gamaliel's turn to attempt a bit of mind reading. Was this man being obtuse, evasive, dishonest, or ingenuous? He obviously knew things and kept secrets. Gamaliel guessed not all the secrets were of any real use to him or anyone else for that matter. Not anymore. It had simply become second nature to him, given his origin and history.

"Yes, you did. Everyone in the palace, including the queen in whose service the girl had been placed, knew her only as Cappo. You told me her name was Alexandra. I ask you again, how did you come to know it?"

"Suppose I were to say, I asked and she answered."

"I would reply that you have a facile mind for an old man but offer me a poor answer. Not entirely truthful, but close, and certainly one that might fool another. But I do not accept it. There is no reason for you to ask a servant her name, particularly when she already had one." Gamaliel paused and inhaled the scent of citrus. He didn't see any tree and it was late in the season, but the aroma wafted across the garden from time to time as the breeze rose and fell. He studied the old man's eyes again. "Why. I asked myself, would you? And the answer came to me, you wouldn't. You knew her name because…may I venture a guess?"

"Of course, if you understand I may not affirm or deny it."

"Yes of course, but in the end you will." Menahem smiled and said nothing. "The girl arrived at the palace of Philip with her father. He wished her to be hidden away. He feared for her safety at the very least, her life more likely. And with cause as it turns out, as she is now dead. Philip tucked her away in his queen's entourage with instructions to keep her safe and, incidentally, pure. The queen received no other information because, I believe, her husband had by then learned he could not trust her."

"With reason, I think you would agree."

"Exactly. When it seemed likely the queen would flee his palace and bed for that of his half brother, Antipas, he contacted you and asked your help in protecting the girl. Am I right so far?"

"Near enough."

"You are no fool nor do you feel any deep sense of obligation to this gaggle of Herodian descendents with which you are saddled, but you had some respect for Antipas and for Philip. I don't know why for Philip, but as you were raised in Antipas' house you must have something of a bond there."

Menahem only smiled.

"You knew, and Philip recognized that this king, your friend and foster brother, is a weak man and unable to resist the blandishments of his new queen. So he, that is Philip, determined it would not be a prudent course to share anything about the girl with him."

"Yes, that is so. But that still does not explain how I know her name."

"Not yet. As I said, you are not slow and I dare say you would not accept Philip's request without some explanation. He told you, I think, that the girl was the daughter of a very important person and it would be unwise for you to know who. Am I close?"

"Not quite there, but again, close."

"But he had to tell you her name because of the letters. I think later, because of that, you may have worked out who she was. Gossip races around a palace like rats in a granary and eventually it would get around to her father, her uncles, and the pot of intrigue they had cooked up. So, you have at least a thought of who she is and why she was here."

"I do. But it is not one I will share with you."

"There is no need to, Menahem. I already know who she is, where she came from, why she landed here, and that you were the conduit for letters to her, and from her, to her correspondent, that is to say her father in the north, for all but the last one."

"So there you are, Rabban, in possession of all there is to know. Why query me?"

"Not all. One small question about the letters remains. When one arrived, how did she know to come to you?"

"She didn't come to me, as you say. If she were in the chambers I would tell her. Usually I sent for her."

"Sent? Who did you send?"

"Oh, someone who would not question the errand, a guard or another servant."

"So that is it. And now I have all that I need to finish this business, I think."

"If you know all, do you also know who killed her?"

"I do."

"Who?"

"Ah, as to that…"

Chapter XXXVII

Gamaliel dropped his gaze and said nothing. Time passed, how long he could not say. If the old man expected an answer he did not show it but waited patiently for the Rabban to continue.

"I am curious, Menahem…That's not your real name is it? It's one that you took after you arrived here." Menahem's response was a faint smile. "As I was saying, I am curious. How exactly did you come to this place? Did you say you were traveling and the late king found you? What?"

"I intended to travel to the east, far to the east, in fact to India. I left the Kingdom of Aksum, south of Kush, and crossed by sea to Elath."

"From Africa, then."

"Yes. There I engaged some Idumean guides to take me through Arabia. They know the oases and the routes through the deserts and keep them secret. For a price, they would keep my journey a secret as well. We had to stop in Petra to re-provision and buy camels before going on our way. It was while I lingered in the City of Stone that Herod found me."

"Found you?"

"I had treasure in my baggage. My companions betrayed me. They gave me up in return for a part of it. The king took the rest."

"Why did he want to take you?"

"All this happened a long time ago, Rabban. The reasons are no longer important or relevant. It is enough to know that at that time, my life could be exchanged for a king's ransom. This Herod did not need the money but he did have a use for me—a political use, you could say."

"You were how old then?"

"No more than ten and seven."

"I see. That would put this trip you were making after the battle of Actium."

"After that by a bit. As I said, it happened a long time ago. What was current then has faded into the mists of time. No one cares anymore about Antony or Octavian or…. I did see the great Augustus once, briefly."

"And your mother?"

Menahem started back. First fear, then resignation crossed his face. Gamaliel raised his hand and shook his head and smiled.

"You do know now that I know who you are? I believe I know the rest as well. I can guess who the girl was, and the reason for her end, and your role in all this."

"Is any of that useful knowledge do you think? At the remove of a half century, knowing who I am can be of no use to you whatsoever. And now that the girl is dead, knowledge about her is equally useless. Rabban, take some advice and let it go. Turn me over to the Prefect and let us be done. I have nothing left to hold me here."

"I would like to but I cannot. I am not made that way."

"More's the pity. Then you must go catch your murderer. Turn him over to this new puppet that Rome has yoked us with and be done with it." Menahem paused and stared off into space for a moment. "Out of curiosity, just how did you work out who I am?"

Gamaliel removed the coin he'd carried in his belt for days and placed it on the bench between them next to the knife. "I found this coin along with some others in the bath. I could not figure out what relationship they bore on the murder. I subsequently decided they had none at all, but I worried about them for days anyway. Then, when I first interviewed you, you turned your head momentarily, enough for me to catch your profile. I knew I had seen it before, but I also knew I had never met you, indeed had only seen you at a distance. It took me several days, past Shabbat, in fact, before I remembered. They say you had a striking resemblance to your father. Then I had it, because, if the coin can be trusted, you still do. But even so, I hesitated to believe it. You were supposed to be far away or long dead."

"Believe me, Gamaliel, there are days when I wished the latter were the case. So, you know, or think you do. Please grant me a great favor and allow me to stay dead and buried."

"Your secret is safe with me, if you wish it to be."

"I do not care one way or the other. I am rapidly approaching my promised three score and ten. I cannot last much longer. I have no value to anyone anymore. Perhaps to be displayed as another of the rarities from Africa. Have you ever seen an elephant, Rabban?"

"No, I confess I have not."

"Well, if you ever do, you will find it to be a far more fascinating study than this old man."

"You sell yourself short. Until recently you were important to someone."

"The king? I think not. Not anymore. Oh, you mean the girl?"

"Yes, the girl. You were the only person she knew and could trust and at the end her only hope. You kept her in touch with her father until he died. Or was he murdered too?"

"The latter, I think. The offspring of Herod are a bloodthirsty, incestuous lot. And coming from me and my past, that is saying something, don't you agree?"

"By incest you mean what, exactly?"

"Aside from this new queen marrying her brother-in-law, is he not also her uncle, as was her first husband."

"It is not unlawful for a niece to marry her uncle. So the notion of incest is moot."

"Tell me, Rabban, this is your field if I'm not mistaken, how is it lawful for a man to marry his niece, but a woman may not marry her nephew? I have followed this religion of yours now for fifty years and I cannot make any sense of it."

"I have neither the time nor inclination to dispute with you, Menahem. It is enough to know that hundreds of years have been spent studying the Torah in an attempt to discern the mind of the Lord and the collective wisdom of the brightest minds over those years have so spoken."

"In Egypt, before Octavian arrived, pharaohs married their siblings. Men were usually pharaoh, but women could be and either way the sister or brother ruled with pharaoh and as spouse."

"You would know, of course."

Again Menahem merely shrugged and waved a dismissive hand. "The thought, you see, was to keep the blood line pure by wedding sisters to brothers, cousins at least. You would say that is incest, no doubt, but I see uncles and nieces wed in this land and suggest you draw a very fine line in the matter."

"And you, Menahem, were you ever married? Are there offspring and grandchildren living in the land of Herod?"

"None that I care to mention. Married? Herod had decided notions about that possibility. I never lacked for company, if that is what you are searching for, but marriage and heirs? No."

"Enough. The antics of kings and queens, their offspring, and the thin edge of Talmud is not a thing we need to waste time any more on. It is what it is."

"Yes, and that, my friend, is the definition of life in these dying cultures. And so we must endure them even as we watch them fall away like castles made from sand."

"Dying? How?"

"It will not collapse right away, Rabban, but the eagle that was once Rome is rapidly devolving into a guinea fowl. The majesty of your Moses has slipped into a quagmire of petty rules, and laws. Disputes between rival interpreters of it will slowly suck you down. Mark my words, Rabban. And remember they come from one who witnessed the mightiest empire in the world founder, fall, and disappear into the Nile. Gaze long and hard on your golden Temple for your generation will be the last to marvel at its glory."

"That borders on heresy, old man!"

"You wish it so, I am sure, but if you have correctly divined who I am, then you know I come from a prophetic race. What I say is true. Put your house in order. Collect your books and scrolls and put them in a safe place against an upheaval of everything you hold dear."

Gamaliel sat quite still, visibly shaken by the old man's words. He heard echoes of the other prophet, the one beheaded due to Antipas' weakness, and he feared he'd been given a glimpse into the future.

"You are mistaken, Menahem. Take your knife and resume your place in the king's household. I will detain you no longer. I will have the girl's killer before Shabbat and I will return to my studies in the sure and certain knowledge that what we determine here in this city at this time will last a thousand years."

"What you will spawn here will and more, but not as you think, Rabban."

Menahem stood, bowed, and left. Gamaliel would never see the old man again, and years later would wonder at his last words.

Chapter XXXVIII

Gamaliel remained rooted to his bench. He watched the old man disappear into the palace's dim interior. Time seemed to stand still. The citrus that had wafted past them as they talked seemed to depart along with the old man. Gamaliel tried to wrap his mind around what he'd just heard. He knew the races from northern Africa, and Egypt especially, were given to claiming powers they neither possessed nor understood. One had only to have the most cursory knowledge of the area and its people to figure that out. Queen Cleopatra's miscues, errors in judgment and bad alliances alone could fill a dozen scrolls ten cubits long. And everyone knew that the Jews in Alexandria, even the most faithful, insisted on reading Holy Scripture in Greek. Gamaliel mourned the fact that many of their rabbis could hardly read Hebrew at all, even if they had wanted to. They did not have the Word in the language of the Lord. But for this man to suggest no, predict the end of Jerusalem, King David's city? Surely not. Foreign nonsense. He heaved himself to his feet and followed Menahem into the palace. He needed to speak to Chuzas one last time before he headed home.

He found the steward in the kitchens having words with a servant who had dropped a salver of roasted quail on the floor. The king and his guests waited in the Great Hall while their dinner sat in an untidy but savory pile on the floor. The aroma of the seasoned game filled the room and made a difficult situation at least passable for Gamaliel while he waited. The birds were retrieved, wiped, re-spitted, and returned to the fire pit for a few moments more, presumably to restore them to a condition thought fit to be consumed by royalty. Gamaliel suppressed a smile. No one, it seemed, could avoid expediency, not even a king.

When Chuzas had finally managed to set things moving in the right direction again, the food repositioned on a clean platter, wine in tall cruets, and all sent out and away, Gamaliel managed to draw him aside.

"I need to leave some things with you, Chuzas. Have you a safe place where you could secure them?"

The steward assured him that he did. He had access to the king's strong box, not his personal one, of course, but the larger one in which various treasures used in the court were stored including the gold chalice used when the king thought there might be an attempt to poison his drink or when he wished to impress visiting royalty—sometimes both. Anything the Rabban left with him would be safe in that box. Satisfied, Gamaliel handed him the leather pouch containing the items he'd brought from his home, Agon's pendant, the letters, the seal, and some of the coins.

"Place these in the strong box for me and then I will need a decoy, Chuzas. I need a lure, if you will, to tempt a killer to show himself."

"You have already arranged a trap, Excellency. What now, another?"

"Not a trap, a fishing expedition, a ruse. It is time to force our killer's hand. If we do not catch him soon, another murder may take place. Also the king, the Prefect, and both their entourages, including you, are scheduled to pack up and leave the city soon. I am running out of time."

"Is that such a bad thing? Rabban, I do not wish to sound callous, but she was only a servant girl, as far as anyone knew. If her killer is not found and punished, it would be a shame, but beyond that is there any reason to press on if the household and the Prefect remove themselves from the city?"

"Am I to assume that is the prevailing attitude in the royal apartments?"

Chuzas nodded. He took the pouch. "I know it will not alter your thinking. Whether that of a king or slave, for you a life is a life, but I felt I needed to say it. What sort of lure will you require?"

"Something moderately heavy and round, about the size of the dead girl's pendant."

Chuzas cocked his head and thought a moment. "I can lay my hands on a bronze medallion which bears an image of the Temple on one side and a tetraskelion on the other. We give them to important visitors sometimes. Will one of them do?"

"Perfect. Take this purse and bring me a medallion. Then I must be on my way."

Chuzas returned after a short pause and handed Gamaliel a bronze medallion which had a silk ribbon affixed to it. Gamaliel detached the ribbon and returned it to Chuzas. The metal bauble he slipped into a worn cloth sack he'd acquired from the kitchen when he'd gone in search of the steward. It still felt slightly oily from some greasy previous usage and smelled a bit rancid, but it would have to do. He bid Chuzas a farewell and stepped into the street. The walk east would take him no more than a quarter of an hour. His house sat nearly at the foot of the Temple in the Lower City and directly east of the palace. Antipas had a smaller palace closer by, but since his marriage to Herodias, he had taken to staying in the larger, and older one built by his father. Gamaliel measured his pace so that anyone who wished to overtake him could do so. That was the point, after all.

He had crossed about half the distance to his house when the first two men made their appearance behind him. The walls that divided the Upper City from the old city of David were in sight when the attack came. As he had hoped, it was not violent. The first two men sidled up behind him; crowding him toward the curb A third man then approached him, his head down as if in deep thought. He collided with Gamaliel and at the same moment the man on his right jostled him so that he staggered into the man on his left. In the next instant he felt the quick searching fingers and heard the apologies from the men who'd bumped into him. If he hadn't known what they were up to and, in fact, had done he would have thought their words sincere. The entire operation took only moments. He'd been relieved of the cloth purse and its medallion. What the killer would do when his accomplices returned with one of the king's honorifics reeking of rancid grease, he could only guess. But now his prey knew where he stood, knew that Gamaliel knew the significance of the pendant, and that if he wanted it, he'd need to be bolder. It wasn't just Gamaliel who was running out of time.

He made it to his house without further incident and sat alone to eat his supper in the smoky light of his multi-wicked lamp. He felt very satisfied with his day's work. Tomorrow, before he returned to the palace to set his trap and expose the killer, he would drop in on Loukas. There were aspects of this developing story that had serious gaps. The physician would know the history and could fill them in. He would need all the pieces if he had any chance in persuading the Prefect he'd discharged his assignment as ordered.

For the next several hours, until his lamp died, he thought through what he needed to do, with whom, and when. He went over the plan repeatedly. So much depended on Chuzas. He wondered if he might have put too much reliance on the little steward whose loyalties were divided at best. He could not afford a slip-up of any sort. He drifted off into a troubled sleep shortly thereafter.

⟨⟩⟨⟩⟨⟩

As Gamaliel suspected, one man could barely contain his rage on viewing the prize his lieutenants brought to him. He threw the bronze medallion across the room where it bounced against the wall with a clang and rolled under a crate. He swore at the three men he'd sent into the streets to waylay Gamaliel. They had allowed that stupid old rabbi to make fools of them. The three apologized and shrugged their shoulders. After all, they said, they had done exactly what he'd asked them to do. They had followed and accosted the man, taken his purse, and brought it and its contents back as ordered. Surely he did not think they would stop and inspect the bag before fleeing or ask the old man if he would mind certifying the item they'd stolen was the one they'd been sent to retrieve?

The man cursed them violently and told them to be still. He sat heavily on an upturned barrel and tried to think. Time was running out. The king would leave for Tiberias within days. The Rabban would turn whatever he had discovered over to the Prefect who, unlike the old Jew, would be smart enough to figure out the whole of it. Whether he would do anything did not matter, the pendant would be lost to him and that would create another set of problems.

His earlier reconnaissance of the Rabban's house did not hold out much promise for a forced entry by anything less than a dozen men. He did not have a dozen men. He had only those three that he could employ without causing some difficulties. It was possible, of course that one or two of the other guards could be enlisted but that entailed risks—and costs. In any event he had no guarantee that the item was even on the premises. It could be with the goldsmith or locked away somewhere in the palace.

He needed time and of course, that was the one thing he did not have. He pointed toward the stairway leading back to the main portion of the palace and sent the men away—all but one. He had no more use for them. Once out of earshot he turned to the one man still standing. "My old comrade in arms, you will take care of those fools for me?"

"Of course. There is no need for witnesses to remain where they might become an embarrassment later."

"Good. So what do I do now?"

"If the old man did not have the pendant with him, or the purse he normally used, isn't it likely that both are still here? That he has hidden them in the palace somewhere?"

"I considered that. Of course he has. He will have put it aside. But where? I cannot search the whole palace."

"The old man did not move about much so finding it could be possible. He did spend considerable time with the king's brother Menahem. Is it possible he left it with him?"

The man scowled, concentrating. He looked up. "Find out for me, Geris. Your reward is as dependent on a successful outcome as mine. You do understand that. Don't you?"

"Of course."

Yom Sheni

Chapter XXXIX

Gamaliel stopped at Loukas' house before putting into motion the series of events he hoped would deliver Cappo's killer to him. He needed to know things about the politics and the satrap rulers of the various portions of the Empire. He'd been taught some bits, but residents of an occupied nation find it difficult to appreciate the history of their suppressors however glorious it may assume to be. Loukas, on the other hand described himself as a citizen of the world. He would know about these things and in some detail. At least Gamaliel guessed he would. He'd known Loukas only as an acquaintance and in a professional way prior to this business at the king's palace. And until that event threw them together it was all he wished to know of him. But the last few days had made him curious about the man.

He was at home when Gamaliel trudged from his house south of the Hulda Gates to the northern edge of the city.

Once seated on benches outside he said, "Loukas, forgive me for my inattention. I thought I knew you but now I am not so sure. Our conversations of late make me doubt my first impression. I have always assumed you were a Greek in fact as well as inclination. Was I wrong? Are you Jew or Gentile? I ascribed your attitude as that of 'Fearer of the Lord' only. So I took you for a Greek and a pagan in search of learning."

"Did you? Well you might. For all intents and purposes I am as you thought, Greek. That is so only because of the happenstances of my childhood. My youth, you see, was wrenched from me as was my family. One day we lived together, the next we were scattered over the countryside. And as this happened to my family, no rabbi or priest came to deliver us. So, I am today what circumstances have made me. My early upbringing ceased to exist."

"I am confused. What sort of past? Are you saying you were Jewish at one time? Are you now?"

"A fair question. Very well, I am a Jew by birth but a skeptic by inclination, if you follow me. But I have none of the fire or faith of my former co-religionists. My childhood circumcision marks me as one of the covenanted but little else. Do not look so shocked, Rabban. I am not unique in this as you must know."

"I am not shocked, only saddened and you are right, there are many like you. I worry how the Nation will survive because of it."

"The Nation? Come, come, Rabban, surely you know that more Jews live beyond the boundaries of Israel than within it. Alexandria alone rivals this city in its total of the children of Father Abraham."

Gamaliel did know but it was not something he liked to dwell on. The thought of so many Jews outside the immediate influence of Jerusalem and the Temple worried him as it did the Sanhedrin. Loukas drew a breath and launched into his narrative.

"My family history is neither unique nor particularly interesting. Like many people, that is to say the marginalized of the Empire, my father was crushed by heavy taxes levied first by the Empire, then by local regents and governors, and finally, a host of agents and bullies. He was a leather worker, or tried to be. It was a skill passed on to him by his father. His survival depended on the tiny margin of profit between the cost of hides and the price he received for the goods he made from them. That margin grew smaller every year and when it finally disappeared, he could no longer pay his taxes. He borrowed from moneylenders against the hope of better times, but in the end, defaulted on his debts.

"There is no mercy to be had from either tax collectors or the moneylenders. The former are a pox on the Nation, the latter worse, but at least with them there can be no illusion about what is expected. As my father had no assets to seize and no wealthy patron to turn to, his family, my sisters, mother, all of us, were sold into slavery. I was very young so that all I remember of that day was the wailing from my mother, sisters, and even father as we were carried off in as many directions as there were of us, to live and die in strange places. I have no idea where they were sent and I have never seen any of them since."

"This is true?" Gamaliel knew it probably was. People did not lie about those things—family being the cornerstone of the society. He also knew that this man's story could be told a hundred times over on every street corner of the city and in every market place in every village and town across the Empire. There was only one relief from poverty. You sold yourself or you died.

"Yes, but you see I was one of the lucky ones. My master turned out to be a physician practicing his skills in Antioch—that would be the Antioch closest to us, just to the north in Syria. We have a peculiar habit of using place names over and over. It can be confusing. At any rate my master, like many of the well educated of the day, maintained a tolerance to all religions and philosophies that might be foreign to his own and, indeed, sought them out for study and discourse. I must tell you, Rabban, he was severely disappointed when he discovered that I, though a Jew, knew so little of my faith."

"He was disappointed? Why did you know nothing of your upbringing?"

"Please understand, my father was a Jew of the Diaspora, always living on the edge of poverty, and therefore little inclined to attend synagogue or instruct his son in the faith. I knew something of the Torah and the lives of David and Solomon, but not much else about the God of Abraham. What little I now know, I gleaned later, much later as I sought to settle the unrest in my soul."

They sat a moment. Gamaliel waited for him to continue, unsure if he intended to or not.

"My life was spent in the homes of the wealthy and privileged citizens of the Empire safe by virtue of their status from the crushing oppression borne by the rest of us. It also meant they were blind to the suffering they and their kind brought on others. They were conditioned by their society and upbringing to expect privilege as an inherent right of citizenship and birth. Wealth, as I have said to you on another occasion, insulates one from one's actions. It is an axiom of power, I think, and the cause for most of the suffering in the world. Can you imagine a world where the rich had to share the sufferings of the poor?"

A picture, a very different picture of his friend began to form in his mind. "That is a very democratic thought, Loukas. You are a Greek after all. No, an Athenian. You are a student of...what's his name...the teacher who is said to have drunk the hemlock for corrupting the youth of the city."

"Socrates? Not hardly. So, when I was in my thirteenth year, when I would have become an adult had I been raised in the faith, my master made me his apprentice. I was a good student and soon found myself constantly at his side. He taught me how to compound his potions from the extensive pharmacopoeia of the time. I soon learned the subtleties of diagnosis, the treatment of agues, fluxes, and the myriad illness and traumas that plague us. I became a better than average bonesetter. By my twentieth year, I was often sent to see the sick and suffering in my master's stead, particularly those whose financial condition suggested they might not be able to pay the Healer's Fee. When they saw it was me and not my master, they usually did not.

"It was a good life, all things being considered. My only regret was that when that good man, in his turn, fell ill, I was powerless to save him. My inheritance, if you can call it that, was my freedom, his name, *Lucanus* in Latin, and his practice, such as it was. So, I accept no religion beyond that of Asclepius. I have no spiritual inclinations, nor have I received instruction in any of the many religious offerings of the day. But I retained, deep in my soul, memories of an angry Moses coming down from the mountain and despairing at the sight of the children of Israel worshipping a golden calf, memories of David and his sling dropping the mighty Goliath, and of a mysterious Isaiah singing about a new day and the Coming One. I read what I could find."

"Read? In Greek? The Septuagint?"

"Indeed, the bits and pieces of it made available from time to time. Those books are costly to own, you understand, but much easier on the eyes than your Hebrew versions, if you must know. So there you have it, Rabban. I am, like so many living in David's city, poised and waiting for what comes next, but not necessarily committed to it, whatever it may be."

"To what comes next? I don't understand. Something is expected?"

"You wait for a messiah, do you not? The pagans who linger at the fringes of the faith expect something to happen, are sure of it, in fact. Perhaps it is the brooding Roman presence that creates this need for something dramatic. You do not have to be a Jew to long for another Moses to lead you out of bondage, you see. There is a tension in the air, Rabban. You are too deep in your scrolls to feel it, but it is palpable to the rest of us."

Gamaliel slouched back in his chair. Loukas was beginning to sound too much like Menahem.

"If you say so, Physician, but I did not come here to discuss the apocalypse with you. What can you tell me about Egypt?"

"Egypt? That is a sudden change in conversational direction. Why Egypt?"

"I wish to know its recent history, back six decades or so."

"You wish to know about the Roman connection and the destruction of a great empire at the hands of Caesar Augustus, then only Octavian. Where shall I start?"

"With the battle of Actium or thereabouts and all that followed. Then you must tell me all you know of Cappadocia."

"I don't think there is a connection between them. Why the two?"

"I have some thoughts that need either confirmation or erasure."

"Ah then, this may take a while."

Chapter XL

"It is fascinating you bring these two questions to me at the same time, Rabban. They are both tangled up in the Roman civil war that broke out after the assassination of Julius Caesar and in very similar ways. The assassins, after Brutus' death and under Gaius Cassius, occupied the eastern provinces, while Antony and Octavian settled in the west and south. Cassius put an end to the rule of Ariobarzanes III and his brother Ariarathes in Cappadocia. But he lost the battle of Philippi to Octavian and Marc Antony, who will next be found cavorting with the Queen of the Nile. The new order, as is their habit, decided to shift the power to someone they could rely on more readily and elevated the high priest of Comana as the new king. That would be Archelaus, the father of Glaphyra, who became the wife of Alexander who…well, you see the picture."

"I'm trying to. It is confusing to say the least."

"More so as her mother was also named Glaphyra and she was married to an Archelaus as well at one time or another. The princess moved around quite a bit. So, Cappadocia was expanded even more when Octavian disposed of Antony and his Egyptian Queen and became Emperor Augustus and sole ruler. He added parts of Cilicia to the country. Then his successor, Tiberius, turned Cappadocia into a province of the empire and sent Archelaus packing and appointed Quintus Veranius governor. At the same time he unofficially folded portions of

Cilicia, Galatia, and Antiochus into it thus making it extend from the Euxine Sea in the north to the Middle Sea. The new governor, by the way, was adjutant to Germanicus who is, I have it on some authority, that is the rumors from the city across the sea, the father or grandfather of Tiberius' successor. The 'Little Boots' we spoke of before."

"My head spins, but Cappadocia is a prize then?"

"Indeed, almost as great as Egypt. It controls the trade routes to the east and the trade routes to and from the south all the way into Africa, intersect the east-west ones as well. To control those roads that send goods east and west, north and south is a 'pearl of great price' in the eyes of a man whose ambitions run to kingship. And furthermore, as a land in and of itself, it is extraordinarily rich and fertile—vineyards, fruit of all kinds and its Caesarea is a capital to rival any in the Empire. And then the landscape, they tell me, has those amazing great phallic stones which the Romans seem to admire for some reason. A phenomenon I prefer not to analyze."

"Really? I had no idea. I think I have spent too much time with my nose in books and papers. Everyone knows these things?"

"Not everyone, no, but those who need to, must."

"Yes, I see. Some of my confusion arises from the dual practices peculiar to royalty in general, intermarriage and murderous plotting. Herod's line in particular has several instances of nieces attached to their uncles and sometimes serially. And this Glaphyra seems to turn up everywhere in the line."

"Perhaps she was a great beauty."

"Perhaps. Cleopatra is said to have been rather plain."

"But she had other attributes. Maybe Glaphyra shared some of them."

"Are you really so carnal or do you say these things only to goad me?"

"A little of both, Rabban, You were saying?"

"I was elucidating the commonalities associated with those royal houses, Egypt's and Herod's—and Rome's as well, for that matter. They all have a habit of executing perceived threats to their power. Brothers, sons, wives, mothers-in-law, and relatives in general, it doesn't seem to matter. The mere appearance of a threat seems to be sufficient. That practice seems especially to have preoccupied the late King Herod nearly as much as the huge building programs he'd launched."

"So now you know the substance of royalty in our time. Is there anything else you need?"

Was there? Whether to the south and east, north, or west, the exploits of these rulers—Cleopatra, Archelaus I and II, Princess Glaphyra, Antony—including those which were only rumored and did not involve a Roman of importance, were enough to make his head spin. Nevertheless, Gamaliel had taken it all in. He sat back, educated, slightly confused, but at the same time pleased with himself because he felt sure now he'd correctly figured out almost all of the important parts on his own. The few bits he did not know and had just learned either did not matter, or confirmed what he'd already surmised.

It had taken longer than Gamaliel expected for Loukas to work out the tortured history of Egypt's last days as an empire in its own right, and almost as long to sort out the complexities of the Cappadocian royal family. But it was as if the last veil had fallen away from his dancer and he could see the naked truth at last. He smiled inwardly at the metaphor. He was certain Loukas would have envisioned a different sort of dancer and a much more graphic nakedness. He smiled and left his friend with a promise to return and speak more of his faith or lack thereof. Loukas nodded and bid him farewell.

It took him nearly an hour to make his way back to the palace through the throngs of people in the streets. It would be the last big day of Feast of Tabernacles and some were making the most of it. Others were already packing and preparing to leave. He did make one last stop at Agon's shop. He had no news for him but hoped he might receive some from the jeweler instead.

"The captain of the guard stopped in again, Rabban. He seemed very curious why you had visited me. Is that a concern?"

"That would depend on you. What did you tell him?"

"Nothing that could compromise your investigation. Enough of the truth to keep me safe and enough embellishments on it to keep him guessing, I hope. He asked specifically—well, not specifically, that would be a stretch—about the pendant. At least that was my understanding of what he was after. He asked about this and that and did an 'oh, by the way' mention of it more like."

"Did he indeed? I wonder. Should I be surprised at that? What did you tell him?"

"I told him you had shown me a pendant, but we determined little or nothing about either its owner or its significance and you put it aside."

"That is true enough. The one I have is the one you made. The one put away, on the other hand, is a key piece to solving this murder and tells us a great deal about the victim. Thank you for your discretion, Agon. I regret to tell you this, but I may have to call on your services again when the murderer is revealed and there is a hearing."

Agon grinned. Gamaliel hurried on to the palace. He did not want to be late setting his trap.

⟨⟩⟨⟩⟨⟩

Gamaliel met Chuzas and Barak outside the palace gate as usual. He quizzed Chuzas closely about the day's plans. He needed to know the position of all the players in his little drama and be reassured they had been correctly placed and were ready. Informed that they were, he entered the interview room. The game was on.

The room had not been altered in any way since he'd last visited it. He would have been nervous if it had. More nervous, actually, for in spite of his apparent calm exterior his heart pounded and he had to concentrate on controlling his breathing. This was not the sort of undertaking a Talmudic scholar would normally engage in, even as a fantasy. Not for the first time he wondered where it would lead him and if he'd ever be the same after all this was over and done.

He waited patiently until he heard the tongue click that signaled that Chuzas had taken his post. Gamaliel walked to the chair in which he had been sitting off and on for days and took his place at the table as if waiting for someone to join him. He placed the replicate pendant on the table and sat back. Somewhere off to his right he thought he heard the scrape of a foot on a step, or perhaps a tile. Did he? If so, would the man dare? Gamaliel waited.

Time moves most slowly when you least want it to, he thought, and right now time moved at the pace of resin oozing down the bark of a pine tree. He tried not to fidget, to signal his impatience. It should happen soon but was he ready? Patience he had in abundance when it came to studying Holy Writ. There was never any need to hurry the Lord, nor did he wish to. He paused to savor every word and every nuance of meaning like an Epicurean rolls his food and wine around on his tongue. But this was different. The man must act soon. He glanced at the door set in the lattice to his right. Would the prey dare make a move while the hunter waited? He clenched his teeth and willed himself to think about all the possibilities. The killer might be bold enough to burst in, snatch up the pendant and flee, perhaps leaving him dead or dying. Why would he not? A witness would be the last thing a killer would want. His plan, indeed his life depended on the likelihood that the killer would employ some ruse, some trick to get what he wanted. And then there was Gamaliel's counter ruse. If all the pieces were in place…were all the pieces in place?

The noise of a commotion out in the corridor interrupted these thoughts. As nearly as anyone could tell, it came from some distance away but it seemed to be drawing nearer. He sat up and twisted in his seat to face the door. The noise grew louder, which diverted his attention away from his vigil. He stood and stepped toward the commotion. His expression had changed from cool anticipation to genuine annoyance. Barak burst into the room.

"Rabban, you must come at once," he gasped and pointed toward the door.

"Come? Come where? Why must I come? This is a very bad time, as you know, Barak. We have important business to attend to here. We must speak—"

"But, Excellency, this cannot wait. There has been a terrible accident. Indeed, it might be another murder."

Gamaliel rushed out of the door, leaving the pendant behind and unguarded. The killer, it seemed had finally gotten his chance.

In the corridor, the two men stopped and listened.

"The captain of the guard has been told?"

"Yes, Rabban. He positioned his men as you expected and waits in the cellars."

"Excellent."

They moved away toward the kitchens to investigate the cause of the uproar. Sure enough a woman lay on the floor, a red stain spread from the area of her forehead across the tiles. Gamaliel knelt and searched the body for signs of life. He asked questions of the few people in the room, most of whom looked either confused or frightened and all were uniformly tongue tied.

Again, time slowed to a near standstill as they waited. Gamaliel leapt to his feet.

"The pendant! I left it on the table," He yelped and dashed back the way he'd come, panicked.

After the Rabban and Barak cleared the room, the woman who'd been lying on the floor stood and wiped the red wine from the floor and her face, then sat to drink what remained of it from a wooden cup.

When Gamaliel arrived at the room, the door to the right hand area stood open and the pendant was gone. Chuzas rounded the corner right behind him.

"It was as you said, Rabban. The man came through the door, snatched up the pendant and disappeared back through it to the cellars."

"And he was?"

"As you said, the man Graecus."

"Describe what he wore."

"Ah, again it was as you predicted, a loose tunic and cloak and, oh yes, leather boots. They were red."

"Not a Greek then."

"Sir? Not a Greek?"

"Boots, my friend the physician tells me, are not the foot covering one commonly sees on or in Greece or its subdivisions. Boots, particularly those dyed in bright colors, are the preferred foot covering of those tribes and residents to the north, like their ancient enemy, Persia. So, probably not a Greek."

Chapter XLI

"Send me the captain of the guard and his next in command, Chuzas, and be sure to wear your badge of office. I would recruit the king for this if I could."

"I believe he would be willing to do as you ask, Rabban. I had to tell him what you had planned. I'm sorry."

"You told him? But why?"

"I am not seconded to you as is Barak. I serve at the pleasure of the king. For better or worse, he is my master. To not tell him what had occurred in the past and what would soon occur today would be both disloyal and traitorous. He assured me that he never had a problem with your investigation, and in fact, wishes to help."

"But he chastised me. You heard him. He made it very clear he wanted no interference from me at all. He denied any further interviews. He—well we did have that chat, so—yes I see."

"He had to keep the queen pacified. We all had watched your interview that day and the queen seemed upset. She muttered something like, 'As bad as the Baptizer.' Well, you can see how that might go. But then, in his defense you saw how he reacted to her letter to Pilate. He will be with you when you talk to the captain, I promise."

"It would be better, I think, if you and the king take up places behind the lattice. Do not say anything or reveal yourself unless things go badly. Otherwise, I want you both to hear the whole interview."

Chuzas left the room through the door that led to the royal apartments. Gamaliel waited until he heard the scrape of chairs and the sounds of the steward and the king settling in to wait. He hoped the king would stay quiet and wait until he'd finished querying the captain. Barak, accompanied by Geris and his second in command, arrived. The two guards seemed short of breath, which would have been their expected state under the circumstances. After all, they had chased the thief/killer through the cellars and…but where was the killer? And what had happened to the pendant?

"Captain, where have you put our man? Is he locked away in a storeroom? Where?"

"I regret to say that he has slipped the noose, Rabban. I am sorry, but your man has escaped."

"How can that be? You had men posted at every possible exit from the cellars. You did post your men?"

"Yes I did, and yet, he has eluded us, I fear."

"That will not sit well with the Prefect, you know."

"I am sorry, but he is gone and taken the pendant."

"Has he? Well, that is too bad, isn't it…losing the pendant. It was a vital piece of our investigation. Tell me, how do you know about the pendant?"

"It is the one the girl always wore is it not? He took it, correct?"

"That was not my question, Captain. I asked, how did you know that he took it? No one but the king's steward, Barak, and I knew the pendant would be in this room today. Who told you?"

"Why…When I was asked to post the guard someone said that it was to catch the killer and he would have…someone said something."

"No one said anything about the pendant or mentioned its importance either."

"I think you are mistaken, sir. He, I mean, we all knew."

"All, did you indeed? Do you know what I think, Captain? I think you are a liar and are complicit in the girl's murder and have been since day one."

"Sir? How can that be? I am the king's own guard. I do not go around killing servant girls."

"No, you probably don't, but you did know or suspect that she was not just an ordinary servant girl. You didn't know what or who she might be at first, but you knew she received letters from someone outside the palace. From time to time Menahem used you or one of your guards to fetch her to him and you all saw, or could have seen, the letters exchange hands. Therefore, you also knew she could read. More importantly, you had contacts back in Cappadocia that you guessed might be interested in those facts."

"I have no idea what you are talking about, Rabban. I hold your position in the highest esteem. That and your age give you sanctuary from anything I otherwise might do to you, but I protest."

"Protest all you like. When I am finished here you will surely benefit from having rehearsed your claims of innocence when you answer to the king's court. Now tell me, who is Graecus?"

"The Greek gentleman? I have told you that already. He is an envoy seeking a trade agreement from the king they say. It is not my place to know these things, sir. I only secure them when they are in the palace."

"Not good enough. He was many things, but Greek was not one of them. No ordinary Greek would wear bright red leather boots. His papers, when we have a closer look at them later, will undoubtedly prove to be forgeries. That part doesn't matter at the moment. What does concern me is your connection to him. I believe you communicated your suspicions about the dead girl to someone in Cappadocia. Shortly afterwards you were asked if the girl happened to wear a particularly configured pendent. It was after that that this Graecus arrived at court and this Attic tragedy began."

"You are mistaken, Rabban. I know nothing of what you charge here and nothing you have said here can be corroborated. I am sorry your suspect has fled, but that will have to be the end to it."

The captain shuffled his feet and looked around the room. Gamaliel smiled and said, "This man is your next in command, is he not?" He turned to the second guard. "Tell me, how did your captain post the guards to capture the man when he fled from the basement?"

"Well, we were posted at all the exits, sir."

"All? Did not the captain assume responsibility for at least one of them?"

"Yes he did."

"And that one was the area nearest the kitchens, I suppose. Good, thank you. Another question, when you searched the cellars, did not your captain also assume responsibility for that same area?"

"Yes."

"One final question. This one is really for you, Captain. You reported to me that Graecus was spotted hiding out with the pilgrims outside of the city. Why did you not bring him in at that moment?"

The captain's expression turned stony. Gamaliel returned to speak with the second man.

"Were you aware the Greek was camped outside the walls?"

The man hesitated and glanced at his superior officer out of the corner of his eye.

"Sir, I—"

"You do not need to answer that. This man has no authority here," the captain cut in.

Gamaliel flashed Pilate's ring at the men. "You are mistaken in that, Captain, in fact I do, but that is beside the point. What is to the point is that you colluded with the man called Graecus. You were the one who went to the girl that night and told her that Menahem waited for her in the bath with a letter. You delivered her to her death and you allowed the man to slip by you just now."

The captain studied Gamaliel. Did he think to fight or flee, brazen it out, or confess? All this confrontation business was new to the Rabban. He felt a small surge of exhilaration and wondered if, by some quirk, he was beginning to like it.

"So what will you do? The man is gone and the pendant with him. This man here," the captain jerked his thumb at the other guard, "will say nothing if he wishes to see his wife and child again, and you…well, I think it likely you may suffer a fatal accident when you fall down those steps that lead to the cellars. You should not have attempted to capture the man yourself at your age. Very foolish thing to do. I will report this accident to the king and he will be most upset and—well, the Prefect will not like this outcome either, but soon we will all leave the city and you, the girl's murder, and her killer will be forgotten."

"Ah, but you are wrong, Captain. You posted your guards so that the man might escape. I posted ones of my own to prevent that from happening. We have your pseudo-Greek in custody. You are finished, my friend. You would be wise not to make your fate worse."

The captain grabbed Gamaliel by his tunic and shoved him toward the open door and the cellar steps behind it.

"Stop right there!"

The king and Chuzas stepped through the left-hand door. So it did open. How very convenient.

Chapter XLII

Pilate made Gamaliel wait nearly an hour on the Antonia Fortress steps before he joined him. It was a petty thing to do, but he was the Emperor's Prefect and he would demonstrate to the Rabban his position and importance and incidentally his impatience with the Jews' refusal to cross the doorstep of people they referred to as Gentiles. This Rabban would not enter the Antonia Fortress. Pilate had had the same difficulty when he wished to meet with the High Priest in the past. These stiff necked Israelites were more trouble than they were worth. He'd said so on more than one occasion. What god or goddess had disliked him so much to have him posted to this land of holy men and fanatics? He'd already been chided by Rome several times for his alleged disrespect for their culture and norms. So, he honored their peculiar scruples, but he felt no need to make them comfortable in them. After what he considered to be a suitable passage of time he stepped into the courtyard and greeted his reluctant investigator.

"You have unraveled the puzzle, this time for certain, Rabban?"

"I have, Excellency."

"Good. So we are done. Who was responsible for the servant girl's death?"

"I must first clear up two things with you. It is a matter of some urgency that you dispatch your agents at once to apprehend a man who, while he resided in the city, that is to say the palace, went by the name of Graecus."

"He was called the Greek?"

"Yes. He is not Greek in fact, but he passed himself off as being of that race to disguise his origins and motives."

"But why should I waste men and time on this man?"

"You asked me to find the killer, I have. It is this pseudo-Greek and his accomplice, the captain of the palace guards."

"Really? The king's own guards? Ah, well, as you may have discerned, I set you that task only to put your king in my debt, you could say. It was never material to me for you to actually solve it, you know."

"I know that, Excellency. What I do not know, however, is why you bothered."

"It is always wise, Rabban, to have powerful men indebted to you—one way or the other. You obviously mistook my intent at first, Rabban. I have no abiding interest in punishing a man for killing a mere servant girl. I would have, of course if he were to be delivered to me, but to pursue him for the death of a servant? I think not. If I would do that, the jails would be filled with most of the owners of slaves and servant masters in the country."

"She is dead, murdered, and deserves justice."

"Pah! She is only one of thousands who find themselves in such situations. She is undoubtedly better off where she is now."

"I will concede that from your point of view, her death may not require any further action. I do not agree with it, but I understand it. Your reasoning, however presumes she was, as you say, a mere servant. That is the second thing you should know. She was no mere servant girl. Please, sir, dispatch your men while there is still time."

"Not a servant? What then?"

"I will tell you in a moment but it is important this man be brought in. Excellency, your agents, please. This man, who foolishly believed he could pass himself off as a Greek but in his vanity could not bear to be without his ostentatious leather boots, must be taken. Chuzas and a handful of palace guards now hold him, but the guards suffer from a divided loyalty at the moment as they are holding their former captain prisoner as well. If he can prevail on them to free him, I fear our Greek may slip away as well. I need your men there so as to encourage the king's men in their duty."

Pilate studied the rabbi and scratched his head. This man was no fool and he seemed unnaturally eager to see the thing done. He frowned at the thought of having to yield to the Rabban. He did not like underlings to argue with him much less order him about. But this was the Rabban and his reputation for veracity had never been questioned. If he thought capturing the Greek important, it must be. He left and gave orders to a tribune who'd been waiting in attendance to mount a detail of soldiers and remove themselves to the king's palace and arrest the man known as Graecus. If by chance, he had slipped the noose and they failed to apprehend him there, they were to send dispatches to check all the roads leaving the city all the way to the Cappadocian border. Then he turned back to the Rabban.

"Now tell me. What do you mean, no mere servant girl? Who was she?"

"It will make more sense if you allow me to begin at the beginning. Might we have something to drink? It has been a long day."

"You will share hospitality with me? Am I not a pagan and what...unclean under your law?"

Gamaliel shrugged. "I hope you will not tell anyone, Excellency. There are times when if one is presented with a dilemma one must exercise a flexible spirit."

"Indeed? You are sounding a bit like a Greek yourself, Rabban." Pilate had a flask of wine and cups brought. He poured two cups and handed one to Gamaliel. "And now?"

"And now, I will tell you an amazing story, Excellency." Gamaliel sipped his wine and paused to collect his thoughts. "First there is the matter of the pendant I found in the pool. Then there is the knife which someone wished me to believe was the murder weapon, and there is the putative Greek."

"The knife was not the killer's?"

"As I tried to indicate to you earlier, it was not. That took me off on a tangent for a time and nearly foiled any chance I had to solve this thing. As it happened the physician had doubts about the weapon as well and then, luckily, the wife of Chuzas came to tell me that her husband was jealous of Menahem and it became obvious who had placed the knife in the pool."

"But why?"

"To bring disgrace on Menahem."

"But why would he do that?"

"That is another story and one I do not think will interest you. It has to do with a rabbi from the Galilee who has gathered followers, one of whom was the wife, Joanna, and the other this old man, Menahem. Chuzas came to believe it was Menahem who first led his wife astray and he thought if Menahem were accused of the murder, his influence would wane and the devotion his wife showed the rabbi disappear. He, like you, believed nothing much would be done to one who killed a mere servant girl, but Menahem would be ruined and perhaps banned from court."

"You wish the steward to be punished for his deceit?"

"No, thank you. Like you, Excellency, I too, understand the benefits of having someone in one's debt. Chuzas will keep me informed of the goings on in the court, information I will find most useful."

"Very good, Rabban, you become more like us with each passing moment."

"With our late king in mind, I prefer to think that you have become like us in that regard. Very well, here is the nut of the fruit. This girl, whose name as it happens was Alexandra, came to this land, or more properly was dispatched to this land, by her father from Cappadocia."

"Her father? Am I to take it this parent was someone of importance?"

"Yes and no. He might have been had he lived. He was the Archelaus about whom you spoke when you first charged me with this commission. You thought he might have come to the city. Your informants were either mistaken in the precise *who* was arriving, or they were deliberately misled. We will never know for certain."

"I am starting to be confused, but please continue."

"Your suggestion that the man in question was in the city led me first to think that Menahem must be this Archelaus. He is a bit older than I would have thought, but I considered it a distinct possibility. But I was disabused of that when I first saw him."

"Why was that?"

"It was the way he looked when he turned his head away. I knew that profile. I had seen it before and recently, but could not place where. Later, I remembered. So had you, I dare say."

"Me? When?"

"In the past, possibly in person, and certainly on some coinage that would have passed through your hands at one time or another."

"Please be clearer, of whom are we speaking?"

"Indulge me for a moment more, Excellency. I want to return to the girl and the pendant. It is more important to you and to your Caesar to have a complete and clear understanding as to what occurred, who was responsible, and the measures you personally took to prevent a potential international incident."

"That is a great deal of information in one sentence, Rabban. International incident? Truly? Measures *I* took?"

"Yes, *you* took. You are the Prefect. You ordered the investigation against most people's better judgment including the king, and you just sent your men to apprehend the killer of a princess."

"A princess? I suppose you best proceed as you wish."

Gamaliel withdrew the pendant from the pouch at his belt and tossed it casually onto the low table which stood between them. Its golden surface glowed warmly in the fading afternoon sun.

"You will see I do not exaggerate. This murder has, as I suggest, far reaching implications and yet is essentially the story of this pendant, who wore it, and why."

Chapter XLIII

Pilate scooped up the pendant and studied it. He turned it over and did the same to the obverse. He dropped it back on the table. "I can see nothing out of the ordinary here, Rabban. There is some writing on the front and back and a rendering of a lion's head in the middle. Not a very good one at that. The writing, I take it is in Hebrew, correct?"

"You would say a dialect, but that is a small point. If you look carefully, it is also repeated in Greek and Latin. At least I am assured it is Latin. I do not read your tongue, Prefect, so I cannot say for sure. Anyway it is what it says that makes it important."

"Do not play with me, Rabban. I will enjoy your company and hear your story, but I refuse to play guessing games. Tell me directly what is so important about this that you believe a report should be sent to Caesar about it. That is what you implied, is it not?"

"Indeed. A report to the emperor might be appropriate or it might not. It is for you to decide." He picked up the medallion and read.

Given this day in the seventeenth year of my reign to my grandson Archelaus. It shall be a symbol of his authority to act in my name…

Gamaliel turned the pendant over and continued.

In all things in heaven and earth.

"Then there is the name of the person who bestowed this item, *Herod, King of Israel.* The lion is his emblem. This medallion or pendant was worn by the dead girl. It was given to her by her father but not in the form you see it here. I found it in the bath, you see, where I presume it had fallen when she was killed. I believe it was the reason she died. Her killer wanted that bit of jewelry very badly. The killing was secondary and I now believe accidental to his desire to obtain the medallion."

"Why didn't he simply take it from her? She was a slip of a girl, an easy thing for a man to overpower."

"Several reasons. I believe that was his intent, but he had another task to perform first."

"And that was?"

"He needed to deflower her. If she was no longer a virgin, she would be considered damaged goods and that meant that the likelihood someone would marry her greatly diminished. Her line, and thus any pretenders to the throne that could come from it, would end with her."

"Throne? What throne?"

"Cappadocia at least."

"I am lost. Go back to the rape. She would not be marriageable, you say? You are a strange people, Rabban. So he rapes her, then what?"

"He was, I think, most probably one of those men who routinely abuse women, especially young virginal ones, anyway. He decided he would force her first and then take the pendant from her neck. It was a serious mistake"

"She fought him?"

"It would seem so. In the struggle he attempted to cut the thong to which the pendant was attached. He held her head underwater to disable her, I assume, and as she struggled to breathe her head jerked forward at the precise moment he attempted to cut the thong and instead of merely slicing through the leather, he slashed her neck as well. Slashing upward, not down. That misled the physician and me, for a time. Because the wound seemed to be downward from right to left as he faced her, we assumed the killer used his left hand, but in fact he attempted to cut the thong and her throat, you could say, got in the way. The rush of blood must have startled him and the pendant slipped from his fingers and into the depths of the bath."

"And he didn't want to go into the water to retrieve it? That seems rather fastidious for a man accustomed to cruelty."

"I do not think it had anything to do with fastidiousness, Excellency. Barak, the man you assigned to me you recall, had the night watch. He entered the area at about the time this man would have gone after the pendant. The killer fled and with the uproar that followed, could not return to retrieve his prize. He tried on later occasions, but, as you know a guard had been posted and then when I had the bath drained, I found the piece and it was too late. All he could do after that was to hope no one would recognize it for what it was and that he might be able to steal it back later."

"He needed the pendant? Why?"

"Ah, that is a question the answer to which I can only guess, but I believe it would have to do, as I said, with the attempt by remaining sons of Alexander to seize the throne of Cappadocia. For the killer, it had to do with collecting his fee."

"Fee? You've lost me again, Rabban."

"Bounty, then. I believe the captain of the guard, Geris, sent word to Cappadocia of his suspicions that the girl might be royalty. I do not know what the relationship was between the two men, but you can find that out when you have them in custody. So, Geris, in turn, sold this information and subsequently was paid by agents acting for Tigranes and/or Alexander II to travel to Jerusalem, pose as an emissary from some court in Greece, violate the girl, and return with the pendant. How he managed to get it was of no consequence to his employer or employers. If he could simply steal it, well and good, but any means to an end would be acceptable."

"I understand that this bit of gold once belonged to the missing son of Alexander. Am I to understand that while Alexander was a candidate for assassination, the grandson was not?"

"It would seem so. Our late great king was a complex man. He willingly punished those whom he believed stood against him, innocent or guilty. But those who he believed did not, he treated fairly. Whole families were not punished for the sins of one of their members."

"I don't know what our late and no longer lamented Julius Caesar saw in him."

"Oh, he was extremely good at what he undertook and I doubt your Caesar cared a fig how he ran his court. Tribute is the measure of success in his world, and Herod the King was very generous. Do not forget, he also won the favor of Marc Antony, Queen Cleopatra, and Octavian, or Augustus, as he came to be. Say what you will, Antipas' father knew what he was about."

"If you say so. I grant that he was a builder. Continue."

"So, it happens this child was the daughter of Archelaus. I can now tell you that he is dead, poisoned by his brothers who, I surmise, had in place a plot to replace their grandfather, the King of Cappadocia who died a decade ago after Tiberius exiled him."

"You're telling me that a pair of Herod's decedents thinks they can seize the throne of Cappadocia? That is patently absurd, Rabban. What fool would challenge the might of the Syrian Legion?"

"I believe they are waiting for the death of the current Caesar. As that seems a near certainty they will step in during the inevitable struggle for succession that will follow and then swear loyalty to the most likely winner."

"There will be no struggle."

"Then that will be a first. At any rate, Archelaus apparently fell out with his brothers and refused to be party to the plan or he might have had separate ambitions of his own. Either way what he knew placed him in jeopardy. When he sensed something amiss, he enlisted the help of his friend, ally, and cousin, Philip. He sent his daughter to him for protection. Philip placed her in his wife's household, but did not reveal to anyone who she was or why she was there. When Herodias left Philip for Antipas, the girl came along as well. As with all things associated with this extended family, nothing is ever simple."

"So she was the great-granddaughter of Herod the First. She was seen as a threat? To whom?"

"Primarily to the remaining brothers. Their opponents, and there would be many, would happily use her as a rallying point for a civil war, or in this case an attempt to reestablish the kingdom forfeited by the first Archelaus. We may never know for sure. Those who lust for power are a confusing and unpredictable lot, but one thing is certain, anyone who so aspires, must have some connection to the throne they covet. A prince is best, but a princess will do. A son of a princess would be marginally better."

"Did she know?"

"I think it unlikely. She never knew her grandfather, and would not be the object of discussion in Cappadocia, I think."

"So she did not have to die?'

"Without the pendant, she had no proof of her relationship and who would believe a woman and a damaged one at that? So, no, she did not have to die."

"But one thing I do not understand. Why did not everyone know this? Surely if they saw the pendant on her neck, they would know or at least guess."

"That is the question, indeed. They did not see it because it was hidden. Her father, to protect her, had an overlay of material put on the medallion that completely covered the inscription and the gold. He did it to protect her. Her identity, you could say, was hidden in plain sight only to be revealed later at an appropriate time and place."

"So her uncles, acting on the information of the...you did say the captain of the guard?"

"Yes."

"Sent this man, posing as a Greek, into Antipas' court to relieve her of her identity." Pilate drank from his cup. "She needn't have died."

"Again, no, she needn't have died."

"And if you, that is to say, I, hadn't been able to capture, or at least identify her killer, it might have gone badly with me in the Senate."

"Possibly."

"I am in your debt, Rabban." He drank again. "You said something about this Menahem. What did you mean?"

"Ah. I said I recognized him, yet I never met him before. I thought I had seen him recently, in fact, but that could not be."

"But you had?"

"I had. So have you—often."

"So you said. When? I do not attend on the king's court."

Gamaliel tossed a coin on the table next to the pendant. "Here, on the obverse of this coin."

Pilate picked it up and frowned. "It is the face of the same Julius Caesar of whom we just spoke."

"Yes."

"And? Am I being thick headed or are you playing games with me again?"

"It is said that Queen Cleopatra's son, Caesarion, bore a striking resemblance to his father whom Antony, among others, claimed was Julius Caesar."

"By the gods, Rabban, you cannot be serious."

"It is so, Prefect. Rumors of the young Pharaoh's fate are many and varied and perhaps mythical—he escaped to India, he returned to Octavian who had him garroted, he was slain by the Nabataeans. It appears, however, that Herod, who as I said was no fool, saw an advantage in holding him. He had conquered Nabataea with the support of Cleopatra already. He had cast his lot with Antony after the death of Julius. As luck would have it, Caesarion was on his way east through Idumea and passing through Petra. I believe a servant betrayed his identity for money. Herod trapped him and brought him into his court. The man, boy really, then had no choice. Accept Herod's hospitality or Octavian's vengeance. Herod thought of him as an asset in the games he played. If he needed to curry the favor of Octavian, he had a die to cast. If not, he could do this one last favor for his late and former allies and protect the son. And, who knew, he might need him in the future."

"And now that asset is mine."

"If you have use of it, it would seem so."

"Was he ever married? Were there children? If so, that might add another complication or advantage. He is very old."

"I know of no offspring. If there are any, and he denies there are, and unless they sprang from a noble family, they would have little or no value, much less be in a position to make a claim."

"That's so. Many years have passed since Actium and with Augustus dead and Tiberius, as you just noted, failing, I doubt this asset is of much use to anyone now."

"Yet even old coins retain value when spent in the right market, Excellency."

"As you say. Thank you. I am impressed, Rabban. I did not take you for a solver of mysteries. How did you do it?"

"You remember our first encounter when you charged me with this business? We spoke glancingly about the Princess Salome and her alleged dance wearing only seven veils and I wondered what the Baptizer's fate might have been—"

"Had she been wrapped in eight and so on. Yes, yes, so?"

"My mystery was like the princess, only not so beautiful. I went through all the bits and pieces. I asked questions. I thought about what I had learned from my interviews. Finally, one by one, the veils fell away. When I acquired an account of the fall of Egypt and the more recent history of Cappadocia to the north, the seventh fell away. All that was left was the business of the basement and the Greek."

Pilate's eyebrows crept up his forehead. "What about the basement?"

"It was where the man was hiding. I needed a means to lure him out. Once that was done, my eighth veil dropped to the floor. I saw all. And on that note, Excellency, I must take my leave." Gamaliel slipped off Pilate's ring and handed it to him. "With respect, Excellency, it is my sincere hope you will have nothing more to occupy my time, now or ever. As you said, you are in my debt—doubly so, I should think."

"Be off, Rabban, I will not bother you again."

Would he not? Gamaliel wondered and prayed it would be so.

Epilogue

Four of Gamaliel's students waited for him when he returned to his work. He couldn't be sure how many, if any, would be there and was gratified to still have them in place and eager to engage. His week-long absence chasing after a killer combined with the Feast of Tabernacles had disrupted the routines of both teacher and students. But he was happy to be back doing the thing he loved best. He spent the morning with them and at noon sent them away to attend to the other duties they were called to. One paused at the door as if to speak.

"So, Saul, is there something you wish to ask me?"

"Not ask, exactly. To consult, more like. I have a problem set for me by the High Priest."

"Ah, I see. Without knowing the nature of the problem, my advice is to keep some distance from Caiaphas. I know he comes from a family proud of their ascension to the position and I have known and been a colleague of his for years, but it has been my experience that the position he holds has within it the seeds of a man's destruction. I do not know why. It may be that it comes from the fact that the position has slipped over the centuries from being held by descendants from the line of Aaron to whomever can curry political favor." Gamaliel looked up at his student and saw the astonishment in his eyes.

"But the High Priest…how can we think of him in such a way?"

"I am sorry, my son, I spoke too soon and perhaps too harshly. I am no longer young like you and I sometimes see the world with an eye that is clouded. Experience should make it clearer, but it doesn't. So, what is the problem the High Priest has burdened you with?"

"He has not yet burdened me with anything, Rabban. He only asks me to consider joining him as part of the Temple staff. I would have thought that was an honor and would like to accept but I am afraid it will interfere with my studies, you see?"

"Ah, so that is it. And what would he have you do as a member of his inner circle?"

"He is concerned about the burgeoning number of itinerant rabbis roaming the countryside and the laxity of their teaching. He wishes me to join him so that the older, more experienced members can launch an assault on some of them."

"He is concerned about more than one itinerant rabbi?"

"Yes, although he seems particularly focused on one, a man from the Galilee, or someplace like that."

"I see. And he wishes you to pursue this man?"

"Not I, no. He has set Ehud to work on that one. He has a plan to bring him down, he says."

"Does he really? What might that be, I wonder? Did he say?"

"Not in any detail. I gather he thinks there is one of the rabbi's number who is weak and he plans to suborn him somehow—money or a bribe, perhaps. I believe he thinks there is enough evidence of blasphemy to punish him."

"Punish? Really, Saul, consider. If you were this rabbi and believed in what you are doing as he must, would a flogging be enough to stop you? Or jail?"

His student frowned and shook his head. "No, probably not. How brave one will be is something one never knows until tested, but no, I would not. The High Priest will have to find some other means to silence this man. And since the Romans have taken away our right to execute criminals or heretics I cannot imagine what that would be."

"Well, as unlikely as it seems, the High Priest might attempt to provide evidence of sedition and remand him to the Prefect for crucifixion."

"The High Priest hates Rome as much as the rest of us. Is that likely?"

"I have a rule, Saul. With the High Priest as with the Lord, all things are possible"

"Well, all this assumes there will be sufficient witnesses brought forth to testify about both. He thinks this disciple will do that."

"But the High Priest does not want you to take that job on?"

"No. He has other duties for me."

"My advice to you is this, do as you think best, of course, but I believe you would benefit most from another year or two with me. But if you do go to the Temple, do not allow yourself to be drawn into the High Priest's mania about rabbis that do not meet his standard. It can only lead to trouble."

"I don't understand. The Law is the Law and it cannot be compromised."

"Is that what I teach, Saul? Don't I teach that the Law is from the Lord for the guidance of men? Too often we think we must do the Lord's thinking for him rather than listening for what he has to say to us. The High Priest means well, but he is like a stubborn camel that has slipped its lead. Instead of following the path already charted for him, he has taken it into his head to break a new one."

"You do not like the High Priest?"

"On the contrary, I do. I have known him most of my life. He works very hard at his job in very difficult circumstances. I would never doubt his sincerity, but in some things he can be like that camel. For example, this rabbi he is so addled about. My advice to you and to him is, leave him alone. Martyrs are always more attractive than the real thing, you understand? Let it be and it will dry up like the Salt Sea in the summer."

"But if it doesn't?"

"I can't say what he should do then, or you either for that matter. I think I would ask myself if it won't go away, what does that signify? And then, act—one way or the other."

"You would seek him out?"

"Probably not. I will be frank with you, Saul. I have no interest in any of this. I wish only to continue to live my life and study my scrolls until I die. I have no further ambition. It is your decision how to deal with upstart rabbis and self-proclaimed messiahs as it will be your generation that will be affected by them in the end."

"You do not think it is a good plan to pursue this man through his disciple?"

"I think it is a very stupid idea. Sorry, that is probably too strong. I think it ill-advised."

"All this, of course, assumes something will come of it."

"Yes, and what is the likelihood of that happening?"

Appendix

Those of us educated in the United States are, or perhaps more properly were, taught our history from a distinctly Eurocentric point of view. We know something of the royal families of England, France, and maybe Spain, and a bit about the Roman Empire and its successor, the Holy Roman Empire. We have the dates for the Norman Conquest, Columbus sailing from Spain. We learned the foibles of Henry the VIII, Louis the XIV, and secretly hoped the Three Musketeers really existed. American history veers off from its European roots but the reference points remain much the same.

Julius Caesar is a familiar figure to us because some of us suffered through his Gallic Wars in Latin I and almost all of us were required to read Shakespeare's play by that name. We may also have read his *Antony and Cleopatra*. And if not either of those, saw the film with Richard Burton, Rex Harrison, and Elizabeth Taylor. (Some few of us are old enough to remember a dishy Claudette Colbert as Cleopatra—in black and white and by all accounts, in a somewhat better rendering of the story.) And Greek mythology was and perhaps still is deeply embedded in our understanding of both western literature and its culture.

However, for most of us "of a certain age," what we know of Mid-Eastern history of that time period must be gleaned from ancient texts like *Josephus,* and the Bible. A very few of my generation could even spell *Gilgamesh* much less have read it. The Bible is generally viewed as a source from which one seeks spiritual guidance, but has only coincidental historical content, and *Josephus* was not on anyone's summer reading list. Consequently, we sometimes miss the fact that these two threads of history are importantly intertwined.

Herod the Great, the instigator of the slaughter of the innocents, as the Bible reports among other things, and Cleopatra, Queen of the Nile, pharaoh, and consort to both Mark Antony and Julius Caesar at one time or another, were contemporaries, allies against common enemies, and occasional rivals for the income to be earned from tolls collected along the King's Highway that began in Africa's Rift Valley and ran the length of their respective countries.

Herod the Great

b. 73 or 74 BCE, d. 4 BCE in Jericho

Herod secured his place as King of Israel with sponsorship of Julius Caesar and he was an ally of Marc Antony. At his death, his kingdom was divided between his heirs, most notably Herod Antipas (the Herod cited in the Passion Narrative and the man who had John the Baptist beheaded at the behest of Herodias' daughter, Salome—she of the infamous "Dance of the Seven Veils.") The other mention is of Philip, Herodias' first husband, and then we learn later of Herod Antipater and Herod Agrippa.

Herod ruled as Client King of the Roman provinces of Judea, Galilee, and Samaria. He was described as "a madman who murdered his own family and a great many rabbis." Whatever else may be said about him, one must add that Herod the Great, once friend to Julius Caesar, Cleopatra, and Antony, and who somehow managed to retain power after Octavian's victory, had to have been a very savvy politician.

William Barclay writes, "He murdered his wife Mariamne and her mother Alexandra. His eldest son, Antipater, and two other sons, Alexander and Aristobulus, were all assassinated by him." (*The Daily Study Bible Series: The Gospel of Matthew*, vol. 1, 2nd edition [Westminster Press: 1958], 20) History records that of the two murdered sons by Mariamne, Alexander had two children by Herod's niece, Glaphyra, from his line stemming from his marriage to Malthace. Some believe there may have been a third child, perhaps a daughter, but there is no record of her or his name. A son, Archelaus, is the author's invention as is his history.

There is also a dispute about Philip, not just the spelling of his name (one L or two) but his marriage. Some scholars question the claims made in Mark's Gospel that he was married to Herodias and had a daughter, Salome. Or that Herodias subsequently divorced him and married his half brother, Antipas. An alternate version has him married to Salome, his niece by Herodias' marriage to someone else. This book holds to the traditional view and that Mark had it right, or near enough. A second problem lies with the repetition of the name itself and confusion with another Philip, the Tetrarch, a near contemporary with a similar marital history (to a niece). And finally, Salome is a name which compounds the problem further as it pops up frequently as well in the royal line and elsewhere.

The intermingled lines of the royal family begun by Herod the Great also create problems for many, particularly this author, who would sort through them in search of a pattern or a direction. Not only do the lines cross but the names duplicate frequently. Thus Philip the Tetrarch was not, it seemed the same as Philip Boethus who was at one time, also a Tetrarch along with his half brother Herod Antipas. Or, then again, perhaps he is. And it must be reemphasized not all scholars would draw up the "family tree" as shown at the front nor would they agree on the names, dates of birth and deaths, or succession.

Lest one is tempted to shake one's head at the seemingly incestuous and tangled mess set forth in the "family tree" illustrated at the beginning of the book, one should pause a moment and consider the royal families of Europe. At the outbreak of the First World War, for example, the primary combatants were England, Germany, Austria-Hungary, and Russia. Nicholas, Tsar of Russia, George V, King of England, and the Archduke of the Austro-Hungarian Empire, and Wilhelm, the German kaiser, were cousins. They were also related by blood and/or marriage to the King of the Belgians, the royal families of Greece, Prussia, and half a dozen other greater or lesser principalities scattered across the continent. Royalty, it seems, is reluctant to share power outside the family.

The Egyptian Connection

Cleopatra, Queen of Egypt, was Herod's contemporary, ally, and sometime rival in the area. At first she ruled as pharaoh with her father, then with her brother to whom she was briefly married as was the custom with the Egyptian royal family, then alone, and finally with Antony by whom she bore three children who later, after her death and the suicide of Antony, and with the sponsorship of Octavian (Augustus), ruled elsewhere as kings and queens in their own right.

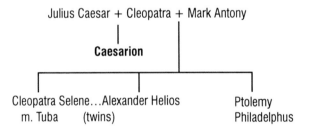

Cleopatra Selene married Tuba, King of Mauritania. After her death, Tuba was married briefly (for a year) to Glaphyra (the same woman who was previously married to Alexander, Herod's son who was assassinated by his father). She left him to marry Philip the Tetrarch, not to be confused with Philip Boethus (the Philip of the New Testament) also her uncle and also son of Herod. Go figure.

Caesarion was alleged to be the son of Julius Caesar and Cleopatra. Mark Antony published a document, *The Donations of Alexandria*, which supported the claim and to which his rival, Octavian took exception. Whether this precipitated the battle of Actium or was simply the last straw in the strained relationship between the two men, we do not know, but Octavian did indeed fight a civil war with Antony and won. Both Antony and Cleopatra committed suicide and the seventeen-year-old Caesarion was elevated however briefly to pharaoh.

The fate of Caesarion has never been satisfactorily determined. The generally held view is that he was captured by Octavian and assassinated in order to remove a potential rival. Other versions have him escaping through the Eastern Sudan (modern Ethiopia) through Arabia to India with great treasure. Some hold that the Nabateans, who had been conquered by Herod the Great, killed him as he made his way east, in order to curry favor with Octavian and perhaps rid themselves of their overlord (Herod the Great) who, after all, had been allied with Antony.

In summary, because of the repetitive use of the same names, both female and male, the near incestuous intermarriage of relatives, near relatives, and the uncertain historical record, your guess is as good as any when it comes to sorting all this out. (But don't tell the Scholars I said so. They are a determined lot and do not like outsiders tampering with their ~~opinions~~ facts).

Cappadocia

Cappadocia is part of Anatolia and lies east-central in the great plain that forms modern Turkey. Its history is not dissimilar to that of Egypt in that it boasted a royal family that traced its lineage back into antiquity, to King Midas of mythic fame, in fact. Its last king, Archelaus, was (or was not) in Herod's line, and did produce a daughter, the peripatetic Princess Glaphyra. As a Province of the Roman Empire it was considered a prize.

Though its borders varied from time to time, the country always straddled important trade routes east and west. The routes running north and south intersected these routes. Thus treasure from Africa and India (and east of that) passed through the country in all directions. This feature should never be underestimated. Trade formed a vital part of the Empire. Indeed, Herod the Great and Cleopatra frequently clashed over who would control which part of the road that originated in the Rift Valley of Africa and coursed northward along the Jordan branching westward at Magdala or eastward and on to Syria and thence east to the sea or westward to India and beyond. It also turned west through Cappadocia. Saint Paul would have used a portion of one of these roads through Capernaum on his way to Damascus. A trip, many say, that changed the course of history.

The name for the eastward extensions, "The Silk Road," was coined by Ferdinand von Richthofen in the mid-nineteenth century, but these routes existed from about 200 BCE onwards with occasional closures dependent on the political conditions at the time.

It is reported that the cost of goods traveling along these trade routes could increase as much as a thousand fold from their point of origin to their destination, so often were they taxed or the caravans that carried them forced to pay tolls and license fees. The Nabataeans were said to offer alternative routes eastward through the Arabian Desert. They kept their routes secret, that is to say the location of the oases along the way. Anyone attempting to cross without this special knowledge risked certain death before reaching the Gulf of Aden. Herod conquered them as much for these routes as to establish his hegemony over the area.

Torah

The Law: The first five books of the Bible, Genesis, Exodus, Leviticus, Numbers, and Deuteronomy (the written Torah). Also included was Oral Torah, interpretations of the Mosaic Law by men like Gamaliel accumulated over many centuries.

Some students also include the Psalms because of the teaching value as well as their use in worship.

N.B. *These are notes put together by an author who claims no expertise in the complexities of ancient history or religious thought. He is, first and always, a writer of fiction. Take them for what they are and nothing more.*

To receive a free catalog of Poisoned Pen Press titles, please contact us in one of the following ways:

Phone: 1-800-421-3976
Facsimile: 1-480-949-1707
Email: info@poisonedpenpress.com
Website: www.poisonedpenpress.com

Poisoned Pen Press
6962 E. First Ave. Ste 103
Scottsdale, AZ 85251

FEB - - 2013

CORE COLLECTION 2012

CPSIA information can be obtained at www.ICGtesting.com
Printed in the USA
BVOW011425020812

296916BV00003B/21/P